HENRIETTA BRANDON

Sonia Prentice (née Bowring) was born in Liverpool in 1922. Her family soon moved to Surrey, where with short interruptions she has lived ever since. She was educated at Benenden School in Kent. In the Second World War she worked in the Naval Section at Bletchley Park. In 1948 she married Ronald Prentice (d.1984). She has three children and five grandchildren. Her first novel, *The Wager*, was published in 2001 by Hollytree Books.

GW00359327

SONIA PRENTICE

Henrietta Brandon

HOLLYTREE BOOKS
HB

First published in Great Britain in 2003 by
HOLLYTREE BOOKS,
Henhaw Farmhouse, Coopers Hill Road,
South Nutfield, Redhill, Surrey, RH1 5PD.

ISBN 0 9541174 1 7

This book is a work of fiction.
Names, characters, places and incidents are either
a product of the author's imagination or are used fictitiously.
Any resemblance to actual people living or dead,
events or locales is entirely coincidental.

Typeset by M Rules, London.
Printed and bound by
The Cromwell Press, Trowbridge, Wiltshire.

I would like to thank my daughter, Caroline,
and my daughter-in-law, Nina, for their invaluable help.

FOR
RONALD

CHAPTER 1

"Well, Julia, I've news that will please you! Our friend and neighbour, Charles here, has driven over to request permission to pay his addresses to our little Louise! What do you say to that, my dear?"

Sir William's cheerful countenance was wreathed in smiles as he ushered his visitor into his wife's drawing-room. Lady Sedley, looking up from the piece of embroidery on her lap, the threaded needle still poised in her hand, was hard put to it to conceal her triumph; with a gracious smile she expressed her surprise and pleasure to the tall, handsome man bowing gracefully over her hand. Neither of the gentlemen could have been aware that her needlework had lain disregarded at her side until the moment when the low murmur of men's voices outside the room had reached her ears and had heralded their approach; ever since the footman had announced that Captain Sir Charles Gresham, formerly of his Majesty's Royal Navy, had called to see Sir William she had sat in her chair by the window filled with a mounting impatience, glancing frequently at the long-case clock by the door.

Sir William continued, "Charles has said all that is proper, my dear. I believe we can entrust our little girl to him and so I have told him."

"I can assure you, Lady Sedley, that your daughter's happiness would be my first consideration if she should do me the honour of becoming my wife." They were unexceptionable sentiments but the calm, even faintly ironic tones in which they were pronounced hardly conveyed a lover-like ardour.

Lady Sedley set aside her work and rose to her feet in a graceful movement, saying soulfully, "We had not expected to lose our daughter so soon, my dear Charles, but a mother must not be so selfish as to stand in the way of her child's happiness." Glancing up into Gresham's face, she was disconcerted to observe a cynical gleam in the very blue eyes that were looking down at her, and thought with a faint feeling of alarm that he was not a man who could easily be deceived. An uncomfortable recollection passed rapidly through her mind of the various stratagems that she had employed during the London Season, now just ended, to bring her lovely daughter to the notice of one or two members of the aristocracy. Not that her endeavours had had the slightest effect upon her daughter. Louise, possessed of a strongly romantic nature, had felt no inclination to bestow her smiles upon a middle-aged Marquis, nor did the wealthy but dull heir to an Earldom excite her interest. She had betrayed an alarming tendency to prefer the company of young and penniless members of his Majesty's armed forces and it was a relief to her mother that the Season had ended without her having formed an ineligible attachment.

As the daughter of a Baron, Lady Sedley had initially aimed higher than a mere baronet but the Greshams were an old and respected family, and, moreover, the baronetcy was not a new creation; there had been Greshams at Gresham Place since the thirteenth century. She had therefore been pleased and surprised when, in London, Charles Gresham had paid a marked attention to Louise, going beyond anything that politeness might have required from him as a near neighbour in the country. Looking at him now, at his tall well-made person, and easy manner, she was not surprised that her daughter had shown a shy pleasure in his company and conversation.

Announcing that she would find Louise and bring her to the drawing-room, Lady Sedley bade her husband entertain their guest in her absence and quitted the room in a delightful flurry, her head full of wedding plans and at the back of her mind rejoicing in the knowledge that her daughter happened to be wearing that day a particularly becoming sprig-muslin morning dress.

She discovered Louise in the old schoolroom absorbed in 'The Romance of the Forest' by Mrs Radcliffe, and even in her present elated mood found herself obliged to censure her daughter for filling her head with romantic nonsense. "But never mind that now, child." she said impatiently, smoothing back a tendril of Louise's hair, "Such a delightful surprise – Sir Charles Gresham has called this morning, has been with Papa and has offered for you! He is with Papa now in the drawing-room and waits to speak to you."

Her blue eyes wide with astonishment, Louise stared at her mother, a faint flush rising to her cheeks. "Charles Gresham! Charles Gresham wishes to marry me?" She felt a strange sensation of excitement mingling with her surprise; if this were so, how well he had concealed his feelings for her: there had been nothing in his manner when they had met at Almack's or had attended the same routs and balls that would have led her to suppose that he cherished a secret passion for her. She had been, indeed, slightly in awe of him, and had believed him to be often bored by the London Season and by the endless frivolous chatter and gossip. She remembered with a romantic shiver those hooded eyes in his sun-tanned face, fine lines etched about them from his years at sea, and wondered again what had changed him from the carefree youth that she remembered as a little girl.

As these thoughts were passing through her mind, her mother was drawing her towards the door, "Such a handsome man, child. Of the first consequence! A most flattering offer. I believe you have been concealing your sentiments from me, sly little puss!"

Uncertain, Louise hung back, her pretty face flushed with excitement and perplexity, "Indeed I have not, Mama, I had not the least notion of his intentions! To think that he loves me – perhaps for years has been secretly hiding his passion!"

"Passion!" Lady Sedley spoke crushingly, "My dear Louise, we are speaking of marriage, of an alliance between two families, of position and settlements. Not of some girlish romantic day dreams! If you accept him you will be married to a man who will treat you with every consideration; I believe him to be sincerely attached to you." Despite these damping words, her daughter followed her out of the schoolroom her head in a whirl with just the very thoughts that her mother had so roundly condemned.

Sir Charles Gresham, looking down into the youthful, smiling face upturned to his, felt a pang of something resembling remorse. Lady Sedley, after a few well chosen words to bridge any awkwardness that might have existed between her daughter and Sir Charles, had removed herself and her unwilling husband, saying in a downright manner, "I don't scruple to leave you alone with Louise, my dear Charles."

He had taken Louise's hand in his own firm brown one and said formally, "I have long held you in the highest regard, Louise. I believe, if you will do me the honour of becoming my wife, I could make you happy and I would exert myself to the utmost to do so!"

She had blushed and smiled and had accepted, murmuring, "Oh Sir Charles! I am quite overcome!" and had looked hopefully at him expecting a passionate declaration of his feelings. It had not been forthcoming. He had felt her surprise and disappointment at his un-lover-like attitude as he had bent to kiss the little hand resting in his. Now he said ruefully, "My dear, I fear you will find me sadly lacking in romance. I should at least have sworn to terminate my existence if you should have refused me."

She laughed a little nervously, she was never quite sure when he was serious or not, and said, "Indeed no! Why, you are the most romantic figure imaginable – to have served under Admiral Hood – to have been wounded in the service of your country."

He retorted with a trace of irony, "But such a paltry wound, my love, now if only I had lost an arm or a leg." For a moment he thought, with wry amusement, that she would make a serious reply to this sally, for there was a look of consideration on her face, then she caught sight of the expression in his eyes and opened hers wide, saying reproachfully, "I believe you are funning, Sir Charles. How can you do so at such a moment?"

He only smiled then said, "Our betrothal will give the greatest pleasure to my mother. She has long wished me to marry. Your parents, too, I am confident approve for you will still be living near to them after we are married."

These sentiments, though agreeable to hear, did not in any way conform to Louise's ideas of romance, but the man who uttered them and stood close beside her embodied in his handsome person every young girl's dream of a hero. Confidently, she told herself that having concealed his feelings for so long, it was not easy for him to declare his love for her. It was, however, a relief to both parties that within a short time Sir William and Lady Sedley returned and, on becoming formally acquainted with the news of the betrothal, were vociferous in their pleasure; Sir William, having shaken Gresham warmly by the hand, gave his daughter a brief embrace and declared himself delighted, rather spoiling her pleasure by remarking in a jovial manner that he had not supposed her to have had so much sense in her pretty little head.

Sir Charles took his leave of them in a mood which accorded ill with his role of successful suitor; by the time he arrived home an air of gloom had settled upon him. The sight of the handsome manor-house, built by a Gresham ancestor in the reign of Charles 2nd, did nothing to lighten his state of mind. A younger son, he had never anticipated inheriting his father's title nor this splendid property set amidst the foothills of the rolling down-lands of Sussex. Rather, he had chosen to make a career in the Navy and had never regretted his choice, even when, while serving as a midshipman under Admiral Hood at the crucial battle of 'The Saints' near Dominica, he had received a wound in the thigh and had been fortunate, indeed, not to have suffered the loss of his leg. Since then he had risen rapidly in the Service and had received his first command as Captain of a ship-of-the-line the previous year. It was during a period of leave, while his ship was re-fitting, that his parents had learned of his brother's death.

Marcus Gresham had been killed in action in India, where his regiment had been engaged in the fighting in Mysore. The news had broken his father's heart and within three months the sorrowing parent had followed his elder son to the grave, having extracted, on his deathbed, a promise from his reluctant heir to quit the Navy and take up the life of a country gentleman. There had followed for Sir Charles a period of acute boredom; his mother, prostrate by her double loss, had shunned society and, submerged in the deepest mourning, passed her days within doors accompanied by an elderly cousin whose kindness of heart was only exceeded by her lack of any sense of humour. Frustrated in his desire to play his part in the naval actions which must surely follow France's declaration of war against England and Holland at the beginning of the year, he had striven to immerse himself in country affairs and to learn about the management of his unlooked for inheritance. Deciding to alleviate his boredom by a brief period in London, he had hired lodgings in the vicinity of St James's Street and had been surprised to find his mantelshelf become crowded with an impressive number of invitations. It was while attending a ball at Devonshire House that he had been presented to Miss Louise Sedley and had recollected at once his neighbour's pretty little daughter whom, nine years before, he had teased, and treated with all the good-natured contempt of a young man enjoying the life of a naval officer.

Louise Sedley, now nineteen years old, had fulfilled her earlier promise and was generally admitted to be a notable beauty. Small, fair-haired, with large soft appealing eyes and a retroussé nose, she had captivated a host of admirers during her first London Season. She had smiled shyly at Sir Charles Gresham and had found his indolently commanding manner and assured bearing an exciting contrast to the callow young lieutenants and ensigns whose peacock-bright regimentals had hitherto attracted her interest. There was something about Sir Charles that had intrigued her and led her, in the succeeding weeks, to weave about his unsuspecting head a whole host of mysterious stories.

Sir Charles, hoping that the acquisition of a wife and the subsequent rearing of a family might in some part reconcile him to the loss of his career, had noted the guileless simplicity of Miss Sedley's manner and her sweetness of nature. These attributes, combined with the circumstance of her having been born and brought up in the vicinity of Gresham Place, had encouraged him to believe that marriage with his neighbour's charming daughter might be the solution to his problems.

Sitting alone after dinner in the panelled dining-room at Gresham Place, drinking his port and gazing moodily at the portraits that surrounded him, he wondered again if he had acted rightly. Such a marriage of convenience was common enough and certainly he had said nothing to Miss Sedley that might lead her to believe that he cherished a 'grande passion' for her, but nevertheless the uneasy feeling persisted that Miss Sedley was the possessor of a strongly romantic nature: was it, therefore, fair to her for him to bring to their marriage nothing more than an affectionate regard?

The August evening being fine and warm with the promise of a full moon, and finding no relief from his thoughts, Sir Charles decided to drive himself down to Shoreham, a distance of only ten miles, where his yacht, 'Ariel', was being fitted out with a new mainsail; the remainder of the evening could always be spent in the company of one of his many acquaintances in nearby Brighton, who, following the example set by His Royal Highness, the Prince of Wales, were recruiting their forces after the rigours of the Season by enjoying the sea air and agreeable society of that fashionable resort.

Earlier that day, as dawn was breaking over Dieppe, Henrietta Brandon stood on the quayside staring down apprehensively at the French fishing smack bobbing gently on the morning tide. So this was to be her final means of escape from the perils of revolutionary France. When the terrifying news had reached her home near Paris, that armed citizens were on their way to arrest the Brandon family as

English spies, her mother's maid had persuaded Henrietta to leave the house immediately. Her brother, Philip, had been out in the woods, shooting, and to warn him had been impossible without a dangerous delay.

Henrietta looked down ruefully at the stained and creased coat and ill-fitting breeches which she wore, for Jeanne had insisted that Henrietta should at once dress herself as a boy for her own protection. She had been arrayed in Philip's outgrown garments, family papers hidden in an inner coat-pocket and other clothes pushed into an old valise, which now lay at her feet. With a wry smile, she imagined her mother's face if she could have seen her daughter now. But Mama was, thank God, away in Switzerland on a visit to relations – at least she was safe there.

The journey from Ville D'Avray had been a nightmare for them all. Jeanne's cousin had driven the cart, with Jeanne beside him, and Henrietta had been hidden in the load of cabbages and bales of straw that the cart contained. Several times they had been stopped, questions asked and staves and pitchforks thrust into the loaded cart, once narrowly missing Henrietta's foot. They had hardly paused in their headlong flight even to eat the food and drink that they had snatched up at departure.

On board the 'Marie-Claire', the skipper, a dark-visaged man in a blue jersey, emerged from below deck and began to coil one of the stout ropes that littered her deck. Glancing up at the sky, he noticed the little group standing above him on the deserted quayside: a burly countryman in smock and breeches, a middle-aged woman respectably but plainly dressed and between them a slim youth, whose dishevelled appearance belied his pale aristocratic face and bearing. There seemed something familiar about the countryman and when the skipper heard his name called, he mounted the stone steps and joined them. It was indeed his old friend, Pierre, not seen for many years, who, after a fond embrace and much back-slapping, drew him to one side and began to speak urgently to him in a low voice. Henrietta and Jeanne looked towards the two men, too

16

exhausted to do more than watch silently. They saw at first the fisherman shake his head but finally, after a further discussion, with a shrug of his shoulders, he nodded, spat, and taking from Pierre's hand a bulging purse, came back towards them.

"For old times sake, I'll do it." he grunted, with a scowl towards Henrietta, "Not that I hold with them accursed English, but I reckon this lad's too young to do this country any harm." And beckoning her to follow him, he descended again to the deck of the fishing boat.

Slowly Henrietta turned to her companion, her eyes filling with tears which she hastily dashed away, and gently touching the maid's cheek, she murmured in her ear, "How can I ever thank you, my dear, dear Jeanne? I should never forgive myself if I have endangered your life, and Pierre's too."

Jeanne flung her arms around her and drew her close. "My little one," she whispered, "You must have courage. No-one must suspect. Now you are Philip Brandon and you must forget the existence of Henrietta until you are safely in your grandfather's house."

An hour later, when the 'Marie-Claire' was ready to sail, two roughly dressed men pushed through the throng of people who were going about their daily business upon the quayside, and came to stand above the fishing vessel. Both had tri-coloured cockades in their caps and the elder of the two wore a sash of the same red, white and blue across his body. It was he who called down in an authoritative voice, "Hey there, Citizen Latour! Here's one of these damned aristos, on the run and a foreigner at that. An accursed enemy of the state! It's your duty, Citizen – your duty to our glorious Republic – to lay any information about such persons before the proper authorities. And I, Citizen – I, Henri Dupont – as head of the local Revolutionary Committee, am that authority." His loud voice had attracted the attention of those standing nearest to him and there was a low growl of approval.

The fisherman spat eloquently over the side, "What in the name of God would the likes of me know 'bout enemies of the state?" He made a rude gesture, "Come and look for yourself, Citizen, if you wish, but hurry about it – tide won't wait for no-one."

The man with the sash descended importantly to the deck and gazed around him, eyed with surly disgust by the other members of the crew. The heavy fishing nets lay neatly in the stern, ropes carefully coiled and everything was clearly ready for departure. Citizen Dupont bent his head and climbed down the companion-way to the cramped cabin below deck and disappeared from view; some tense few moments passed, while the onlookers held their breath – but Dupont was alone when he reappeared and the crowd emitted an audible sigh, disappointed to be deprived of their prey.

"Satisfied, Citizen Dupont?" There was a brief nod in reply. The man of authority cast a final disgusted glance around him and returned to the quay, and moved slowly off, clearly, by the expression upon his face, someone would suffer for the false information that he had received.

The coast of France was almost invisible to the naked eye when Gaston Latour at last raised a corner of the folded nets. The 'Marie-Claire', her bows lifting in the rough water, had made good speed since they had set sail from Dieppe with a brisk following wind. The pitching of the boat had had its effect, however, on the woebegone figure that emerged from what had proved to be an effective, if uncomfortable, hiding-place; even the hardened old seaman was moved to pity, "Victuals is what you need, my boy, victuals and a brandy."

She shook her head, appalled – at that moment even the arrests and executions that had precipitated her escape seemed to have paled into insignificance before the present miseries of the heaving deck; but when a loaf of bread and a bottle were brought to her she forced herself to eat and drink and found herself the better for it. For the remainder of the voyage she remained on deck, perched on a coil of rope near the foot of the mast and even recovered sufficiently to be able to admire the skill of the crew as they moved about their tasks. As the sun began to sink, she saw for the first time the cliffs of her native land and found herself curious to see for herself this country about which her father and her old English nurse had spoken so often.

Their arrival off the little port of Shoreham some hours later appeared to attract little attention: the 'Marie-Claire' flew no flag to identify her nationality and they anchored discreetly offshore. The dinghy which transported Henrietta to the beach turned back as soon as she had set foot on land, leaving her alone, valise in hand, in the gathering dusk, looking about her with interest. Straightening as best as she could the cravat knotted about her throat and brushing the dust off her coat, she set off purposefully in the direction of an inn whose sign, portraying a dolphin, she had observed swaying in the wind by the waterside. For the first time she consciously recognized the difficulties that now lay before her: shelter she must have for that night and in the morning the means to reach her destination; all this without possessing any save French money, hardly acceptable currency in time of war! Preoccupied with these thoughts, she failed to notice two figures, who detached themselves from the deep shadows formed by the projecting wall of a nearby building and followed her with swift silent steps

Sir Charles Gresham left his drinking companions and sauntered out of the brightly lit taproom of the 'Star' inn, bending his head to pass beneath the low lintel of the doorway, and stood for a moment on the threshold of the snug hostelry while his eyes became accustomed to the darkness. In the inn yard his groom, Benson, was patiently holding the heads of a fine pair of bays. Sir Charles was about to cross to his waiting curricle when he heard a youthful cry of distress, swiftly muffled, and the sounds of a scuffle close at hand. On the far side of the highway, in a lane leading to the harbour, he could discern two figures bending over what seemed to be a bundle lying on the ground; then he saw a cudgel raised and at once moved quickly towards them, with a speed that was surprising in one whose manner was habitually indolent.

The two ruffians, looking round at the sound of his footsteps, must have glimpsed the silver-mounted pistol in his hand for, seizing some object from the ground, they took to their heels and disappeared into a narrow alleyway and were lost to sight. Sir Charles, reaching the spot, slipped his pistol into his pocket and stood looking down; a youth, wearing buckskin breeches and dusty boots, lay face downwards at his feet. He was relieved to hear a low groan from the boy and, calling to Benson to bring him a light, he dropped on one knee and gently turned him onto his back.

The groom, ordering a stable-boy to mind the horses, took one of the lighted carriage lamps and brought it to his master, while Sir Charles began to loosen the cravat at the boy's neck. Suddenly he saw the boy's eyes open, to stare blankly at him, then widen with alarm; he felt his hands thrust away and the victim struggled to sit up, exclaiming weakly, "*Mon Dieu! Qu'est ce qui se passe? Qui êtes vous?*"

"By God! A damned little Frenchman!" Sir Charles gazed with something between disgust and amusement at the figure before him.

"*Non, non – Pardon!* – I should say – No, sir!" a hurried voice replied, "I am English! But it is true that I have come from France – it has been my home." Henrietta could not see her rescuer's face clearly in the dim light of the lamp, but she found herself somewhat reassured by the calm, deep voice which had spoken to her, regardless of the sentiments expressed by it. Still confused by the sudden attack, she struggled to her feet and was thankful to feel his hand at her elbow supporting her. Her head was aching violently as she straightened herself and looked around her for her valise. To her relief she saw it lying nearby and would have bent to pick it up had not Sir Charles, commanding Benson to take charge of it, announced his intention of returning with her to the inn so that the extent of her injuries could be ascertained.

Saying in a matter-of-fact voice, "You were fortunate indeed that I was at hand – I believe these villains are on the watch for unwary travellers." he guided her towards the Star inn and, after one look at his white-faced companion, he demanded and was given a private parlour. As she was led into a side room she had a fleeting glimpse of the startled faces of two young army officers standing at the bar. There, seated upon an oak settle by the huge open fireplace, Henrietta found herself being handed a restorative measure of brandy. Taking the glass in a hand that shook a trifle, she murmured her thanks and looked up shyly into Sir Charles's face. Her eyes met a pair of vividly blue ones, smiling lazily down at her, and she was amazed to discover before her a very tall gentleman dressed in the first stare of fashion from his dark locks cut short, à la Brutus, and perfectly fitting coat, to his skin-tight pantaloons and highly polished boots. So unexpected was this vision in what had appeared to her to be a relatively obscure harbour town that something of her amazement must have appeared upon her countenance as she regarded him over the rim of the wine-glass.

Sir Charles noted the surprise but was unconscious of its cause; he was, himself, experiencing a degree of astonishment: the self-possession of his companion made a strange contrast to his youthful looks, the smooth cheeks and absurdly long lashes that framed his eyes could only belong to one of no more than fourteen, or at most fifteen years of age, if indeed that, yet the worldly-wise expression in those same eyes seemed to belie that impression. He observed a bruise high up on the boy's forehead, near the tangle of raggedly cut, chestnut brown curls that stood out, like an aureole of gleaming bronze about his head; he was a handsome youth, with a short straight, finely chiselled nose and determined chin. His garments bore evidence of hard-wear and seemed over large for their owner's slim person.

Breaking the silence, Henrietta said awkwardly, "I must thank you, sir, for rescuing me . . ." when the door flew open and Sir Charles's two erstwhile drinking companions burst in.

"By Jove, Charles, what the deuce are you up to now?" demanded Lieutenant George Frensham, the younger of the two subalterns, while eyeing Henrietta disapprovingly through his quizzing glass, "Why, damn it, man, it was only last week that you were giving a lift in your curricle to some old gypsy woman! Who the devil is this young stripling?"

His fellow-officer, who seemed a trifle unsteady upon his feet and was staring owlishly at Henrietta, said solemnly, "You know, you'll have to be careful, Charles, my boy – making a habit of helping people – you don't want to be thought like that devilish queer Spanish fellow, who went around tilting at windmills!"

"Tilting at windmills?" George Frensham guffawed and emptied the glass in his hand, "It's you that has windmills in your head, Rupert!"

During these exchanges, Henrietta could not help but recollect ruefully that her presence, as a young female, in a private parlour of an inn in the company of a strange gentleman and two young officers, both well in their cups, was extremely improper. She could only be thankful that she had not been rescued by either of these foolish young men. How strange to think that they were representatives of an army greatly feared by the French. Indeed, it was hard to imagine either of them performing great deeds of valour on the battlefield.

Meanwhile Sir Charles, sighing patiently, said, "The boy has been set-upon by a couple of ruffians. I can hardly abandon him now. Meanwhile I should like to have a few moments in private with him, if you please, so that I can discover his destination."

Looking with extreme disfavour upon Henrietta and muttering, "You know your business best, no doubt, Charles." and "Don't say we didn't warn you, my boy!" George and his companion departed with all the solemnity of the partially drunk.

Sir Charles looked enquiringly at Henrietta, who now began again to speak, determined to let no tremor in her voice betray her anxiety. She must, at all costs, appear to be of the masculine gender. "My name, sir, is Philip Brandon and I am just now escaped from France, and sailed from Dieppe early this morning aided by friends." she shivered, "You see, I hope to find a home with my grandfather, Lord

Hartfield." Hopefully, she added, "Perhaps you are acquainted with him? For I understand he lives in these parts." Unconscious of the strange expression upon Sir Charles's face, she began to search in the pockets of her coat, and, finding them to be empty, looked up aghast, exclaiming in dismay, "Dear Heavens! My papers! My money! Whatever shall I do? They are gone – stolen!"

Sir Charles frowned, and raised the quizzing-glass that hung by a ribbon about his neck in order to survey his young companion more closely; Henrietta found something infinitely chilling in the action.

"You do not believe me, sir?"

"If Lord Hartfield is your grandfather, may I ask you your father's name?"

"My father is dead, sir, murdered by the mob two years ago. He was the Honourable John Brandon, second son of Lord Hartfield."

It was clear to Sir Charles that the boy resented having his word doubted and found himself impressed; he lowered his glass and sighed. The boy was watching his face anxiously. What a fool he would be, Sir Charles thought, if he further embroiled himself with this young stripling and yet the arrival of this self-styled Philip Brandon was a strange coincidence. He felt his interest and his pity aroused and said suddenly, with amusement in his voice, "My name is Charles Gresham. I believe you must stay in my house tonight, young Brandon! Tomorrow I shall inform your family of your arrival. You see, my dear boy, we shall soon be kinsmen for, if what you say is true, then you are a cousin of my future wife!"

CHAPTER 2

It seemed to Sir Charles that dismay was the predominant emotion that appeared upon the boy's face, dismay mixed with something akin to embarrassment. Had he before him an impostor after all?

Henrietta found herself in a dilemma; not for one moment had she imagined that she would be obliged to continue her masquerade for more than a few hours in England, nor that she should become acquainted with any person with whom she might later be connected. She cast a surreptitious glance at the stranger from under her eyelashes; it was difficult to read his thoughts. He seemed to be regarding her with indifference and certainly gave no sign of having penetrated her disguise. She wondered if she might trust him with her true story – the temptation to do so was strong – but, she told herself, she knew nothing of this man, and with neither money nor papers to prove her identity she would be powerless in his hands. Besides which, it would be vastly more entertaining for the moment to continue her role as a boy. In spite of the hazards of her escape and of her journey, she had to admit it had pleased and amused her to find how readily she had been accepted as a member, however youthful, of the sterner sex and during these last days she had experienced a heady freedom she had never known before.

Sir Charles, aware of some inner doubt that was troubling his young companion, broke the silence by suggesting that, as a journey of some ten miles lay before them, they should depart without delay.

"Explanations, Philip – for so I shall call you – can wait until tomorrow, when you will have had a good night's rest!"

The good sense of his suggestion prevailed with Henrietta; she stood up, declaring as she did so, "I am infinitely grateful, sir. You have been more than kind. A strange chance, indeed, that you are so intimately connected with my family. For my part, I have no knowledge of its members." She gave a little Gallic shrug and continued with a chuckle, "Of me they know nothing!"

Henrietta had little recollection of their drive along the winding Sussex lanes. By now the moon was up, illuminating the undulating contours of the Downs, but before they had covered more than a mile her head had dropped forward on her chest and Sir Charles, glancing sideways at his passenger, became aware that his young companion had fallen into an exhausted slumber. He thought wryly that he would be presenting his bride-to-be with an unexpected surprise and, from what he knew of Miss Louise Sedley, one which should appeal to her romantic nature: it was not every day that one acquired a new unknown cousin escaped from heavens only knew what horrors from across the Channel! Whether the other members of her family, notably her cousin, Hugo Brandon, would be equally enthusiastic was another question.

Waking with a start as the curricle halted, Henrietta looked around her with sleepy interest as the bulk of a large building loomed up beside the carriage. A footman opened wide a massive oak door set beneath a pillared portico and warm, golden light streamed out into the courtyard.

"Down you get, my boy, the sooner you are in bed the better for you!" Sir Charles, alighting, strode into the house, an action that reminded Henrietta as she scrambled down, that, in her masculine role, it was only natural that no assistance in descending from the carriage would be forthcoming. Once inside the panelled hall with its lofty ceiling, she was too engrossed in studying her surroundings to feel any qualms about her future. The butler, who had been waiting up for his master's return, bowed impassively when informed that an unexpected visitor would be staying the night and, directing the footman to take Henrietta's shabby valise to a guest-room, enquired whether Sir Charles would be wishing to partake of any refreshment.

The latter turned to Henrietta, with lifted brows, "Are you hungry, young Philip? I seem to remember at your age I was perpetually sharp-set."

"No, sir, I thank you, but – forgive me – it is sleep I require."

Sir Charles looked down into his companion's face where eyes larger than ever in a face now drawn with exhaustion gazed up at him apologetically.

"Off to bed with you then, my boy – we'll talk in the morning." He watched, with a frown, Philip's slight figure mount the stairs behind Cummings. In what future drama had he involved himself, he thought with an inward groan: Hugo, with his ever-increasing load of debts, if rumour be true, would move heaven and earth to obstruct any claimant to his expected inheritance. Well, at the least, it would add some excitement to a damnably dull existence.

The following morning Henrietta was awakened by a knock on her bedroom door, immediately followed by the entrance of an elderly manservant holding a tray bearing a cup of chocolate and slices of bread and butter. Clutching the bedclothes close to her chin as he set the tray down beside the bed, she responded with a shy smile to his "Good-morning, sir!", then, as he drew back the curtains and the daylight flooded in, she enquired anxiously, "What o'clock is it? For I fear I have slept prodigiously late."

"The stable-clock has just struck ten, young sir," was the response, "and I've a message for you from the Captain. He says that he has to ride out on estate matters and will join you for a nuncheon shortly before mid-day." As he spoke, he was collecting Henrietta's discarded garments and boots and observing her anxious eyes following his movements, announced kindly, "I'm Morton, the Captain's valet and it's best I give your clothes a press, young lad; they ain't fit to be seen in this state. I'll soon have all shipshape." Upon his departure, Henrietta enjoyed her breakfast and wondered, with some apprehension, who her host and rescuer might be. The manservant had referred to him as 'the Captain', perhaps he was an army officer. Certainly he had appeared to be on intimate terms with the young officers at the inn.

However, when Morton returned with her clothes, now well-pressed and brushed, and Henrietta asked him in which regiment Captain Gresham served, he looked positively affronted, "Captain Sir Charles Gresham, His Majesty's Royal Navy!" he said proudly, "Served as his personal steward five years or more, I did. The Captain had to leave the Service – more's the pity – when his elder brother was killed in India. And I'll tell you something – the Navy lost a fine officer then!". He looked at Henrietta with a comforting smile on his weather-beaten face and said, "You'll be all right with the Captain, my lad. There's many a midshipman has been thankful to be under his command. He never allowed no place for bullies in his ships." To Henrietta this seemed re-assuring news; her host was evidently a compassionate man where the young were concerned, and, shortly afterwards, she arose and began hastily to dress herself. It was to be hoped that assisting a male guest in his toilet was no part of the duties of her host's manservant.

Descending to the hall, once dressed, Henrietta saw through the window a terrace that ran along the back of the house and below it a parterre with gravelled walks and an abundance of flowers, all bathed in sunlight. Beyond were lawns and borders descending to a shrubbery through which she could glimpse the sparkle of water. So this – all that lay before her, was an English garden. She found a door, which opened onto the terrace and went outside. It was, indeed, so strange and so different to their property in Ville D'Avray where all had been shabby and in need of repair. Looking back at the house she noticed in particular the soft colour of the mellowed brickwork, the tall windows and steeply inclined roof. Resolving to explore the garden, she followed the paths, discovering a circular dovecote, standing alone, and a large ornamental pool with a fountain playing in the middle. There was also an extensive kitchen garden, orchards and glasshouses, all in excellent repair. How fortunate she had been, she reflected, to have been rescued by the owner of such a splendid property and a person clearly of some kindness. Now she must discover how soon she would be able to continue her journey to her grandfather's house.

It was by now, she reckoned, approaching mid-day and she returned to the house, eager to find out how soon she might depart, for it would not be so easy to sustain her masculine role in the cold light of day. Upon enquiry, a footman in the hall directed her to the breakfast parlour where she found her host already seated at a table, upon which ample supplies of ham, cheeses and loaves of bread, as well as jugs of beer and cider had been laid. Sir Charles, looking up from the newspaper open beside his plate, wished his unexpected guest 'good-morning' and indicated a chair beside him, saying, "Help yourself, Philip, I feel sure you must be devilish hungry."

Henrietta, inwardly amused to realise that as a boy she was no longer entitled to the respectful politeness of a gentleman towards a lady, took her seat and helped herself from the dishes. No man would rise to his feet at *her* entrance under present circumstances! Sir Charles soon withdrew his attention from the newspapers and, smiling at Henrietta, enquired whether she had slept well. Upon hearing her grateful affirmative, he requested some account of her history and that of her father, who, he said, by all accounts was believed to have died long ago. A thoughtful expression upon her face, Henrietta began to recount her history with an engaging candour. It was a sad tale.

Her father, the Honourable John Brandon, a man with a fatal predilection for the gaming tables, had fled to France following the unfortunate death of his adversary in a duel and from that moment all contact with his noble family had ceased. In France he had married the daughter of an eminent but impecunious academic at the

University of Paris, and, being unable to rid himself of his dangerous addiction to Faro and Hazard, had lived a precarious life with his wife and two children on the property she had inherited near Ville D'Avray, a village on the outskirts of Paris.

"We were happy enough, sir, though it was a hard life for my mother, then tragedy entered our lives!" She looked down at her hands and continued in a low voice, "It was nearly a year ago – my father was arrested in Paris – for what reason we know not – and before he could even be brought to trial, the mob broke into the prison where he was held. He was massacred, sir, along with his companions!"

She looked up and, for a moment, thought she saw a look of anger in Sir Charles's normally tranquil expression but he only enquired gently, "And what followed for you and your family?"

Her face vividly revealing her feelings, she remembered the past months and days. She told him of their ever-growing alarm at the events in Paris and throughout the country; how, early that year, a Revolutionary Tribunal had been set up, sending out its members, armed with extraordinary powers, into the provinces. There many so-called suspects had been rounded up and jailed. Worst of all for the Brandon family, the declaration of war upon England at the beginning of the year had heralded the start of a country-wide hunt for English spies. A positive spy-mania had swept the country and, in due course, while their mother was absent on a visit to relations in Switzerland, it had come to the ears of their faithful servants that a group of patriotic citizens were at that moment on their way to arrest the young Brandons and bring them to justice.

"My brother was out in the woods, shooting, when the news came! The servants would not let me wait for his return – they hid me in a cart full of cabbages and conveyed me to Dieppe! My mother's maid, Jeanne, came too – her cousin drove the cart – we were stopped several times!" She paused, and there was a look of remembered anguish upon the face that gazed at him.

Charles prompted softly, "And then?"

"They found the 'Marie-Claire' tied up in the harbour – she belongs Jeanne's brother-in-law – and persuaded him to take me to England; of course they paid him well."

"And you had documents to prove your identity?"

"Yes, sir, I took them from my mother's desk – my baptismal certificate, other papers – but now they are gone –"

"Were you not frightened by this journey?"

"Yes, sir, I was greatly afraid – but worst of all – my brother – I know not whether he has escaped – my mother will, I believe, be safe, if she can be warned not to return home, but they are without mercy, these people – the French, they have gone mad, sir." There was a look of horror on the young face.

Sir Charles lent forward and laid his hand on her shoulder reassuringly, "I am confident that your brother will be safe for I am sure that your loyal servants will help him to escape as they have helped you." There was such kind sympathy in his expression that she felt an irresistible impulse to confide in him but, before she could do so, he turned from her and pushed back his chair from the table. His handsome face inscrutable, he said pensively, "And now you must meet your new relations. Have you thought that they may not welcome you with open arms?"

Astonished, Henrietta replied, "Why should they not, sir?"

He hesitated, then said, "Because your father's elder brother died ten years ago. He had no sons and therefore, when the old Lord Hartfield dies, the title and property would have gone to his great-nephew, Hugh Brandon; but now if your father was the second son, then you or your brother will be the heir."

The little face beside him had become very thoughtful, "Indeed, sir, I am sorry for this Hugo Brandon. But I cannot help being who I am. Perhaps he will not care too much." she added hopefully.

Sir Charles stood up, some very real doubts were in his mind, but he said nothing of them to his companion. Instead he made known his intention of sending a note to this self-same Hugo Brandon, informing him of the astonishing arrival in England of a cousin of his, and suggesting that he might care to dine at Gresham Place that day to make the acquaintance of his new relation.

Shortly afterwards, having sent off his message, he found Henrietta in the garden. "Would you care to ride out with me this afternoon, Philip?" he enquired, "I have to see how work has progressed upon some drains that are being dug in the upper field and I suppose that you ride." Thankful that she had ridden astride many times as a young girl, (unknown to her parents), she happily assented and together they proceeded to the stables. On their way there Henrietta found herself, quite naturally, exclaiming on the beauty of the gardens and the splendid views of the countryside. Her enthusiasm drew a surprised glance from her host, who looked into her ecstatic face, eye-brows raised and remarked, "So you are interested in gardens – what a strange boy you are."

She had tried to cover her slip by kicking nonchalantly against a stone on the path, saying in a gruff voice, "You know, sir, I wish, above all, I might have the chance to see a cricket match, for my father often spoke of this new game."

He laughed, "I believe that should be possible. There are matches played in the vicinity."

Henrietta was impressed by the stables. It was clear that Sir Charles loved his horses and took the keenest interest in their welfare. Upon their arrival, he enquired into the progress made in the treatment of the fetlock of his favourite hunter, strained when out at pasture. He then entered into an animated discussion with his head groom as to whether he should arrange to have a neighbour's stallion cover the young mare he had recently acquired. At such frank conversation Henrietta hardly knew where to look and hoped fervently that she had not betrayed her discomfort. She was relieved when a bay hack was brought out for her to mount and thankful, as Sir Charles was still deep in conversation, that it was one of the stable-boys who was bidden to give her a leg-up onto the saddle.

The hour that followed was one of unalloyed pleasure. Sir Charles, mounted on a handsome grey, led her across several fields where there was the opportunity for a canter. Later, following paths beneath the trees, they engaged in amicable conversation about the countryside, about hunting and about horse-breeding in general. It soon became clear to Henrietta that, although the Navy had been Sir Charles's first choice in life, he was well suited to his present role of landowner. How different, it seemed, was the life of country gentlemen in England to that led by well-born Frenchmen. In France they had spent little time living in their splendid country houses and in overseeing their estates where the peasants existed in direst poverty. There, the families in the upper circles of society had spent their lives gathered around their monarch at Versailles or in the capital, dedicating themselves to a life of leisure and neglecting the condition of their tenants. That Sir Charles did, however, grievously miss his former life in the Navy soon became clear to Henrietta when she asked him about his last command and the crew who had served under him, remembering that Morton had told her that he had been the Captain's steward.

"You can have little idea, Philip, of the closeness that exists between all members of the crew in the British navy, regardless of rank. When a ship is in action, every man is dependent upon the skill and courage of his fellow seamen. In my last command, many members of my former ship's crew volunteered to serve again under me. Indeed, my friend Henry Clifton served with me as midshipman, masters mate and lieutenant. Now he has his own command and he has recently honoured me by asking me to be godfather to his son."

When Hugo was shown into the library about five o'clock he found his host and the stranger from France engaged in a game of chess. Henrietta had, by now, come to feel quite at her ease in the company of her new acquaintance. He was leaning back lazily in his chair, watching her bright-eyed face as she surveyed the board, her slim fingers hovering over first one piece, then another. "I believe you have me, sir," she was saying regretfully, "if I move here," she indicated the square, "I lose my Queen, if I move here, I am in check!" She looked up and saw the stranger standing in the doorway and got to her feet. She saw a good-looking dark-haired man of above average height, with penetrating eyes and regular features, his well-marked eyebrows drawn together in a frown.

Charles Gresham rose in leisurely fashion to his feet. His guest's brow cleared as he came forward with a cynical smile upon his lips, saying, "Why, Charles, doing it rather too brown, ain't you! Good God, a Brandon with a French mother and hair that colour. I find that hard to credit!"

"Nevertheless, that's what this young stripling claims to be, no less." Charles put a hand on Henrietta's shoulder and propelled her forward, "Your Cousin Hugo, Philip!"

Henrietta executed an awkward little bow and straightened to survey the forbidding figure before her with an interested and friendly gaze. On closer inspection, she perceived the strained expression upon the new arrival's countenance, the cold, hard eyes that surveyed her with dislike.

"Gracious, so you are my cousin, sir. You resemble my brother, I believe. But I – I have my mother's colouring." she saw the sceptical expression on his face and added, "You see, my maternal grandmother was from Savoy – light brown hair, even blond, is not uncommon there!"

It seemed that Hugo was unimpressed. He was perfectly civil to Charles's guest and asked Henrietta many searching questions about her father but she could see that he was unconvinced. He listened, with a faintly contemptuous smile upon his face, to her story but when he learned of the loss of her papers there was a definite lightening of his mood. The harsh lines upon his face relaxed and from then on he seemed to dismiss her from his notice as not worthy of his attention, and during the dinner that followed his arrival, directed all his conversation to his host.

"Did you hear, Charles, that Letty Lade persuaded Prinny to stand up with her at last Thursday's ball at the 'Ship'? Caused the devil of a flutter amongst the females present! Some of the ladies even left the room in high dudgeon."

Charles grinned appreciatively and turned to Henrietta, "Society does not approve of Lady Lade – she swears like a trooper but she's a devilish fine horsewoman! And," he added, "almost as gifted with the ribbons as her husband – Sir John drives the Prince of Wales' coach for him, you know, and manages his stables."

Henrietta looked her amazement; indeed there was more to follow to astound her – it seemed that the circle around the heir to the throne of England conducted itself in a manner totally opposed to that which had obtained at Versailles before poor Louis' downfall. Here, indeed, was an informality that would have been totally unacceptable to the French Court.

Frowning at Charles's polite inclusion of the young boy in the conversation, who, to his eyes, merited no such courtesy, Hugo continued, "By Jove, Charles, you should have been in Brighton last week. You never saw such a sight! There was George Hanger, scarlet in the face – with a jockey on his back – a jockey, booted and spurred, if you please – racing across the Steine against a fat bullock!"

"Good God! Don't tell me he won?"

Hugo laughed, "The bets had to be called off, for the bullock was distracted by the crowd that had gathered and couldn't be brought to the finish! I thought his Royal Highness would die of laughing."

As Henrietta listened, entranced, she rapidly formed the opinion that her new cousin, however disagreeable his manner to her might be, was undoubtedly a member of the raffish circle which appeared to surround King George's successor; how her brother would have enjoyed his company!

It was after the butler had placed a decanter of port on the table and left the room, that Charles dispatched his young guest to the library, saying in an authoritative voice, "You will find our talk of local affairs devilish dull I fear, young Philip! Look around the shelves and find yourself a book to amuse you!" When the door had closed behind Henrietta, Charles turned to Hugo, one eyebrow raised quizzically, "Well, what do you think? A strange story, is it not?"

"Quite unbelievable!" was the flat reply. "Good God, if John Brandon had married and raised a family, why the devil should he have kept it from his relations? More likely he fathered a child on some French fille de joie, that's what I would expect of him from all accounts. And now she plans to make use of the war to further her son's future – no chance of investigating his antecedents at present!"

Charles pushed the decanter towards his guest and said reflectively, "You may be right – yet there's something about the boy – an air of innocence – if there's some trickery about the claim, I believe he's not aware of it. And yet, I have the notion that he is concealing something." He paused and then continued with a faint smile, "You may as well know now, for the announcement will be in the Gazette in a few days, that your felicitations are in order. Your cousin, Louise, has only yesterday consented to become my wife!"

He encountered an incredulous stare from his guest, "Good God, never knew the wind stood in that quarter! I'd no notion you had a tendre for my little cousin." Then, realizing that he was becoming guilty of over-stepping the bounds of politeness, he added hastily, "My congratulations, Charles. I wish you happy!"

"Thank you, Hugo, I believe we shall suit." There was no sign of the ardent lover on his countenance and Hugo Brandon wondered what lay behind that faintly bored manner. He found Charles Gresham something of an enigma. Why had he extended his patronage to this young upstart? Better by far, he thought, if the brat had been left penniless, unconscious even, in some alleyway in Shoreham.

Bidding his guest farewell at the front door later that evening, Charles recollected Hugo's nephew, now on holiday from Eton and a young gentleman of an enterprising nature. "Send George over tomorrow," he suggested, "it must be deucedly dull here for a boy of Philip's age."

Hugo laughed shortly, "Certainly, if you have no objection to having your peace entirely cut up. Never knew such a boy for getting into scrapes. Keeps a pet stoat and let it loose in the kitchens last week – caused the devil of a row!"

Charles smiled reminiscently, "I've had plenty of midshipmen of that variety under my command! I believe I shall survive."

Despite the fears that haunted her night and day for the safety of her brother, Henrietta found that she was enjoying her unexpected stay at Gresham Place. She delighted in the rambling old house and its furnishings of a pleasantly faded elegance held a greater degree of comfort and informality than anything comparable in France. There was, she found, a considerable difference. There the houses of the wealthier circles of society contained furniture of a more elaborate and decorated style, gilded and inlaid. Here, polished oak predominated, although some more recent pieces were of carved mahogany and rosewood.

The following day, she accompanied Sir Charles upon a further visit to the stables and was introduced to several of the horses regarding them with interest from over the doors of their loose boxes. On their return to the house they heard the sound of horses' hooves in the drive and soon after, as they were nearing the front door, George Brandon arrived. Followed by his groom, a dark, stockily built boy of about sixteen astride a well-bred chestnut came into view. Springing from his mount and throwing the reins to his man, he strode up to Charles, his hand extended in the friendliest of manners, exclaiming, "A capital invitation, sir, for I have been bored to tears!" He then seized Henrietta's hand in his and shook it vigorously, saying as he did so, "By Jove, I envy you – escaping from France – what a lark it must have been."

Striving to conceal her involuntary wince at his strong grip on her fingers, Henrietta retorted wryly, with what she hoped was an air of nonchalance "Well, yes, it had its moments of excitement." She cast an appraising glance at the youth but found nothing in his frank, ingenuous countenance to alarm her.

During the luncheon that followed directly upon his arrival, George cross-examined Henrietta with unconcealed relish upon every detail of her flight. Laughing heartily at her description of the perilous moment when a national guardsman had stuck his bayonet amongst the cabbages missing her foot by inches. He seemed quite unable to comprehend the real dangers of her situation. He then proceeded to entertain them with a series of anecdotes concerning the last half at Eton, at the same time doing ample justice to the well-laden table. Henrietta, listening to him with a mixture of horror and fascination, felt from time to time the colour rise in her cheeks at some of his warmer stories and hoped fervently that her companions were not aware of her embarrassment. At the conclusion of the repast, Charles suggested to his companions that they might care to try their hand at fishing – perch and carp abounded in the lake and there was, he said, every chance that their efforts would prove successful.

Relieved that the projected pastime for the afternoon was one with which she was familiar since her childhood, Henrietta nodded happily to the two enquiring faces turned towards her and professed herself to be delighted to take part in a sport to which she declared herself to be addicted. Some time was spent in the selection of suitable rods and the choice of bait that would be most efficacious in tempting their quarry but finally the two young Brandons set forth in complete amity for the lake, which lay upon the farther side of the spinney beyond the pleasure gardens. It had become a remarkably hot day, the sun beating down from a cloudless sky, and it was not long before both young people found it necessary to remove their coats and waistcoats and cast off their cravats. So, by mid-afternoon, it was in shirts and breeches that they were seated a short distance apart on the northern bank of the lake, contentedly trying their luck and adding to the growing catch of quite reasonably sized fish in the basket. Perhaps the incident that followed would have occurred in any case, given time: fishing, for George, was hardly a sport which sufficed to employ all his abounding energy. However that might or might not have been, the advent on this peaceful scene of the two schoolboy sons of one of Charles' tenant farmers was the signal for an abrupt change of occupation.

Rupert and James Cope, coming along the lakeside from the direction of the Home Farm, greeted George Brandon with enthusiasm. Having been introduced in an airy fashion by George to the stranger, whom he described as being a fellow just arrived from that blood-soaked revolution in France, they dutifully admired the catch and, viewing the youthful foreigner with a suspicious eye, pronounced fishing to be a deucedly dull business. A suggestion that a swim in the lake would be very much more to their liking was vociferously agreed to by George who, instantly throwing aside his rod, began to unbutton his shirt.

Henrietta, appalled by the turn of events, stood up hastily, saying in a firm voice that as far as she was concerned swimming in such muddied and brackish water would be beyond anything disagreeable, and announced her intention of an immediate return to the house. As she uttered these words, she saw with alarm total disbelief on the three faces turned towards her. Rupert, the elder of the Cope brothers, a fair-haired giant of a boy, exchanged a wicked grin with his brother and said loudly, "Never heard of a Frog that didn't like the water!" This witticism was greeted by convulsive laughter by James, and George, who had at first felt some obligation to support his host's guest, found himself unable to keep a straight face and let out a whoop of mirth. It did not take Henrietta more than a moment to realize that three such adversaries would not have the slightest difficulty in forcing her into the water if they so desired, and she began hastily to pick up her discarded garments. It was too late! With one accord her companions moved to encircle her, their faces alight with mischief and that wish to torment so distressingly prevalent amongst young males, and advanced towards her. With a desperate lunge, she threw her coat over James's head and thrust past him, dodging George, who made a grab at her arm. She heard the sound of tearing cloth and fled panic-stricken up the path by which they had come. There came

38

cries of "Gone away!" and "Tally Ho!" and she heard behind her the thud of feet in hot pursuit.

Charles pushed his chair away from the writing table and, leaning back, stretched out his long legs and clasped his hands behind his head. He gave a heavy sigh and gazed out of the window filled with disgust that irksome estate business should have kept him indoors on such a glorious afternoon. How different his life had been before he had been obliged to resign his commission – no doubt the Navy would soon be playing an ever more active part in the war and he was to have no part in it. He stirred restlessly, brooding upon the follies of Prinny's boon companions in Brighton with whom Hugo consorted. One could not but be amused at their antics – and yet it was a sobering thought that his future monarch appeared to prefer the company of such fribbles, even to be more interested in the cut and colour of uniforms than in the tactics of warfare. Putting aside these reflections, he thought of his young guests down by the lake and, envying them their carefree existence, decided to pay them a visit and see if the fish were rising. He crossed the gardens, then, as he traversed the track which skirted the wood, he heard shouts ahead of him. Rounding a bend in the pathway, he suddenly encountered a slim figure, running headlong, who charged straight into his arms and would have fallen had he not clasped the slight body to him. He could feel pounding heart-beats through the thin shirt pressed against his chest and looked thoughtfully down at the head of dishevelled curls tickling his chin, his eyebrows raised.

Henrietta's only sensation was one of relief. She clutched at Charles's coat with urgent hands and looking up at him, eyes wide with fright, exclaimed, "Help me, sir! D-don't let them catch me!" Before Charles could discover the meaning of these cryptic words, her pursuers came into view, George in the lead, closely followed by the Cope brothers, all emitting various hunting cries and clearly in the best of spirits.

"Well done, sir! Headed him off!" George, his face red and perspiring, beamed at Charles.

James explained with a grin, "We can't let a Froggie miss a swim on such a lovely day, sir!"

Charles looked around him at the eager faces, then down at the apprehensive one so close to his own. He loosened his hold and gently detaching the clutching fingers from his sleeve, said lightly, "Can't allow you to ruin my coat, dear boy. My man, Morton, wouldn't care for that, y'know."

Henrietta flushed and straightened up, muttering in a determined voice, "I won't swim, sir – and no-one shall make me!"

Charles, observing now the torn sleeve, the slim, bare arm visible at the shoulder, frowned and said brusquely, "And why the devil should you swim?" Then, addressing her three tormentors, who had begun to look considerably aggrieved at being deprived of their prey, he added pleasantly, "I came to suggest a visit to the stables, George, – bought a three-year-old last week, a prime bit of blood and bone. Come and see what you think of him." No better diversion could have been suggested: Charles Gresham was well-known in the neighbourhood as a first-class judge of horseflesh and George could not but be flattered to have his opinion sought; there was an immediate and enthusiastic move towards the stables, the prospective immersion in the lake of the foreign visitor quite forgotten.

Henrietta found herself left alone on the path, and as soon as she was certain that the stable party were out of sight, sank down onto a fallen log at the side of the pathway, finding her legs strangely unwilling to support her. It was proving more difficult than she had expected to sustain her masculine role and she acknowledged to herself that she must endeavour to present herself at her grandfather's house as soon as possible and there end her masquerade. Conscious of a certain reluctance to leave Charles Gresham's protection, she wondered what he would think of her when he learned of her true identity. It had been strangely tempting to confide in him for there was a real kindness about him and he inspired trust. But, if he knew her age and sex, that must change his attitude towards her and she would be, after all, completely in his power. It was a frightening thought, and she resolved that, come what may, she must continue in her present role.

That evening after dinner, when the tea-tray had been brought in and the cups of tea duly poured out, Henrietta sat a little forward in her chair and began diffidently, "Sir – I believe –" then stopped short, scarcely knowing how to continue and found herself being surveyed lazily from beneath lifted brows. Her host made no effort to prompt her and there was something disconcerting in his dispassionate gaze.

All the remainder of that day since the departure of the ebullient George, she had been conscious of Charles's gentle cross-examination about her life in France. It had been difficult at times to answer his questions and it had only been by the exercise of all her wits and the substitution of Philip's boyhood for her own that she believed she had avoided giving away inadvertently her own identity. How fortunate that her mother's admiration for Mary Wollstonecraft's educational theories had resulted in Henrietta's comprehensive schooling. At least she would not betray herself by lack of familiarity with classical languages, history and other subjects commonplace for any schoolboy but universally considered unsuitable and unnecessary for girls.

She began again, "I believe, sir, that I should trespass no longer on your hospitality. If it would not be too much to ask –" she hesitated, "Perhaps you would be kind enough to advance me some funds so that I may travel to my grandfather's house." Before he could reply, she added hastily, "That is, of course, if you would trust me to repay you, sir."

Charles examined the young face regarding him earnestly, the brown eyes meeting his gaze squarely, and was conscious of a certain tenseness in his companion's attitude. Observing his guest's hands clenched tightly on the arms of the chair, he replied affably, "When you leave here for Lord Hartfield's house, my dear Philip, my carriage shall convey you there. However, before that happens I would wish you to make the acquaintance of your aunt, Lady Sedley, and her daughter."

"The lady you will marry, sir?"

"Yes – she will wish to meet you while you are here. And Lady Sedley will know whether Lord Hartfield is residing in Gloucestershire at present."

"What is she like – Lady Sedley?" Henrietta enquired, striving to achieve an air of nonchalance; she was rapidly becoming more and more uneasy at the prospect of meeting any further relations while still masquerading as a boy.

Before he replied, Charles took a pinch of snuff in a leisurely manner and looked at her thoughtfully, "A proud, ambitious woman – dotes on her son," he said shortly and added with a smile, "Miss Sedley has quite a different character – you will like Louise."

Henrietta nodded her head vigorously, "Indeed, if you say so, sir – I don't doubt it." As she spoke, she thought to herself hopefully, that, if this Miss Sedley should prove to be someone that she could trust, she might be able to confide in her.

CHAPTER 3

Louise Sedley sat gazing into space, her hand poised above the virgin sheet of writing paper. At last she wrote "Dearest Charlotte . . .", then paused again, caressing her cheek with the feathered tip of her pen, lost in a pleasant daydream. It had been her intention to inform her dear friend, Miss Charlotte Maitland, of the exciting news of her betrothal but it was essential to find the right words to convey a sufficiently romantic description of the secret love she believed her future husband to have nourished for her all these years. Charlotte, she knew, would enter into all her feelings on the subject, not like Mama who took a sadly prosaic view of life.

It was Lady Sedley who entered the morning room at that moment, a letter in her hand and upon her face an expression of satisfaction. "Dear child, such a delightful invitation!" She sat down near Louise, her normally severe countenance softened by a fond smile as she contemplated the charming picture that her daughter presented with her golden curls falling each side of her face and cascading down her back. "Charles has sent a note inviting us to dine at Gresham Place today. He writes of a surprise – can it be that he has purchased the *Ring*! Oh my dear Louise, how glad I am that your brother will be here to join in the festivities. He will be returning home this morning."

While expressing her pleasure with sparkling eyes at the invitation, Louise could not help feeling that Francis would add little to the gaiety of the occasion. Taking after his father rather than his mother's side of the family, Francis Sedley's passion in life was sport: fox-hunting was his great love and his days were spent in country pursuits. Not for him the pleasures of the Season except under duress. He had little time for the ladies and the awkwardness of his manner did not make him a favourite amongst the fair sex.

"Your pale pink muslin for tonight, my love – or perhaps the white embroidered gauze? – I believe I shall lend you my pearls!" Lady Sedley reflected seriously upon these weighty matters, frowning thoughtfully.

Her daughter was scarcely attending. She thought shyly how strange it was to think that she was to marry a man of whom, inspite of their earlier acquaintance, she knew so little and looked forward with pleasurable excitement to the evening. No doubt, he would, that evening, reveal to her and to the world something of the love for her that he had concealed for so long.

A commotion in the hall, a loud voice and jovial laughter announced the return of Mr Francis Sedley to the parental home following a week's absence visiting friends in Gloucestershire. He strode into the room, whip in hand, two excited spaniels leaping at his heels. Kissing his mother and sister affectionately he then flung himself down onto an armchair and demanded to be told the latest news.

Lady Sedley, adjusting the frills of her cap which had been cast awry by such a wholehearted embrace, smiled fondly at her son and announced in a voice of great satisfaction, "My dear, Charles Gresham has offered for your sister and has been accepted by her. The announcement will be appearing shortly in the Gazette ."

"Well I'll be damned! I beg your pardon, Mama." Francis's countenance had lit up as he turned his ruddy-complexioned face towards Louise and exclaimed enthusiastically, "Excellent news! Best pair of hands in the county and a bruising rider to hounds, you couldn't have done better, little sister."

Even Lady Sedley felt a shade of irritation at this inapposite comment and Louise, flushing angrily, retorted, "As if I care for such things. Really Francis, how can you be so lacking in proper feeling?"

Her brother, however, was unrepentant, "Wouldn't like to see you married to a skirter – a man who's good with horses will make a good husband."

Lady Sedley, foreseeing the start of an undignified quarrel, intervened quickly, "I am pleased you are returned today, Francis, for we

44

are to dine at Gresham Place." She observed her son's dusty top-boots and breeches with disfavour and added repressively, "You had best ring for Richards, and change your garments for some more suited to a lady's drawing-room!"

Her son grinned not in the least discomposed. Getting to his feet, he ruffled his sister's hair and, whistling to the dogs to follow him, removed his tall, raw-boned person from their presence and was soon heard mounting the stairs two at a time, shouting for his valet.

Henrietta, having used her best efforts to present a neat appearance inspite of the meagre resources of her wardrobe, entered the drawing-room well in advance of the arrival of the guests. She found her host, a vision of sartorial splendour, standing before the window gazing out. He turned on hearing her footsteps and subjected her to a slow scrutiny through his quizzing glass as she approached him. She looked up at him as she drew near and said anxiously, "Will I do, sir? This coat – it is wretchedly shabby – is it not?"

There was a gleam of a smile in his eyes as he replied in a grave tone, "Quite shocking!" Then, letting his glass drop, he added, "And your cravat! My dear Philip, it is nothing short of a disaster!"

Henrietta went across to the large gilt-framed looking-glass over the mantel-piece and stood on tip-toe to inspect the offending article of clothing. Charles came to stand behind her and taking her shoulders, turned her around towards him, tilted up her chin, and began to rearrange the crumpled cravat. She stood still, looking confidingly up into his face as with deft fingers he adjusted the bow of starched muslin, at the same time very conscious of his closeness to her. Having finished his handiwork, he remained for a moment staring down at her with an expression that she found impossible to read: there seemed to be amusement in his face and something besides. For one instant she felt faintly uncomfortable – then he turned away and sat down to await his guests.

He stood up and came forward when, shortly afterwards, the butler opened the door with a flourish and announced the arrival of Sir William and Lady Sedley, Miss Sedley and Mr Francis Sedley, in a voice that managed to convey, by some subtle modulation of its tones, that the news of his employer's betrothal had already reached the servant's hall. Henrietta, masked by Charles's tall person, rose to her feet from the corner of the sofa where she had been sitting and waited hopefully. Having greeted his guests in a calm and civil manner and obtained a shy smile from Louise as he kissed her hand, Charles turned, and gesturing towards Henrietta, desired Lady Sedley to make the acquaintance of his young guest recently arrived from France and residing in his house; adding with a smile, "You see Lady Sedley, my young companion claims to be your cousin, Philip Brandon!"

Coming forward to make her bow, Henrietta approached a tall, thin woman, fashionably dressed with aristocratically aquiline features, and an expression of extreme surprise mingled with disbelief in her prominent eyes. At the same time she observed with a fleeting glance the astonished faces of a heavily-built older man wearing an old-fashioned wig and a tall, bony-faced youth, both peering over Lady Sedley's shoulder; at her side stood a small, fair-haired girl of about her own age – a girl of extraordinary beauty, with large, soft, appealing eyes and enchantingly delicate features. It was the girl who was the first to speak. Louise stretched out her hand in a friendly gesture, saying, in an expressive voice, "Why, Sir Charles – so this is to be your surprise! You poor boy – Cousin Philip, I should say – what terrible times these are for your country."

Lady Sedley, having mastered her astonishment and permitted Henrietta to kiss her hand – an action which the latter performed with an air of embarrassment which rather served to confirm her apparent lack of years – remarked austerely that she would prefer to hold some conversation with young Master Brandon before committing herself to some relationship of which she had been, until that moment, completely ignorant. Seating herself on the sofa, she indicated to Henrietta that she should occupy the place beside her.

It was at this moment that Hugo and George Brandon were ushered into the room, the former looking not best pleased to see before him a gathering which had every appearance of being a family party: a party, moreover, which seemed to have at its centre the very same young person whom he was determined should not be acknowledged in any way as a legitimate member of his family. They crossed the room to join the group by the fireplace and Hugo, bending down to pay his respects to Lady Sedley, murmured in her ear, "So you have met your Cousin John's by-blow – I cannot think what Charles is about." It was said in a low voice, but Henrietta was near enough to catch the final word. She flushed angrily but before she could say anything, Hugo moved away quickly to speak to Louise and she was obliged to speak to Lady Sedley, who, to do her justice, was looking at Henrietta more with pity than disgust. Lady Sedley, having evidently decided that it was beneath her dignity to enquire too closely into this boy's antecedents, confined her questions to the means by which Henrietta had escaped from France and, most particularly, how she had become acquainted with Sir Charles Gresham. Lady Sedley's eyebrows rose ever higher as she heard of the rescue at Shoreham. Privately, she hoped that her future son-in-law was not in the habit of making such quixotic gestures. She could not avoid feeling that he had betrayed a lightness of mind and lack of judgment which she considered quite deplorable and she looked across at him, where he was standing in conversation with her husband, with decided disapproval.

Louise had greeted Hugo's arrival at her side with pleasure. She was fond of her good-looking, rakish cousin and looked forward to receiving his felicitations on her forthcoming marriage: she was not to be disappointed.

"Charles is a devilishly lucky man!" he told her, "I had no idea – must have suddenly struck him that such a jewel lived so close by."

Louise opened her lovely eyes wide, "Oh no, Hugo!" she murmured, "A long-standing attachment," she shook her head mysteriously as if she could have said more if she had wished to do so.

Meanwhile Sir William and Francis Sedley were deep in conversation with Charles. George had described to them in glowing terms the most recent addition to the Gresham stables and it was only the announcement that dinner was served that put an end to such an absorbing topic. At the dinner-table Henrietta regretfully found herself seated at the foot of the table and as far as was possible from Sir Charles. However, as he had placed the Sedley ladies one on each side of him, at least it also removed her from their immediate presence. She had a strong feeling that they were far more likely to subject her to a detailed scrutiny than were the men and she was not entirely confident of being able to carry off successfully her impersonation at close quarters. At first she was able to enjoy the succession of dishes in peace for her neighbours at the table. Sir William on the one hand and George Brandon on the other, had continued their equine conversation, drawing both Hugo and Francis into the discussion. She still marvelled at the substantial nature of English meals – the fillet of veal with mushrooms and high sauce, the pigeons and asparagus, roasted sweetbreads and apricot tart as well as an array of syllabubs and jellies.

Sir William, a kindly man, suddenly took it into his head to address a remark to the young boy beside him, "Devilish goings-on in your country, my boy!" he shook his head and added loudly, with all the contempt of a loyal subject of his Majesty King George the Third. "Cut off poor old Louis' head – shockin' affair – believe they're murderin' all manner of people! Don't know what things are coming to these days. But the French, y'know – can't expect much from *them*, eat frogs and snails, so I'm told – but you'd know all about that, I dare say."

Henrietta found it difficult to make a sensible reply to this chauvinistic outburst, and, torn between amusement and irritation, nearly choked over the mouthful of wine that she had been about to swallow. A friendly thump on the back from George did nothing to restore her composure and feeling all eyes at the table fixed on her, she said defiantly, "There are many evil persons in France, sir but there are many, likewise, who are good and kind."

Lady Sedley said in a quelling voice, "Such conduct can not be condoned by decent people!" as she looked around her.

There was something so absurdly inappropriate in this comment on the recent terrible events in that poor country that Henrietta looked helplessly at Charles and saw in his eye a spark of amusement as he said, "Quite so, Lady Sedley – a dashed ill-bred set of fellows over there!"

Lady Sedley, helping herself generously to a dish of mushrooms, remarked repressively in a low voice, "I am at a loss, my dear Charles, to understand how you came to invite this young person to stay under your roof. It is not, I believe, a connection that I shall wish to continue."

"But Mama, such a young boy!" Louise interposed eagerly, smiling with approval at her betrothed, "How could Sir Charles have abandoned him – what horrors he must have witnessed, what scenes of misery endured!"

Charles looked from the one face, alight with interest and compassion, to the other, whose set lips proclaimed a barely concealed irritation. "The boy was without money or papers, Lady Sedley. If he were indeed to prove to be related to your family I should have felt myself sadly remiss if I had not extended my hospitality to him."

"No money or papers!" A triumphant gleam was in Lady Sedley's eye, "I fear you have been hoodwinked, sir. An impostor certainly! No kinsman of mine would travel in such a harum-scarum manner." and, having roundly dismissed 'Philip Brandon's' claims, she turned the conversation to more agreeable matters.

When the ladies had retired to the drawing-room, Charles had suggested, in a tone which had firmly indicated the absolute necessity of compliance, that George and Henrietta should remove themselves to the garden and there beguile themselves with an archery match on the lower lawn instead of enduring the boredom of the older generation's conversation. It was not a recommendation that found favour with George. At sixteen, he considered himself quite old enough to enjoy the delights of masculine company uninhibited by the presence of the ladies. He followed Henrietta out onto the lawn with an expression of disgust and during the following half-hour gave vent to his offended feelings by treating his unskilful opponent's efforts with the greatest contempt. By the time that this uneven contest had ended and Henrietta and her disgruntled companion had entered the drawing-room, the gentlemen had rejoined the ladies and were requesting Miss Sedley to entertain the company by playing the pianoforte, at which she was an accomplished performer. Little persuasion was required. Louise was fond of music, nor was she averse to sitting at the instrument, well aware that the many branched candelabra cast a becoming light upon her face, while Sir Charles turned the pages of music for her.

She had just commenced a spirited rendering of a minuet, her audience all attention, when a footman entered the room and addressed a few words to his master in a low voice. Sir Charles, standing beside the instrument, permitted a faint expression of surprise to appear on his face as he nodded his head in assent, and bent forward to turn a page. Henrietta, who had found her eyes drawn to the betrothed couple, wondered vaguely what had been said to provoke just that look. She did not have to wait long for the answer. The double doors of the drawing-room were thrown open, the footman announced in a loud voice, "Mr Philip Brandon!" and a tall, handsome young man in a long great-coat, with romantically flowing, dark locks, appeared in the doorway, looking around at the assembled company from beneath angrily frowning brows.

The silence that followed was broken by a cry of delight and, before the startled eyes of Sir Charles's guests, Henrietta flew across the room and threw her arms around the stranger's neck, kissing him fervently on both cheeks. He, however, remained frowning down at her joyful face, his hands on her shoulders, saying in a voice stiff with disapproval, "My God, child, what the devil are you doing here?"

Louise was the first to find her voice; gazing wide-eyed with astonishment at the new arrival, she exclaimed, "If you are Philip Brandon, sir, then who is this boy?"

Hastily Henrietta turned to face her, pressing the young man's arm warningly, "You must forgive the deception, Miss Sedley." She tried to appear nonchalant, "This is my elder brother, Philip, whom I thought I had lost, and I – I am really his younger brother, Henry Brandon!"

There was a startled pause, then Sir Charles spoke from his place by the piano, "I believe you should more justly say Miss Henrietta Brandon," he said pensively, an underlying amusement in his voice.

CHAPTER 4

Lady Sedley broke the scandalized silence. Raising her lorgnette to her eyes, she surveyed Henrietta from head to foot with the utmost disapproval and pronounced in icy tones, "Quite disgraceful! A most shocking want of conduct!" Whether this censure was directed solely at the young girl was not entirely clear for the affronted glance that she cast at her future son-in-law disclosed a mind filled with the gravest suspicions.

Her husband, who had been standing beside his son, warming his coat-tails before the fire, was heard to mutter in his off-spring's ear, "Dammit, Francis! Can't make head nor tail of this – devilish queer set-out, what!" To which came the reply, accompanied by a broad grin, "Why Papa, It's plain enough! Our so-called cousin's sailing under false colours! So here's a to-do – and one that Mama will not care for one little bit!"

Meanwhile Louise, still seated at the piano, looked up at Charles, a slight frown marring the smoothness of her lovely brow, "*Henrietta*, Sir Charles?"

"Yes, my love, desperate times require desperate measures, it's not the first time that a masculine disguise has proved necessary for a female to escape from France. Miss Brandon will need all your support now, I'm sure." He seemed calm and faintly amused which served somewhat to reassure her, although she still looked shocked.

As he crossed the room to greet the new arrival, Hugo Brandon stepped forward and murmured in his ear, "Damme, you're a devilish deep one, Charles – when and how did you find out the truth of her sex?"

He received no reply. All further comment was halted by an abrupt move on the part of the new Philip Brandon. Pushing his sister roughly aside, fists clenched, he advanced upon his approaching host. With barely suppressed anger, he demanded "Are you Sir Charles Gresham, sir?"

The young man's dark glittering eyes in a lean mobile face challenged Charles's calm blue ones. Observing him with amused surprise from beneath raised brows he replied courteously, "I have the honour to bear that name, sir, and am more than pleased to welcome you to my house."

This conciliatory reply did not, however, abate one jot of his questioner's belligerence. He almost spat out his next words, "I demand satisfaction, sir! – My God, my sister's honour! – How dared you, sir – an innocent young girl –" It seemed as if he was about to strike his host when his sister darted forward. Clutching his arm she demanded in round terms that he stop making a complete idiot of himself. She was so clearly both unafraid of her supposed ravisher and appalled by her brother's behaviour that he was obliged to pause, and in pausing he looked beyond the smiling Englishman and saw what appeared to him a being from some celestial sphere coming towards him.

Louise was a kind-hearted girl and, although at first understandably piqued at not receiving her fiancé's confidence concerning his guest, her pity was aroused by the young girl's plight. Perhaps at bottom she found it hard to believe that the worldly Sir Charles could have discovered any attractions in this boyish, commonsensical young person. She rose from her stool and came swiftly towards the group by the door, her hands outstretched to Henrietta and a smile upon her lips. This was the vision that Philip Brandon saw approaching. He was partially hidden by Charles's tall person and it was only as he fell back a pace that he was fully revealed to Louise. The discovery that this remarkably handsome young man was staring at her with undisguised admiration could not but be delightfully flattering and it was with a pleasurable feeling of her own merit that she took Henrietta's hands in hers, announcing softly, "My dear Miss Brandon, for so I must now call you, we must lose no time in restoring you to female attire for to have been forced to assume such a disguise must have been quite shocking for you – every sensibility must have been offended."

Miss Brandon, it seemed, did not feel the same urgency. Smiling at Louise she remarked cheerfully, "In truth, Miss Sedley, I shall feel quite sorry to change my breeches for petticoats!" Seeing Louise's horrified expression, she added with aplomb, "You can have no idea how delightfully free one feels without them." The only person present who appreciated this exchange was Sir Charles, who gave a discreet chuckle. Clearly Philip was not amused for, momentarily forgetting his desire for vengeance, he turned upon Henrietta with a scowl and bade her, in a very brotherly manner, mind her manners and have some regard for decorum.

"Well, yes, Philip, but you must apologize immediately to Sir Charles, for you are the one who has misunderstood everything – it is Sir Charles who has saved my life when I was attacked by robbers and if it had not been for him I should surely be dead. Moreover he has treated me with great kindness." She turned to Charles as she spoke and said to him in a mystified voice, "I did not think, sir, that you had discovered that I was a female!"

He did not reply. Contenting himself with smiling enigmatically down at her, he extended his hand to Philip, saying, "I am glad you are safely in England and can now take care of your sister – I believe I don't envy you the task!"

It had slowly dawned upon Philip that he had vastly misjudged the situation. Impossible to believe that this fashionably dressed Englishman, so calm and so assured, and with whom his sister seemed to be upon such easy terms, could have abducted her against her will and to have harboured evil designs upon her person. He had clearly misinterpreted the information that he had received from the innkeeper in reply to his enquiries on his arrival at Shoreham, but felt all the resentment that a young man must suffer at being obliged to admit his error in public – especially before this enchanting member of the fair sex who stood beside his sister. However, he took Charles's hand and said grudgingly, "It seems I owe you an apology, sir – I think you must comprehend my feelings – my misapprehension –"

It was at this point that Lady Sedley rose to her feet and approached them. At first outraged to discover that her daughter's betrothed had been harbouring a female under his roof and had had the effrontery to introduce this person to her innocent young daughter, she was rapidly comprehending that there was more to the affair than met the eye. It would be foolish to rush to conclusions which must inevitably lead to the termination of an engagement which had given her so much satisfaction. It was, moreover, excessively displeasing to her to be a mere spectator of these exchanges. She eyed Henrietta's garments with a shudder and turned to her host. "Sir Charles! An explanation, if you please."

"Lady Sedley, I am sure that I can rely upon your good nature to give your countenance to these two unfortunate people. You must understand that Miss Brandon's only hope of escape from France was to take upon herself the identity of her brother. May I now present to you the real Philip Brandon who claims to be your late cousin's son."

The elegant bow bestowed upon her by this good-looking young man, who kissed her hand with all the grace and charm of a native-born Frenchman, went far towards mollifying Lady Sedley's ruffled feelings. She even began to fancy that she could see some family likeness and bestowed a gracious smile upon Philip, saying in a civil voice, "These matters will have to be looked into, no doubt. I was too young to have much recollection of my poor cousin. However, I rejoice for you in your escape from those barbarians across the Channel." It was doubtful whether these unexceptionable sentiments were intended to include Henrietta. Indeed it seemed, for the moment at least, that Lady Sedley preferred to deny her existence. As she spoke the remaining members of the dinner-party had crowded round and a series of introductions in form began. A curt nod was all that was offered by Hugo but was offset by the genial greetings of Sir William and Francis. George, who had been regarding Henrietta with a kind of fascinated disgust, shook Philip's hand briefly and said in a gruff voice, "Welcome to England, sir!" It was the presentation of Miss Sedley that seemed to produce a disturbing effect upon the new arrival. As he raised Louise's hand to his lips, Lady Sedley said, with a warm smile directed at Sir Charles, "This dear child of ours has recently become betrothed to our host and neighbour, Sir Charles Gresham." The young man, retaining Louise's hand in his a fraction longer than mere politeness dictated, drew in his breath sharply and his eyes searched her face.

For her part, Louise bestowed upon him a brilliant smile, "Then we must be cousins, sir!" she murmured.

"Cousins, eh! Well, well, – we shall have to see about that!" Sir William seemed to have recovered from his astonishment. Recollecting his position as Justice of the Peace in the county, he continued in his bluff way, "Got papers and so forth, young man? No offence, what! – But you'll need proof, you know."

"Why, yes, sir – I understand perfectly." Philip drew from his pocket a roll of documents tied up with ribbon and presented them to Sir William. There was an audible sigh of relief from Henrietta.

"I think perhaps a move to your study, Charles?" Sir William was now clearly enjoying the situation and felt himself very much in command.

"Of course, sir!" His host conducted him through a door into the adjoining book-lined room, followed by Philip and a frowning Hugo. Francis and George, after a quick glance at the ladies, followed suit and the door was closed behind them.

Left alone with her new aunt and cousin, Henrietta's only feelings were those of intense relief. To know that her brother was safe and in England and, moreover, that he had brought with him papers to prove the legitimacy of their claim to be members of the Brandon family, far outweighed any sensation of discomfort. Being of a naturally sanguine nature, she felt confident that within a short time she would be able to conquer Lady Sedley's disapproval while her new cousin, Louise, appeared to be already well disposed towards her. She thrust her hands into her breeches pockets in an unconscious imitation of

George and crossed to the fireplace to stand before it, looking with shining eyes at her companions. It was not the most tactful of moves. Impossible for Lady Sedley to ignore this flagrant display of masculine habits and garments; a bashfulness of manner, a sense of shame at her abandonment of feminine modesty might have softened that lady's heart, as it was, she frowned repressively at Henrietta and sat down stiffly upon the sofa, indicating that Louise should take a seat.

Louise's mind was in a whirl. Thoughts fluttered in her head like a flock of birds. Sir Charles – so chivalrous – the handsome stranger, now almost certainly her cousin, and the flattering expression of admiration in his eyes – the boy who was now a girl – so fortunate that her chestnut curls set off her own blonde beauty – it all resembled the novels that she read so avidly. "Mama, our new cousins must surely now come and stay with us." she turned eagerly to her mother.

"My dear Louise," a frigid glance towards the fireplace accompanied her words, "there are many important matters, a great many, to be resolved before any such invitation can be offered. Your papa must first establish the validity of this 'claim'!" Her pronouncement of the word made it sound utterly spurious.

Henrietta was too happy to be offended by these imputations. She already liked all that she had seen of the English way of life, slight though that had been; delightful, too, to make the acquaintance of these English relations. She said confidently, "The good Sir William will know, I am sure, and I am so happy, so very, very happy to be here with my dear Philip."

In the study Sir William spread out the documents on a table, while Charles brought a heavy silver candelabra from the mantelpiece and set it beside the papers. Sir William, his spectacles perched upon his nose, bent forward and read in silence. The others crowded around him, striving to catch a view of a sentence here and there; only Philip stood apart. At length, having read slowly through the pages, he straightened up and cleared his throat, "Seems to be in order," he pronounced, "but some of it written in that damnable French lingo! Marriage lines, baptismal certificate, everything – have to be checked, of course, but I for one see no doubt of it!" He looked over his glasses at Philip, his brows, for a moment, drawn together, then his face cleared. He put out his hand and patted him on the shoulder, "Well I'm damned, a new cousin-in-law! Good God, what will old Hartfield say to all this I wonder!"

"With respect, Sir William, there's more to it than that!" Hugo, grim about the mouth, spoke with ill-concealed anger, "The papers may be in order but who is to say that this is the man to whom they refer. Why, he could have stolen them – the real Philip Brandon may be dead by now for all we know!"

Philip, furious, stepped forward, "Sir! Have a care! You doubt my word? If so, you shall answer to me for that!"

Sir Charles, snuffbox in hand, eyed the young men dispassionately, "Devil take it, no need to fly into the boughs!" He took a pinch of snuff and offered the box to Hugo, "Doubtless John Brandon spoke of his home and childhood to his children, stands to reason." He turned to Philip, "Can you remember any stories that only John Brandon's son would know? Something that would set all doubts at rest?"

"He spoke fondly of his old nurse – Armitage, he called her." Philip's face softened, "I remember he said he had a pony, called Cockrobin – he must have set great store by him, by all accounts – took a toss off him once and broke his collarbone." He looked fiercely at Hugo, "There's much else besides, but why the devil does it matter so much to *you* whether I am the real Philip Brandon?"

"Good God – don't you know?" Hugo, much shaken, was very pale now, "Only a matter of a title and a fortune!" He turned away and threw himself down onto a chair; even a stranger could not have failed to notice the striking likeness between the two furious faces.

Philip, astonished, looked around him and with a shrug enquired, "Of what does he speak? I don't understand. There is an elder brother, is there not?"

There was a chorus of voices. Sir William took up the tale and, amid a confusion of interjections, laid the facts before Philip. The young man was now the one to turn pale. Amazed, he looked around him, his face a comical mixture of delight and disbelief. "To come to this – after all the horrors in France – the knowledge that my life could be forfeit. It is incredible! Can it be true?" He seemed truly shaken and, perhaps for the first time, his auditors were conscious of the dangers from which this young man had so recently escaped.

Sir William, recollecting his wife and daughter who awaited them in the adjoining room, drew Charles aside, "Must join the ladies – what! Damme man, you said you had a surprise for us but I never expected anything like this – no more did you, I collect! But what's to become of these two – must have a word with you in the morning, my boy, when I've talked to her ladyship." He shook his head and added confidentially, "There's devilish trouble ahead, mark my words!"

Whether this remark referred to the reception anticipated by Sir William in the drawing-room or to the future of the refugees from France was not clear. In any event, he carried all off in a manner born of long practice by announcing immediately upon rejoining the ladies that it was high time that they were on their way home – "Can't be sure of the moon tonight, my lady. Call our carriage if you would be so kind, Charles."

"But, my dear Sir William, what is the result of your deliberations?" Lady Sedley interposed irritably with heightened colour, "Are these young people indeed my uncle's grand-children?"

"No doubt about it, my dear! No doubt at all! Puts young Hugo in a devil of a fix." He gave a genial smile to the young Brandons, now standing close together, "Talk of it more in the morning, eh – sort it all out then."

"Papa, may not Miss Brandon return with us?" Louise looked appealingly at her father, who after a swift glance at his wife's stony face, replied hastily, "Better wait until tomorrow, my dear, – sleep on it, what! Besides, she'll wish to be with her brother, no doubt."

"Oh yes, sir." Henrietta looked fondly at Philip, then added hastily, with an anxious glance at Charles, "That is – if Sir Charles is agreeable?"

"We impose upon you, sir." Her brother, signs of exhaustion beginning to be visible upon his countenance, spoke with embarrassment, "But I cannot for the life of me think what else to do –" He drew a hand wearily across his brow.

"No trouble, my dear fellow – a good night's sleep is what you need. As for your sister," Charles looked down at Henrietta with a decided gleam of amusement in his eyes, "I believe she will not be averse to another night as Master Brandon!"

CHAPTER 5

Lady Sedley had passed a restless night and woke the following morning with a strong sense of resentment. How regrettable, indeed, how inconvenient was the arrival in England of these young kinsmen. Nothing, she was determined, should be allowed to cast a shadow over dearest Louise's betrothal to their gallant neighbour. One had to admit that it was unfortunate that Sir Charles should have involved himself in their plight – Lady Sedley hoped devoutly that he would not prove to be a man who acted upon impulse – she shuddered at the thought and putting aside her cup of chocolate, rang for her maid, turning over in her mind the best way to cast a cloak of respectability over Henrietta Brandon's presence at Gresham Court. Certainly many distinguished female refugees had been obliged to conceal their identities in masculine attire – there was the Countess de Noailles received, after all, by no less a person than Mrs Fitzherbert into her own house in Brighton. But, and here, alas, lay the difference! She had not passed several days and, worse, nights in the un-chaperoned company of a man!

"My dear Julia, you have risen unconscionably early this morning!" Sir William, casting aside his napkin, stood up from the breakfast-table and observed with relief that his wife seemed to have regained her habitual composure, adding tactfully as he resumed his seat, "A great pleasure, my dear – not often blessed with your company at this hour."

"Never mind that, Sir William." Lady Sedley was in no mood for pretty speeches, "We shall have to invite them to stay. There must be no scandal of any kind."

"Scandal, eh, my lady? What scandal is that?" Sir William, surprised, paused in the act of conveying a cup of coffee to his lips.

"My dear sir," Lady Sedley helped herself to a thin slice of bread-and-butter and regarded Sir William with raised eyebrows, "If it should become known – and I say 'if' advisedly – that that young girl from France had spent three nights alone in Sir Charles's house – three nights un-chaperoned, as his mother is absent in Bath –" she added in parenthesis, "not only would Miss Brandon's reputation be ruined but it might well appear as a slight to our dear Louise in the eyes of the world."

At Gresham Court breakfast was proceeding in leisurely fashion. Philip, encouraged by the evident interest of his host in the political situation across the Channel, was recounting his experiences of the past months, while at the same time applying himself with enthusiasm to the food laid upon the table. "You see, sir, France is fast sliding into anarchy. The military defeats in the spring and the defection of Doumouriez to the Austrians have revived fears of foreign invasion and counter-revolution. The English are now hated as much as the Austrians and foreigners are closely watched by these *comités de surveillance*. Indeed, there are now many paid secret-agents throughout France."

Charles surveyed the young man with interest, "I am amazed you did not attempt to quit the country earlier?"

"My mother is half French, sir, and brought up in France, she believed that we were safe and feared to leave her homeland. Living quietly in a village where we were known and respected, she thought we would escape the hostility of the revolutionaries. You see, there have been so many rumours, sir, it has been hard to discover the truth. Marat was assassinated, as you may know, in July – it was fatal for the moderates – and the revolutionary committees are now, in effect, masters of life and death."

"If one can believe half one hears of events in Paris, it is hard to credit that any human beings, women even as well as men, could behave in so bestial a fashion."

Philip looked up, a frown creasing his brow, "Sir Charles, people who have been treated as animals will, alas, behave like animals."

"Good God, surely you cannot mean that you sympathize with them?"

"In fact, with the poor, I do." Philip set down his cup, his dark eyes aglow with the intensity of his emotions. Embarking on a spirited indictment of the regime prevailing in France before the revolution, he glanced towards the door, and stopped suddenly in mid-sentence, a frown appearing on his brow.

Henrietta stood in the doorway, for the first time most horribly conscious of the appearance she presented in masculine dress. Her brother was scowling at her not attempting to hide his disgust and it was with a faint flush in her cheeks that she looked at Sir Charles and said anxiously, "Good-morning, sir, I fear that I have overslept and am late."

Sir Charles, resisting the impulse to rise to his feet in the presence of a lady, indicated with a wave of his hand the laden table and said in a friendly voice, "You are by no means late. Help yourself and take a seat beside your brother." His attitude was so comfortingly the same as it had been before the revelations of the previous day that Henrietta was able to take her place in a reasonably composed manner and even managed to pronounce some unexceptionable remarks about the weather while she ate. There was, however, a hint of laughter in his courteous replies that made her look sharply at him, only to find that he was regarding her with an air of amiable attention.

The gentlemen's interrupted conversation re-commenced, and it was evident from Philip's remarks that, while condemning the violence of their actions, he had some sympathy with the aspirations of the revolutionaries. "You must understand, sir, that in former days the privileges of the nobility were immense. Only the *noblesse* could become ambassadors, only they could reach the highest office in the church or command regiments in the army. Worst of all for the people, the aristocracy were exempt from the *taille*, a tax which fell heavily upon the peasants. In addition the local *'seigneur'* imposed upon them the payment of feudal dues

"It is true, sir," Henrietta joined in eagerly, her eyes wide with indignation, "I have seen such abject poverty – men and women without shoes, children ragged and hungry even in the countryside – like scarecrows, sir."

Philip nodded, an expression of anger and contempt crossed his youthful face, "There was one day I shall never forget, sir. It happened when I was a boy, fifteen or sixteen years old. I was in Sèvres, through which the road between Paris and Versailles passes; two little girls were playing at the side of the road, watched by their mother. A farm wagon was trundling by when suddenly a coach-and-four, driven at breakneck speed, came into sight. As it slackened its pace, for there was scarce room to pass the wagon with the children beside the road, a man, painted and powdered, leaned out of the coach window, cursing and shouting to the coachman to put on all speed. The coach, horses at a gallop, drove straight upon the little girls. They had no time to run – they were mown down, sir! I shall never forget the expression of terror on their faces. Then, sir, as the coachman pulled his horses to a walk, appalled, I suppose, at what had occurred, the passenger appeared again at the window, looking back, and one could see it was the Marquis de Jouvain, the owner of a nearby estate, his face contorted with fury. He swore at his coachman for stopping, threw a few coins to the ground and ordered the coach to be driven on to Versailles with all speed! Sir, you can imagine the grief and bitterness of the mother – of the whole village – it goes without saying! When such a man as that went to the guillotine how could one feel pity?"

"The man was indeed a monster!" Sir Charles looked grave, then, observing the expression of remembered horror on Henrietta's face, he enquired by what means Philip had made his escape, determined to direct his companions' thoughts to a less painful subject.

"When I returned from shooting, our servants told me that they had received a warning that men were already on their way to arrest us, and that, thank God, Henrietta had already departed with Jeanne for Dieppe. Having collected together papers and what little money there was in the house, I was hidden by them in the barn that night beneath the hay while the house was searched."

Henrietta was following his words, wide-eyed, "The poor souls, how can we ever repay them?" she murmured.

Philip nodded, "Just so! It seems that inspite of our servants' protestations the house was ransacked and such belongings as we possessed of any worth were taken. The following night I left home secretly on horseback – escorted by André, who lent me his son's papers. We reached Dieppe without incident and I got a passage with the 'Marie Claire' like you."

"Thank God, Mama was safe in Switzerland." Henrietta sighed, then, with a return to her customary cheerfulness, she added with a mischievous smile, "How she would be scandalized if she could see me now, sir, for inspite of her advanced views on the rights of woman, she would not approve of such immodesty as masculine dress."

It was half-an-hour later that sounds of voices were heard in the hall and the butler, opening the breakfast-parlour door, announced that Sir William and Lady Sedley had called and were desirous of seeing his master. "Show them in here, Cummings." Sir Charles, rising to his feet, betrayed none of the surprise that such an early morning call might have warranted.

"Good-morning, Charles! Urgent matters required this intrusion!" Lady Sedley swept into the room, followed by her reluctant spouse. Her gaze moved to Henrietta, who, like her brother, had also risen and a spasm of something akin to pain crossed her ladyship's face as she perceived once more the offending small-clothes; with an effort she murmured, "Good-morning – Henrietta – good-morning to you, Philip!"

"Some refreshment, ma'am," Charles's hand was on the bell-pull, "A glass of Madeira – some ratafia?" but his offer of hospitality was declined.

"This is not a social call, my dear Charles." Lady Sedley said bluntly as, comfortably seated, she began to reveal the object of their visit. "Sir William and I have arrived at a satisfactory solution of the present difficulties that confront us all!"

She glanced towards her husband, who nodded his head admiringly, saying, "Quite so, quite so, my dear. Deuced clever thinking."

Her ladyship continued, "When we return home shortly, Miss Brandon and Mr Philip Brandon must accompany us and stay at the Grange with our family until there has been time to acquaint my Uncle Hartington with the news of their arrival. Indeed of their existence." She added thoughtfully, "No doubt, at that point, other arrangements will be made, for, after all, if and when the documents are proved correct, and Sir William seems confident that they will be, then Philip will be his grandfather's heir." She paused, her gaze resting for a moment upon each of the faces surrounding her, "Now for the tale that the rest of the world shall hear! It will be known that the *real* Philip Brandon was the first arrival at your house, Charles, and that Miss *Henrietta* Brandon only arrived last night to join her brother beneath your roof – thus," she continued, "no scandal can attach to the presence of Henrietta in this house and it need not become known that she had passed several nights here in these –" she hesitated, then continued grimly, "– in these unfortunate garments which, it seems, she was obliged to adopt. Perhaps, Charles, you will be able to instruct your servants to report accordingly to any who may enquire." She sat back, looking around her triumphantly as might a general surrounded by his commanders in the field.

Philip was the first to speak, his handsome face alight with gratitude, "Lady Sedley, I thank you with all my heart. I have been greatly exercised in my mind how to preserve my sister's reputation!" A muffled sound came from Henrietta which sounded remarkably like 'Fustian' but she was clearly relieved to hear that their immediate future seemed assured.

"A masterly plan, ma'am, may I felicitate you. All shall follow as you suggest." Charles, offering his snuff-box to his future father-in-law, added, with a re-assuring smile to the young Brandons, "Miss Sedley, I am sure, will welcome you with the greatest kindness and certainly cannot fail to be enthralled by your tales of heroism and of dangers overcome!"

After such a welcome invitation, it took little time for Henrietta and Philip to collect together their few possessions and to be ready. Lady Sedley had had the foresight to bring with her a voluminous cloak and this was cast about Henrietta's shoulders, concealing her person in its entirety. Philip, dazed at the prospect of rank and wealth so suddenly opened before him, was impatient to be gone but Henrietta had enjoyed her brief excursion into the masculine world and it was with a feeling of some regret that she clasped Charles's hand in farewell, saying, "I owe you a great debt, sir, for your kindness – for my life itself, indeed, when you rescued me." She looked up into his face, her eyes sparkling mischievously and added, "So much trouble I have caused you – I am sure you must be thankful to be rid of me."

"On the contrary, Miss Brandon," he replied politely, handing her up into the closed carriage, "it has been a pleasure to have been of assistance to you and if I am thankful for your departure it is only because I fear, if you had remained longer under my roof, you would have contrived to beat me at chess, and that, I confess, would have had a sadly lowering effect upon my self-esteem."

Although their estates were adjoining, the distance between Gresham Court and the Grange was all of four miles by the winding country lanes. Henrietta and Philip caught glimpses of growing crops and grazing sheep before the carriage turned in at a pair of open gates and continued up a short drive to stop before the front door of a pleasant brick-built house with tall sash-windows and roses growing upon its walls. Upon their arrival, Henrietta had hardly set foot upon the ground, where an assortment of spaniels and a setter were waiting to greet her, than she was hustled through the door by Lady Sedley, past the attendant footman and up the stairs which mounted directly from the flagged hall into the regions above. She had a pleasing impression of light and the scent of roses and beeswax, and found herself ushered into a charming bedroom with pretty chintz curtains and a tester bed.

"There!" Lady Sedley, a gleam of satisfaction in her eyes, sank into a chair by the window and surveyed Henrietta complacently. Henrietta, looking around her with interest, crossed to the window and gazed down into a walled garden, where flowerbeds bordered a lawn and a rustic seat was partially concealed by drifts of rambling roses. "I shall send for Pearson, my dresser, Henrietta – she can be thoroughly relied upon – and instruct her to find all that you require from Louise's wardrobe. How fortunate that you girls are much of a size."

As she spoke there was a tap on the door and Louise, entering the room, flew at once to her new cousin and embraced her fervently. "How truly delightful!" There was such real warmth in her greeting that Henrietta's face glowed with pleasure and she began to feel she might indeed be happy here in this comfortable house, for until that moment, feelings of rebellion against Lady Sedley's high-handed ways were simmering just below the surface.

The entrance of Pearson into her bedchamber had heralded the commencement of a transformation which went far beyond anything that Henrietta had imagined, accustomed as she was to the strict economy of her mother's household. The dresser, a thin, trim figure, almost as fashionably dressed as her mistress, her starched, beribboned cap set upon tight, dark curls, cast inquisitive eyes upon the new arrival and nodded her head briskly, her mind already running over the contents of Miss Louise's wardrobe. "A shocking thing, to be sure, m'lady! And the young lady not quite in our Miss's style, if I may make so bold as to say so – but there – one or two of Miss Louise's gowns which don't become her so well, may prove just the thing for this young lady!"

If these ominous words could have cast a damper upon Henrietta's hopes of achieving a fashionable appearance, she need not have been dismayed. Responding to the challenge presented by her mistress and to a certain prim satisfaction in being the recipient of confidences which would, she knew, not be bestowed upon the rest of the staff, Pearson had indeed proved an efficient, if forbidding conspirator. Only a tightening of her lips, as she had assisted Henrietta out of her coat and breeches, had betrayed any feelings of censure. She had bundled the offending garments together, saying, with a sniff, "You'll not be wanting this lot again, Miss, that's for sure."

She would have removed them from the room to dispose of them elsewhere, had not Henrietta, feeling that her last link with home was about to disappear, quickly replied, "And yet I have an odd wish to keep them, Pearson, for they will serve to remind me of my escape." Taking them from the disapproving Pearson's hands, she laid them onto a chair beside her.

It was more than two hours later that Henrietta was permitted to descend the stairs once more. Certainly Pearson had exercised considerable skill in choosing amongst Louise's dresses. It was not only Louise's fair hair which differed from Henrietta's bright halo of bronze curls, but the former had a soft, delicate fragile look, very different to the straight-backed resolution of Henrietta's slim figure, her decided chin and steady brown-eyed gaze. A simple muslin open-robe had been chosen, finely striped in blue, over a white petticoat with a broad sash of a deeper blue at the waist. A plain white neckerchief completed the effect, while her raggedly cut hair had been trimmed and brushed by Pearson's skillful hands into fashionable curls. It was strange for Henrietta to feel once more the restriction of a boned bodice and petticoats but seeing her reflection in the looking glass, discomfort was forgotten. Never had she been dressed in such modish fashion, and turning to Pearson, she offered her thanks, saying with round-eyed astonishment, "I look so fine, Pearson! Why, you have performed a minor miracle."

Speaking later that day to Mrs Finlay, in the housekeeper's sitting-room, Pearson had condescended to give her reserved approval of Miss Brandon. "And," she confided, with a certain relish, "if this young Miss were to look at the gentlemen with those eyes of hers – as big as saucers – same as she looked at me when I'd finished dressing her – I tell you, Mrs Finlay, she'll break a heart or two around here – no doubt about it!"

"What'll her Ladyship think of that, then, Miss Pearson?"

"Not much, she won't, mark my words!" Pearson permitted herself a grim smile, "Though, I'll say this – Miss Louise and Miss Brandon make as pretty a picture together as you can imagine."

Their toilet completed, the cousins descended the stairs together, arms entwined, Louise in a chemise dress of soft white jaconet muslin, embellished with a breast-knot and sash of palest pink to match her slippers. Hearing voices, they entered the drawing-room and paused in the doorway. A variety of emotions were displayed on the four faces turned towards them. Lady Sedley, seated in her favourite wing-backed chair by the window, was not able to conceal a certain degree of irritation which moderated her pleasure at the undoubted success of Pearson's efforts. The picture before her was a delightful one but she had not anticipated *quite* such a striking result: Miss Brandon was, in her own way, a very good-looking girl, and her ladyship had an uncomfortable presentiment that she was not one to be easily guided. Sir William, frank appreciation writ large upon his jovial countenance, glanced at his wife's face and remarked, with the diplomacy acquired during twenty-six years of married life, "My congratulations, your ladyship, a triumph. Not a doubt of it."

Francis, who had been lounging on the window-seat, sat up straight and exclaimed in an astonished voice, "Good God, Mama – a regular out-and-outer!" then, with a broad grin directed towards his sister, he added teasingly, "Well, sister, you'll not be the only belle of the neighbourhood now!"

However, it was not upon his own sister that Philip's eyes were fixed. A look of intense admiration was upon his face as his gaze rested upon Louise's charming person, an admiration so evident that no one in the room could fail to be aware of it, not least Louise, who blushed prettily and dismissed her brother's teasing, saying, with an affectionate glance at Henrietta, "As if I cared for such nonsense."

"Indeed it is nonsense! Why you are a true beauty, Louise, no man in his right mind could have eyes for anyone else." Henrietta's reply was followed by a slight frown as she observed her brother's expression. Comforting herself in the recollection that he had long been susceptible to female charms, she asked politely of Lady Sedley whether Louise might show her the garden. "I have seen Sir Charles's garden and am quite in love with the English style – so much less formal than the French."

It seemed that the young gentlemen were also of a mind to stroll in the sunshine, for Philip expressed a wish to accompany them and Francis remarked off-handedly, "May as well come with you – for I'm on my way to the stables to see how 'Juno' goes on."

As the four young people crossed the terrace, which lay outside the French-windows, Henrietta remarked, eyebrows raised, "It's the first time I've known you betray any interest in gardens of any kind, Philip!"

"My dear sister, did you not know, as I have most recently discovered, that the English rose is the fairest of all flowers!" Philip had contrived to be at Louise's side as they left the house and as he said these words he cast an admiring glance in her direction.

To Henrietta's surprise, Louise made no attempt to give Philip the sharp set-down, which, in her opinion, he richly deserved; rather, she blushed faintly and cast a shy glance at him from beneath her lashes, then began in a soft voice to talk about the garden and the recent improvements that her father had caused to be made.

Left alone in the drawing-room, Lady Sedley and Sir William exchanged glances.

"I believe, Sir William," her ladyship said thoughtfully, "that it would be as well that you set in hand as soon as possible the necessary enquiries into the authenticity of these young people's claims, and if all proves to be in order, to make arrangements without delay for them to proceed on their way to the Hartingtons."

Sir William, taking snuff, nodded his head, remarking inconsequentially, as he did so, "Handsome young fellow – flattering ways –" he sighed and added, "Silly girl – head full of nonsense!" Snapping his snuff-box shut, he rose to his feet saying with resolution, "I'll take young Brandon to London to see Mr. Forsythe tomorrow, my dear. Better get Hugo to come as well – see that all's right and tight."

"Very well, Sir William, pray make arrangements to do so." Lady Sedley paused, then remarked with a sigh, "What an unexpected upset of our quiet lives."

Henrietta was seated at the dressing-table, brushing her hair and reflecting upon the day's events before climbing into bed when there was a soft tap on the door and Louise appeared in the doorway wearing a modest wrapper over her nightgown and saying in her gentle way, "May I come in, cousin? We have had so little time alone together to talk and there are a thousand things that I wish to say to you!"

"Indeed, yes – we must certainly become better acquainted – I know so little about you all!"

It seemed to Henrietta a golden opportunity to reach some understanding of the relationships existing between the many persons whom she had met in the last few days. Taking her candlestick and setting it beside the bed, she climbed between the sheets and invited to Louise to take a seat beside her on the bedcovers. "Tell me, when are you and Sir Charles to be married?" Henrietta asked bluntly, settling herself against the pillows, this being the subject at the forefront of her mind.

"It is not yet decided for our betrothal is of only a few days duration and the announcement has not yet appeared in the Gazette. Oh, it is like a story from a novel, you know!" Louise continued softly, warming to her favourite theme, "I have known Sir Charles since I was a child and all this time I had *no* idea that he had been cherishing a secret passion for me all those years."

Henrietta felt astonishment and amusement rising within her. The impression that she had received of that gentleman was of a very different nature and certainly not one in which 'secret passions' had any place. "Why do you suppose he did not acquaint you with his feelings before now?"

Louise looked thoughtful, "Perhaps it was because he was away at sea, in the Navy – a Captain, you know – he was wounded once, when he was a midshipman. He is a truly romantic figure, you know."

"Wounded!" Henrietta said quickly, her voice full of sympathy, "Why, how terrible! But one can hardly describe a wound as romantic. How did it happen? Where was his injury?"

"I have no idea." Louise sounded a little offended, "I suppose it was his leg, for he was obliged to walk with a stick at first. Then, last year, his elder brother was killed – he was in the 19th Hussars, you know – and his father made Sir Charles promise to resign his commission and live at Gresham Court."

"But how unfair! Poor Sir Charles." Henrietta frowned, then her face brightened, "But you must love him dearly, I am sure, and that will make up to him for the life that he has had to give up."

For the first time a note of hesitancy crept into Louise's voice. "Do you not think, Henrietta, that we females do not know a great deal about love before we are married – and Sir Charles is so very much the gentleman –" her voice died away.

Henrietta nodded solemnly. Being, herself, so recently emerged from the schoolroom, she hardly felt in a position to pontificate upon the subject, but she could not help but feel some surprise at Louise's remarks. It seemed to her that Sir Charles embodied all that a girl might wish for, tall, handsome and, above all, kind – unbelievable not to have fallen in love with him! To change the subject, she said, "And Francis, has he formed an attachment?"

"Francis!" Louise laughed, "You don't know him yet, that's clear! His only interest is in horses and dogs – Mama can hardly persuade him to come to London in the Season. I cannot believe your brother is like that – and he is so very good-looking." she added.

"Oh Philip! He is a fickle creature, for ever chasing after one girl or another." Henrietta ruthlessly blackened her brother's character and hoped devoutly that he would not become aware of it."

"I believe Hugo has a bad reputation with women," Louise confided, "I have heard Mama speak about it to Papa when she had not known I was by, but he is amusing and attentive and says pretty things." She turned towards Henrietta, wide eyed, and said curiously, "How afraid you must have been when Sir Charles took you to Gresham Court – I vow, if I had been you, I should have died of fright."

Henrietta considered, "No," she said pensively, "I was not afraid then, you see he thought that I was a boy – at least –" she hesitated, "at least I *thought* that he believed that I was a boy." She regarded Louise's enquiring face with a slight frown and added in a puzzled voice, "I don't really know at what moment he discovered that I was not." There was a moment of silence, then a smile lit up Henrietta's face as she recollected the calm, amiable gentleman who had befriended her. "You are indeed fortunate, Louise, Sir Charles is so – so, how does one say it? – Dependable!" she finished triumphantly.

"Dependable!" Louise echoed, in a subdued voice, "Is that how you think of him?"

Candid brown eyes gazed into troubled blue ones. By now the fire was almost out and the candles were burning low; outside in the stable yard the clock struck eleven and Louise stirred, with a stifled yawn she slipped off the bed, "Gracious, I had not realized the hour was so late, Mama would be in a fine taking if she knew that I was not yet in bed." Taking up her candlestick, she bade Henrietta an affectionate "Good-night" and departed.

CHAPTER 6

There had been a great deal of astonishment and pleasurable speculation amongst the household of Gresham Place following the
departure of the young brother and sister from France. Sir Charles
had instructed Cummings to assemble all the staff and inform them of
the real identity of Master Brandon. Furthermore, they were told to let
it be known in the neighbourhood that the *real* Philip Brandon had
been the first arrival in England and that it was his sister, now to be
known as Miss Henrietta Brandon, who had followed him later.

In the servant's hall, this announcement had created considerable
amusement, and Morton, Sir Charles's valet and former member of
his ship's crew, found himself the target of much ribaldry from his
fellow servants. "Thinkin' of setting yourself up as a lady's maid,
eh?" enquired the young footman, "Beats me how you didn't suspect
nothing!"

Morton, however, was unfazed. He was finding it difficult to realize that the young boy that he had attended so assiduously was a
young lady but, nevertheless, he still retained his admiration for the
courage and for the pleasant manners of his charge. "Count yourself
lucky, young fellow-me-lad, that you wasn't ever put in such a situation like that poor young lady. Pluck to the backbone she was."

Mrs Burberry, the housekeeper, was curious to discover at what
moment her employer had realized the true sex of his unexpected
guest. Discussing the subject with Cummings in the butler's pantry
after the meeting, she raised this question and was interested to learn
that Sir Charles, at the dinner table on the previous day, had not
allowed this young person to remain in the dining room after the
ladies had withdrawn. "Seems to me, Mrs Burberry," Cummings
speculated, "he didn't want that young 'un to hear coarse talk or bad

language. Sent her out in the garden with Master George, which, by the way, Master George didn't care for one bit. Ain't that something that gives one pause for thought? I reckon he had discovered that she was a female afore that."

Mrs Burberry agreed and wondered what Lady Sedley and young Miss Louise must have thought of these strange events. "Miss Louise, she's a real beauty, no doubt about that, but this Miss Henrietta – made a handsome boy, she did – and I can't help wondering how she will turn out as a young lady. Makes me laugh to think as how she fooled us all with her boyish ways and strode around as happy as can be in breeches!"

Cummings nodded, "Lady Sedley won't be best pleased, that's for sure. You and I, both, have heard talk from the Grange about Miss Louise and a betrothal: we don't want ought to prevent that. Be the best thing for the Captain. Marriage and a family is what he needs and my lady – why she'd be over the moon if he was to marry."

The morning following their arrival at the Grange, Sir William and Philip made an early start to London, and having, and after several brief stops to change the horses and some refreshments at The Chequers in Horley, arrived at the offices of Messrs Grantley, Forsythe and Simonds by Lincoln's Inn Fields shortly before two o'clock in the afternoon. Hugo Brandon, when requested to attend at the lawyers' place of business, had preferred to meet them there, saying that he wished to drive himself in his curricle. He had in fact remarked bitterly to Charles, whom he had encountered the previous evening, "I'll be damned if I'll sit mewed up for hours with that wretched youth, who looks to ruin all my hopes."

Philip had enjoyed the journey. His first sight of the English countryside had impressed him. The rolling down-lands of Sussex had given place to Surrey woods and hills, the road was good, thanks to Prinny's fondness for Brighton, while the toll-gates were speedily opened for them. The well-kept cottages and gardens which lined part of their route had an air of prosperity and order. London, when they reached it at last, was an unforgettable sight, the splendid buildings, the noise and bustle, the shouts of street vendors, the air of excitement and fashion all made him long to become more closely acquainted with this great city.

Hugo had arrived before them in the dusty, book-lined outer office, where men sat writing at tall desks and papers were piled high upon every available surface. He greeted the newcomers curtly and together they were conducted by the clerk into the inner sanctum of Mr. Amos Forsythe. That gentleman, rising from behind the large desk at which he had been seated, came forward, bowing to Sir William and saying, "A great pleasure, sir! In what way can we be of service to you?"

Sir William, reflecting inwardly that it was fortunate that his and the Brandon family affairs should be in the hands of the same long-established firm of solicitors, remarked with some diffidence that "It was a devilish awkward business," and introduced his companions. Mr. Forsythe bowed to Hugo and Philip, his eyebrows raised enquiringly as he became acquainted with the latter's name.

"Mr. Philip Brandon? Let me see –?" He paused interrogatively.

"Well, that's the nub of the matter." Sir William turned to Philip, "Show Mr Forsythe the papers, my boy, let's see what he makes of them."

Seats were found for all present, while Mr. Forsythe placed his gold-rimmed spectacles upon his nose and read slowly through the documents. Hugo, lounging back in his chair played idly with his quizzing-glass as if indifferent to the proceedings but there was a certain whiteness around his mouth that belied his apparent calm. Philip, visibly anxious, regarded Mr Forsythe intently.

At last the lawyer raised his head, and looked at them over his spectacles thoughtfully. "I believe we have a document in our possession which may have some bearing upon this matter. Permit me to consult my clerk?".

"By all means! By all means!" Sir William responded.

The lawyer rang a bell on his desk and gave some orders to the pale young man who answered his summons. After a short interval a large deed-box was brought in and laid before them upon the desk. Mr. Forsythe extracted a sealed letter. "This, my dear sirs, was entrusted to me some three years ago by a gentleman returning from France. I ask you to read the superscription. The three men leaned forward and read the words, written in faded ink – 'Only to be opened after my death' – and signed in a firm hand, 'John Fortescue Brandon'.

A faint sigh escaped from Philip's lips, "My father's hand." he said softly.

"Open it, open it, my dear sir! There can be little doubt that the poor fellow is no more." Sir William was all impatience. Mr. Forsythe, wielding an ivory paperknife with a flourish, opened the seal and, unfolding the document, silently perused it. There was a tense silence. "I will read this to you, gentlemen, and then you may study it at your leisure." Clearing his throat impressively, M. Forsythe began –

I, the Honourable John Fortescue Brandon do solemnly swear that upon the 26th day of June, 1771, I was joined in Holy Matrimony to Miss Marie-Joséphine Foster in a private ceremony at the residence of the British Ambassador in Paris conducted by the Reverend Miles Everton, clerk in Holy Orders, tutor to one Richard Garfield, of Somerset.

I do also solemnly swear that a son, Philip Fortescue, was born to us upon the 5th day of October, 1772, and a daughter, Henrietta Marie, upon the 21st day of April, 1776.

I make this solemn statement in the unhappy knowledge that the present events in France may place all our lives in danger.

Inspite of the rift between my family and myself, I, herewith, make my last request, that my wife and children be given all the assistance that they require in the event of my demise.

Signed, John Fortescue Brandon.

Witness – SirRobert Callow, of Gadby House, Bourne, Derbyshire.

Witness – Samuel Turner Esquire of Shorne Park, Felbridge, Hampshire. The 20th day of July, 1790.

Mr. Forsythe's voice ceased and he looked solemnly around him, then added in his precise lawyer's voice, "Legally it behoves me to investigate the authenticity of the clergyman's signature and that of the witnesses. But I believe it to be only a formality – although you will understand, there may be a delay on that account. In the meantime I shall acquaint Lord Hartington with the facts as they stand now."

There was a moistness in Philip's fine, dark eyes, Hugo was scowling; Sir William blew his nose noisily, "Very touching, sir! A sad business!" He looked at Philip, "Well, my boy, seems that settles it, what!"

"By no means, Sir William!" Hugo, tight-lipped, glared at the usurper of what he had come to regard as his inheritance. "As I have said before, what *proof* exists, to say that this man is Philip Brandon?"

"Good God, sir, there's a notable family likeness between you! Though," Sir William added forthrightly, "I must admit the Froggie fellow has the advantage of you in looks."

Mr Forsythe, no doubt feeling that matters were getting a trifle out of hand, intervened swiftly, "Sir William, with your permission, I propose to put to this young gentleman," he bowed in Philip's direction, "certain questions which only the son of the late Honourable John Brandon could answer, thus establishing without doubt his claim to the name of Philip Brandon."

Sir William indicated agreement, and Mr Forsythe proceeded, "Can you tell me of anything unusual about your father's person?"

Philip looked thoughtful; then he said carefully, "The top joint was missing from the little toe on his – let me see – his right foot."

Mr Forsythe nodded, "That, gentlemen is correct. I knew the late Honourable John Brandon as a boy, as of course you know, Sir William. There was a sad accident at harvest-time . . . however, let me continue. Did your late father ever tell you anything about the house that he grew up in?"

There was a pause, then Philip said slowly, "I remember he called it Bampton House. He told me of a priest-hole, from the time of Queen Elizabeth, I believe."

Mr. Forsythe leaned forward, "Did he, perhaps, inform you of its exact location?"

"Why yes, I remember it well, – it was so extraordinary. There was panelling between the bookshelves in the library with carving around the fireplace. Very intricate, my father said – representations of acorns, interspersed with oak-leaves, you know. He said that if one counted the acorns on the left-hand side and pressed the third from the top, the panel on that side would slide open disclosing a few shallow steps leading down to a concealed room."

Mr. Forsythe positively beamed, "Gentlemen, I believe that to be conclusive proof! The presence of the priest-hole has always been kept a closely guarded secret. It was only when I was with the late Mr. Simmonds, attending upon Lord Hartington many years ago, that I was shown the means of entry to it – in case at any time papers or valuables should be concealed there – a strange fancy you may say, but the old lord was quite an eccentric gentleman, if you will forgive the expression." He leaned back, placing his fingertips together, and surveyed his auditors with satisfaction.

Hugo stood up abruptly, grim-faced, and turned to his newly acquired cousin, "Be damned to you! This ain't the last you shall hear from me, sir! There's many a slip between cup and lip, by God – and don't you forget it!" With an effort he remembered the civilities due, "Your servant, Sir William, – Mr. Forsythe, good-day to you," and without further word he strode from the room, scowling so ferociously that the senior clerk in the outer room, who had been waiting to escort these important clients to the street door, stepped back in dismay.

In the absence of the gentlemen, Lady Sedley had planned an expedition to Brighton. The proposal was rapturously received by the two young ladies. "The shops in Brighton are excellent, my dear," Lady Sedley informed Henrietta, "and naturally you will not wish to continue in borrowed garments. Besides, although of a size, you are so unlike Louise in colouring and in – in –" she searched for a word.

"In character, in fact!" prompted Henrietta cheerfully, "Louise is gentle and romantic and I, most certainly, am not."

Casting a fond glance at her lovely daughter, Lady Sedley continued, "Louise, too, must begin to purchase her bride-clothes and," she added, "Sir William has bade me frank you, Henrietta, until your affairs are set in order."

She was rewarded by a warm smile but there was an anxious expression in Henrietta's eyes. "My lady, you are so kind – never have I known such kindness as I have received in England. First Sir Charles, now you and the good Sir William. I know that Philip brought some small amount of gold with him from France but I fear that it can hardly be sufficient for our needs. For the moment, as I have no English money, I gratefully accept your offer but we shall endeavour, as soon as we can, to repay Sir William."

Although a person of decided opinions and strong views, Lady Sedley was touched by the honesty of her young guest. "Everything, my dear, will be settled in due course. I have no doubt that Sir William will set all aright. Now we must make the most of our opportunity of an agreeable visit to Brighton."

Thus, in earnest discussion of their future purchases and with frequent appeals to Lady Sedley for advice as to which of the shops would best suit their requirements, the journey passed speedily enough and they were soon entering the outskirts of the town. It was all of absorbing interest to Henrietta, for now she had the opportunity of seeing an English town and observing the English way of life of which she had heard so much from her father.

His Royal Highness's Marine Pavilion was pointed out to Henrietta as they passed. "Rebuilt from the original farmhouse by Henry Holland a few years ago." Lady Sedley announced, and Henrietta beheld a delightfully harmonious building – a central rotunda, surmounted by a shallow dome encircled by columns bearing classical statues, and two flanking wings whose curved bow-windows rose from the ground through both storeys in a most charming and novel manner. Before this edifice, upon a broad stretch of mown grass, Henrietta was astonished to see fashionably dressed men and women strolling. "We shall return here after a light luncheon, my dears, the Steine is a delightful promenade and beside it there are excellent shops and libraries." Even the austere Lady Sedley seemed to be in an expansive mood.

Both young ladies were amazed at the number of uniformed officers amongst the fashionables walking upon the grass. "Why, Mama, it seems every other gentleman is in regimentals!" Louise's eyes sparkled.

Lady Sedley was knowledgeable upon the subject, "A camp was established in Brighton on Tuesday on the west side of the town. The troops marched from Ashdown Forest and were met at Preston by the Prince of Wales, whose regiment headed the column. There is, I believe, to be what is termed a 'Sham-fight' on the downs soon but that, of course, would be quite unsuitable for young ladies to attend."

By now their progress was slow, for the road was thronged with vehicles: phaetons, curricles, gigs and every other kind of open carriage, the horses, for the most part superbly matched and groomed, their harnesses brilliantly ornamented. Before them lay a wide view of the sea, sunlight dancing upon the water and a light wind ruffling the waves. Turning to the right they drew up before the 'Ship' inn where they were to partake of some refreshments before commencing the serious business of the day.

At the end of their meal, Lady Sedley and her two companions were leaving the dining-room when, to their surprise and pleasure, they encountered Sir Charles Gresham accompanied by a young officer. Sir Charles, greeting them with a polite bow, introduced his companion, "Lieutenant Frensham of the 10th Light Dragoons. George – my friends and neighbours – Lady Sedley, Miss Sedley and her cousin, Miss Brandon." At once, Henrietta recognized Lieutenant Frensham as the young officer whom she had first encountered at the Star inn at the time of her rescue in Shoreham and was greatly relieved to discover that he did not appear to have recognized her. The young man, very conscious of the lovely Miss Sedley by her mother's side, plunged into a polite exchange of civilities with Lady Sedley.

It was the first time that Henrietta had been in Sir Charles's company while wearing normal feminine attire and, to her surprise, she found herself feeling strangely uncomfortable and very aware of her changed appearance. He was regarding her with amused approval and finding that they were a trifle set aside from the others, murmured in her ear, "May I congratulate you, Miss Brandon, you look most becomingly and quite in the latest mode!"

Seeing the gleam of laughter in his eye, she responded, with a smile, "Since all of my garments belong to Louise, sir, it does not surprise me that you approve. But," she looked up at him confidingly, "I own I shall be thankful when I am no longer obliged to appear in 'borrowed plumes' – indeed that is the object of our expedition."

Sir Charles, eyebrows raised quizzically, smiled down at her, "And yet, Miss Brandon, you appear to have the uncommon ability of being quite at ease in whatever garments you have borrowed!" Henrietta chuckled, the memory of her recent masculine disguise returning vividly to her mind. She was pleased to discover that the same easy relationship with Sir Charles was to continue now that she was restored to female attire. Indeed, somewhat to her surprise, she felt after all no awkwardness, only pleasure in renewing her acquaintance with her rescuer, a man she had grown to admire.

Meanwhile Lieutenant Frensham was describing to Lady Sedley his recent experiences at Waterdown camp – the downpours of rain and the swampy conditions. "You might well say we were transformed into an army of frogs!" he finally declared with a wry smile. Henrietta, hearing these words and having now discovered that 'frogs' was a synonym for Frenchmen, enquired his meaning. "Only, ma'am, that we were so deucedly wet, you know." He looked mournfully at her and added, "These field-days are quite a puzzle to us subalterns. We are all obedience to our superiors but we cannot comprehend the manœuvres." He continued with a grin, "I have often made enquiries to learn whether the part we were traversing was that of Friend or Enemy but – as I am determined to be an Englishman – I was not so sorry to find that I could not receive positive information upon the subject. As a result, at the conclusion of the day, I made up my mind that we had been the English and had returned victorious!" Lady Sedley looked disapproving and Louise's charming countenance displayed incomprehension, but Henrietta, warming to this disarmingly honest young man, suggested kindly that such a field-day must be an exhausting affair. A comic expression, part amusement, part shame appeared upon the young officer's boyish face. "Well, ma'am, you could describe it as a field-day of rest!" Seeing their surprise, he said ruefully, "For example, we took possession of a range of hills to the south-east of Ashdown Forest. The day was more than comfortably warm and the men were ordered to stand at ease – from standing at ease, they stole to sitting down and, from sitting down, about two thirds of them prostrated their noses to the earth – and, insensibly, fell asleep!"

"Good gracious!" Louise exclaimed, looking mystified.

"After about three hours," he continued, "the first discharge of guns came, and that from naval ordinance, which aroused them from their peaceful death, and with our banners waving in the wind, we marched home again!"

All, save Lady Sedley, could not but laugh at this un-heroic description, but Lady Sedley seemed clearly not amused and announced with tightened lips that it was high time for them to depart. Wondering frostily how Charles could associate with such a remarkably foolish young man, she bade him and his companion farewell with less than her usual affability towards her future son-in-law. The girls made their adieux with genuine regret and the ladies proceeded on their way.

The afternoon that followed was of a highly satisfactory nature to all members of the expedition. They called first on an establishment in Middle Street, where, upon Lady Sedley's advice, Henrietta ordered a riding habit of a dark blue superfine in a fashionable military style. "It is preferable that such a costume is tailored by a man, my dear. For the rest of your wardrobe, we may buy the materials and my own mantua-maker, a most excellent woman, can make them up for you." A linen-draper's in North Street was their next port of call. It had recently been opened by a Mr Champney, the enterprising owner of a like business in Cheapside. Here were displayed a multitude of muslins of every description, both Indian and British, along with a great variety of fashionable printed calicos, cambrics and Irish linens. Louise, her eyes sparkling with excitement, purchased, with her mother's indulgent approval, a length of white gauze embroidered with rosebuds and several yards of dove-coloured Florentine for a riding-coat dress. Henrietta, too, after some serious consideration upon such an important topic, bought several lengths of muslin, of crape and of gauze, as well as warmer fabrics and was astonished that the elegant young men who served them displayed such dedicated interest in their choice of materials.

Leaving North Street they crossed a rectangular plot of ground, designated, so Henrietta was informed, the 'Promenade Grove', where a Public Breakfast was in progress and an immense throng of fashionably dressed people were consuming various sorts of cakes and fruits and meats and sipping tea, coffee and chocolate to the accompanying roar of a military band. "His Royal Highness may well be present later." Lady Sedley announced, as they took some refreshments, "We are subscribers, of course, so have no need of tickets."

Upon reaching the Steine, which was pleasantly sheltered from the sea-breezes, they entered several of the small shops that surrounded it to make some further purchases. They were delighted by the milliner, where some enchanting hats, elegant shawls, neckerchiefs and caps were displayed, as well as gloves and parasols, and also by an emporium for fancy-goods stocked with toys and china, ribbons and lace.

It was while Henrietta and Louise were debating the merits of a trimming of aquamarine silk and one of jonquil yellow that Lady

Sedley, observing an array of embroidery silks, offered to buy for Henrietta the materials for a piece of needlework, "For you will be glad enough of something to occupy your hands if you go to the Hartingtons, my dear." A work-basket accompanied the gift, for which she was prettily thanked and, as they proceeded on their way, Lady Sedley reflected with some surprise that, always supposing that Philip and Henrietta's claims should prove to be true, and after some guidance from herself in the manners prevailing in English society, this girl might well be an extremely eligible 'parti'. After all – to be the grand-daughter of Lord Hartington was not something to be dismissed lightly. She was certainly a well-mannered child.

Mr. Gregory's circulating library was their final destination. Henrietta was surprised and intrigued to discover that one could not only read, buy or borrow the latest novels, plays and poems, one could also purchase materials for elegant pursuits such as painting and sketching. Within its portals too, both sexes alike were engaged in such activities as writing letters, looking through portfolios of caricatures, playing cards or trying over a piece of music. From the library, after a short spell spent in browsing among the shelves, the Sedley party emerged, bearing with them such volumes as had caught their several fancies, 'Cecilia' by Fanny Burney and James Fordyce's 'Sermons for Young Women' amongst them, having been strongly recommended by Lady Sedley – a commendation which only served to make both the young cousins view these improving works with grave suspicion.

The journey home of three well-satisfied ladies was accomplished long before the return of Sir William and Philip from London. Indeed Henrietta had already mounted to her bed-chamber and was about to prepare herself for the night when there came an urgent knock at her door and before she could answer it, the door flew open and Philip was in the room, hugging her to him, his whole person radiant with excitement. "I am accepted, Henrietta – all is well – there was a letter from Papa – in fact – you see before you the heir to my Lord Hartington!" He spun her around, laughing and jubilant. Henrietta, breathless and smiling, begged him to sit down and tell her all that had occurred at the lawyer's office.

Seated by the fire, hearing the details of her father's letter, Henrietta said softly, "Dear Papa, he had a good heart, in spite of all his follies" and sighed, remembering sadly the gambling that had reduced them to a precarious existence, perpetually upon the brink of disaster.

Philip leaned forward and seized her hands, "It is incredible – but it is true – and not only will I be Lord Hartington one day but I will be a wealthy man! Sir William tells me that Lady Hartington was an heiress – some nabob in her family – and now, Henrietta – now I shall have the opportunity of becoming better acquainted with that lovely girl!" His dark eyes alight with ardour rested upon his sister's face and found there surprise and dismay.

Anxiously she asked, "'that lovely girl' – of whom do you speak, Philip?"

He made a gesture of impatience, "But who else could it be – why Louise, of course – she is quite beautiful – an angel."

"But she is betrothed, Philip!" Henrietta was horrified, all her anxious forebodings realized. "And, worse than that, she is betrothed to Sir Charles, to whom our gratitude is due. You must not speak so."

"A marriage of convenience in effect." Philip was dismissive.

Henrietta, staring at him with great troubled eyes, felt herself torn in two. Her innate honesty forced her to admit to herself that there was little sign of the ardent lover in Sir Charles, but then – had not Louise spoken of a long-concealed passion – and, after all, it was not the first time that Philip had thought himself in love. She faltered lamely, "How can one tell Sir Charles's sentiments – we have not been brought up in England – here manners are more restrained –" Her voice died away; what, indeed, did she know of Sir Charles's inner-most thoughts and desires?"

Philip stood up impatiently, "It is useless to talk to you – you are too young. Certainly you owe him a great deal, that is true, but you do not understand these matters."

"Indeed I understand matters of honour, my dear Philip – better, it seems, than you. To repay his kindness in such a way!" Henrietta's eyes flashed with indignation as she rose to her feet and said fiercely, "It is dishonourable to pursue Louise with your attentions – I beg of you not to do so."

The only response she received was a light-hearted laugh. Giving her a brotherly kiss on the cheek, Philip went to the door of her chamber, "You are foolish, Henrietta, you see nothing, nothing at all!" and still softly chuckling he left her.

As Henrietta slowly undressed and prepared herself for bed, her thoughts were confused. It was a relief indeed to know that their identity had been satisfactorily established – no worries in that quarter now – and she might have expected a period of at least some tranquillity. Now all seemed changed by Philip's interest in Louise. Blithely she dismissed out of hand his accusation that she knew nothing of affairs of the heart. Of Sir Charles's affection for Louise she felt reasonably certain – of Louise's sentiments she was less sure – she sensed an element of unreality in Louise's thinking and her romantic expectations were perhaps unlikely to be fulfilled. Henrietta thought of Sir Charles's kind, calm, manner – alas, perhaps he was too reserved, would not feel the ardent wooing of a young female was necessary or expected. She sighed – to her mind there was no comparison as a husband between the tall, elegant Englishman, whose presence gave her the sense of security so long absent from her life, and her wayward brother, all fire and passion, changeable as the wind. She climbed into bed and, as she settled herself snugly beneath the covers, decided that given the opportunity, she would herself try and give Sir Charles some hint as to the romantic expectations of a girl such as Louise; he would, she mused sleepily, be profoundly grateful to her for her advice and with these gratifying thoughts she fell asleep.

CHAPTER 7

When Philip awoke the following morning he found it almost impossible to realize fully the immense change in his future prospects. At home in France he had never had the opportunity to take any part in fashionable society. Thanks to his father's dissolute way of life on the outer fringes of the aristocracy, he had perforce been brought up amongst the bourgeoisie. Educated at home by his mother and the local priest, he had then been employed as a tutor by several families in the neighbourhood and had had no regrets at the time that he was barred by his impoverished circumstances from any close association with people of rank. Rather, he had been intensely interested in the new philosophical ideas that had preceded the many changes in France before the storming of the Bastille and which appealed to his idealistic nature. Despite the terrible situation in France, from which he had escaped so precipitously, he still hoped that there might be a better future ahead for the general mass of people in that country. Now, suddenly, wealth and a title lay before him, as well as a new family of cousins. Now he would be accepted into Polite Society in a country of which he knew at present so little. As his thoughts turned to his new cousins, he contemplated with pleasure the days that lay before him; to be staying under the same roof as the enchanting Louise gave him now the opportunity to become better acquainted with her.

Upon rising, the clear blue sky and the sunshine of that morning matched his sanguine mood in every particular. In spite of Henrietta's warnings, no doubts or hesitations clouded his mind and, after a substantial breakfast, he set himself the task of finding an opportunity of being in Louise's company without the presence of a third party. Fortune favoured him, for at about eleven o'clock he overheard Lady

Sedley's request to her daughter to pick some roses for the drawing-room and observed from the window Louise set out along the garden path wearing a becoming Bergère straw bonnet tied under her chin, a shallow basket on her arm. In a matter of moments Philip had left the house and, wandering seemingly without purpose, eyes alert, soon encountered the object of his search amongst the roses in the walled garden.

"Good-day, Cousin! What a perfect morning – permit me to assist you!" As he took the basket from her hands, his admiring eyes scanned his companion's face and saw with delight a faint blush rise to her cheeks, the soft blue eyes lowered modestly beneath his gaze.

Louise had that morning heard from her mother that Philip Brandon was indeed her cousin and, without doubt, the legitimate heir to the Hartington title. Even in her unworldly mind he had gained in stature. She glanced at him from under her lashes and said with a smile, "I am so happy for you to hear that all is settled now." She added ingenuously, as she began to gather roses, "Why, it is amazingly like a story that I have been reading – the unknown heir arriving from overseas to claim his inheritance. "

It was too good an opportunity for Philip to miss, "I hope he was the hero of your story and that in the end he won the love of the heroine against all odds!" It was said lightly but the look in his eyes as they met hers reflected an inner seriousness.

Louise found her heart was behaving strangely; flustered, she looked quickly away from those dark eyes, her hands moving shakily amongst the roses on the bush and gave a little cry of vexation as a thorn pierced her finger.

"Dear Heavens!" Philip seized her hand and brought it to his lips and, before Louise could utter a word, had kissed it gently.

With a charming attempt at dignity, Louise endeavoured to disengage herself, murmuring, "It is nothing – a mere scratch, cousin." But Philip, retaining her hand in his, drew her towards the nearby seat, where cascading roses formed a sheltering bower, saying,

"Come, Louise, let us sit down so that I may make certain that no thorn remains in your finger."

In preparation for the arrival of the mantua-maker that afternoon, Henrietta had, since breakfast, occupied herself in studying the latest fashion drawings in the long-deserted nursery and making plans for the transformation of her purchases of the previous day into elegant dresses. For her, this was indeed a novel occupation – there had never been, in France, the means available to be dressed fashionably nor, in fact, had she felt much interest in her appearance and had often been censured by her brother for her hoydenish looks. Reading had been her greatest pleasure and had filled her days. Downstairs she heard a bell ring in the servants' hall and thought contentedly that, since she had no acquaintances in the neighbourhood, she would be saved from having to attend upon any morning callers.

She had been given by Louise a charming riding hat, its edges rolled over in a three-cornered style which would be the perfect complement to her new riding-habit and only needed the addition of some trimmings to make it perfect. Deciding that the curled feathers of a particularly delightful azure blue, which she had been tempted to buy in Brighton, would be the very thing, she ran down to her bed-chamber to collect them from where they lay upon the window-seat. As she picked them up, she leaned out of the open window, thinking ruefully that it was truly shameful to be indoors on such a beautiful morning. There below her was the walled garden, its beds bright with flowers, and as her eyes rested on this tranquil scene she was shocked to observe that Louise and Philip were standing close together at the farther side of the garden, Louise's hand raised to Philip's lips. Indignation was rising within her when, to her dismay, she beheld the tall, unmistakable figure of Sir Charles Gresham enter the enclosed garden through an archway in the east wall. By now Louise and Philip had moved to the rustic arbour, and there, seated side by side, he still held her hand in his and was bending over it, their heads close together. Henrietta watched, transfixed, and saw Sir Charles advance a few paces and look around him; he was clearly seeking out some person and, with a sinking heart, Henrietta realized that Louise must be the object of his search. It seemed impossible that he could fail to observe her and her companion and, in a frantic effort to avert an unpleasant scene, Henrietta was about to call out to Sir Charles to distract his attention when it became plain that the worst had already happened. Sir Charles's gaze having fallen upon the young couple, he took a step or two forward in their direction then paused, regarding them, motionless and silent. From Henrietta's viewpoint, she was not able to see his face, but she could well imagine his expression; with a feeling of foreboding she ran from her room and hastened down the stairs.

The thorn having been removed, Louise was about to withdraw her hand when Philip, still holding it in his, said sadly, "So this little hand is to be bestowed upon Sir Charles Gresham – I trust that he realizes his great good fortune – though there is of course no doubt that his lands and your father's run so conveniently well together." and, with a deep sigh, he raised her hand again to his lips and kissed it. Louise had had many admirers since her come-out and had soon learned to flirt a little and accept with composure the flowery compliments which it was the custom for fashionable gentlemen to bestow upon young ladies; but there could be no mistaking the depth of feeling of the young man so close beside her. She had seldom been alone with a man, for Lady Sedley was strict in all matters of propriety, and she felt aware of a strange sensation of excitement coursing through her veins. Her eyes wide with astonishment, she looked up into his face and then, hearing footsteps, glanced beyond him and snatching back her hand, rose to her feet, her flushed face the picture of confusion and guilt.

It would have been hard for the most perspicacious student of human nature to determine what thoughts were passing through Sir Charles's mind as he drew near. To Louise it seemed that his look was stern; Philip, who had also risen, regarded him defiantly and felt a sensation of something akin to outrage when Sir Charles greeted them in his customary urbane manner, saying, "Good-morning, my dear Louise – your servant, Brandon. A perfect day, ain't it?" and stood regarding them easily without uttering another word.

Louise, flustered and profoundly ill at ease, hastened into speech, "So unfortunate, Charles, – I pricked my finger – on the rose-bush you know." She held out her hand in explanation, "Cousin Philip kindly removed the thorn for me." Her eyes were anxiously fixed on Sir Charles's face.

"Indeed!" The latter raised his eyeglass and solemnly regarded the slim finger extended towards him, saying calmly, "But how fortunate that Philip was there to assist you."

Feelings of relief flooded over Louise, at least there was to be no angry scene but behind those feelings, in a corner of her mind, she was conscious of a feeling of chagrin that her future husband should be so indifferent to her well-being, so devoid of jealousy. It dawned upon her how little she knew of this man whom she had agreed to marry. At this moment there was the sound of light, running footsteps and Henrietta came swiftly down the path towards them, although she slowed to a walk when she saw that they had observed her approach. Even before she had reached them she broke into breath-less speech, "Good morning, Sir Charles, how good to see you – is it not excellent news that Philip and I are now officially recognized by our family?" As she drew nearer she was relieved and surprised to see, from the faces turned towards her, that whatever else had occurred before she arrived upon the scene, at least no ugly incident was about to take place. Louise's face was still a little flushed, Philip's countenance bore a reckless, devil-may-care expression which she knew, alas, only too well. Only Sir Charles appeared impassive. What could he be thinking? She realized with a sudden sensation of sur-prise that she had no idea.

It was he who made the first move towards her, bowing politely over her hand and saying, with every appearance of sincerity, "Indeed, I am delighted – but you know, ever since I first made your acquaintance I never doubted your identity." There was an ambiguity about this remark, which made Henrietta look quickly into his face. His expression revealed nothing and his eyes returned her gaze with a blandness which she felt certain concealed his real thoughts and rather served to increase her unease.

Now he was addressing Louise, "I have called because I received yesterday a communication from Bath which will, alas, oblige us to make some minor alteration to our plans." He saw her look of surprise and continued, "I had written to my mother apprising her of our betrothal, so that she should learn of it directly from me, before the announcement appears in the 'Gazette'. I now discover that she and her companion have left their apartment in Bath to visit a childhood friend of my mother's in Wales and have omitted to leave an address with their landlord. It is unfortunate, but I believe we must therefore delay the announcement until I am able to communicate with her – I am sure that you will agree with me that it would be unthinkable that she should first learn the news from the 'Gazette'. Although," he added, "I have not the least doubt that she will be overjoyed at the news that I am to marry."

To Louise, the intelligence of a delay in the announcement of their betrothal, coming so swiftly upon Philip's words concerning her marriage, bore all the interesting marks of an unknown Fate taking a hand in her destiny. She looked up at Sir Charles, with an effort at composure, and replied gently, "Why, but of course, sir, I would not offend your mother for the world."

He looked pleased and for the first time that morning his countenance expressed real affection, as, kissing her hand, he said, "I knew you would understand. But now I must leave you – I have to inspect a roof at the Home farm and Cope is awaiting me – but I will call upon you tomorrow." Turning to Philip and Henrietta, he added pleasantly, "I am glad for you both that all is settled now. No doubt you will shortly be visiting the Hartingtons?"

With an effort, Philip forced himself to reply in a civil manner, "Why, no, sir, our plans are still uncertain."

"Then we shall have the pleasure of your company in Sussex for a while longer." and bowing politely, Sir Charles took his leave of them and strolled off towards the house.

He was standing in the hall, receiving his hat and gloves from the Sedley's butler, a thoughtful expression on his face, when Henrietta came quickly along the passage from the garden, and, with a glance at the manservant's retreating back, said in a low voice, "Forgive my delaying you, Sir Charles, but I wish to speak to you in private. Would you be kind enough to come into the drawing-room for a few moments?" Seconds later, confronting Sir Charles alone in the drawing-room, Henrietta suddenly found herself at a loss for words. She sat down abruptly upon the window seat, running her fingers through her curls in a gesture of perplexity, thereby ruining the effect so cleverly contrived by Pearson that morning, and looked up at Sir Charles's impassive face uncertainly, saying in a distracted voice, "I scarcely know where to begin."

Sir Charles, beholding the anxious face upturned to him, gave a sudden chuckle, "Perhaps, Miss Brandon, it is your wish to tell me that I should set no great store by the touching scene enacted before me in the walled garden!"

She looked startled and her colour rose as she said with amazement and relief, "So you know it is all a piece of nonsense."

He replied calmly, "I did not say that – but I believe it is what you wish to tell me."

She looked puzzled, then brushed the distinction aside, "Certainly it is nonsense – but, in fact, I wished to offer you some friendly advice – being a female, you see."

"Indeed – no doubt you have a great deal of experience." he responded solemnly, but there was so much amusement betrayed in the laughter-lines around his eyes that Henrietta looked at him sharply, then said awkwardly, "To be plain, sir, you are by no means sufficiently romantic in your dealings with a girl like Louise."

"And how, Miss Brandon, do you propose that I should become more 'romantic'?"

"Why, you should pay her more compliments, be more ardent in your manner. How can she know that you love her passionately if you never show that you do so."

Sir Charles looked thoughtful, "And that is what *you* recommend, Miss Brandon?"

"You see," Henrietta continued with more confidence, "Louise sets great store by romance. Now my brother conceals nothing, every passing feeling is revealed . Of course he is foolish beyond permission in his behaviour, but that is all, and I shall speak to him severely and reprimand him for his conduct."

Somehow, at that moment, Henrietta became aware that she had erred; whether it was her proffered advice or whether it was the mention of her brother that had precipitated some change in Sir Charles's mood, she could not be sure. He had been leaning negligently against the mantel-piece, as he listened to her with an air of polite attention. Now he straightened and came across the room to stand over her and something in his manner suddenly reminded her that here was a man who was accustomed to exercise authority – this was, she thought quickly with a feeling of alarm, how a member of his ship's crew would have felt when brought before him on a charge!

"Miss Brandon – no doubt you have the best of motives – but I would be greatly obliged if you would not meddle in my affairs." He added, after a pause, "Though it may surprise you – I am perfectly capable of managing my own life. I should infinitely prefer that you say nothing to your brother or to anyone else upon this subject. You are far too young to have any comprehension of the matter."

Henrietta, though inwardly indignant at his reference to her youth – she was, after all, only two years younger than Louise – felt obliged to apologize, for, as she told herself, she had undoubtedly overstepped the bounds of propriety since her acquaintance with Sir Charles was, it must be admitted, of only a few days duration. It was indeed only natural that he should resent her interference. She still felt, nevertheless, a degree of anxiety – what was he planning to do to avert what seemed to Henrietta to be the possible wrecking of his marriage plans?

She stood up, her brown eyes regarding him frankly and said without hesitation, "Sir Charles, I am sorry that I have interfered and have displeased you."

The stern look on his face vanished and with a return to his normal calm, easy manner he took Henrietta's hand in his, to bow over it in farewell, saying politely as he did so, "Unthinkable that you should displease me, Miss Brandon."

Looking quickly up into his face as he straightened, Henrietta wondered whether she caught a gleam of laughter in his eyes, then dismissed the notion. It was impossible that he should find it a matter for amusement for there was no doubt in her mind that he was determined to brook no interference from anyone concerning his betrothal. After he had departed, Henrietta sat a long time, deep in thought; should she be relieved or rendered more anxious after her conversation with Sir Charles?

Meanwhile, as these events unfolded at the Grange, the atmosphere in Hugo Brandon's household that morning had become increasingly gloomy for, although George had been instructed the previous day by Sir William to make no mention of Henrietta's first appearance as a boy, he had not been able to resist the temptation to tell of the arrival of two unknown cousins from France. The fears of the few remaining servants had been further exacerbated by the return from London of their master, late the previous night, in a savage mood. He had dismissed George peremptorily to his bed and had sat half the night drinking himself into a stupor and biting the head off any person foolish enough to address him.

"It ain't what you might call 'promising'!" Mrs Arnold, a stout, slatternly woman in her late fifties addressed her husband, who shook his head mournfully in response. The immense kitchen quarters wore a neglected air, upon which the half-hearted efforts of two local girls made scant impression. Indeed the rest of the house was scarcely better tended: fine furniture had grown dull with lack of polish and curtains hung in dusty folds, damasks and velvets slowly disintegrating. Upon this depressing scene, the entrance of a slight, elegantly dressed man of middle years, whose fashionable appearance contrasted sharply with Arnold's ill-fitting and well-worn livery, provided a welcome diversion.

"Well, Mr Smales, 'ow is 'e this morning? Or ain't 'e rung for you yet?" Mrs Arnold sniffed disapprovingly.

"Still sleeping!" was the sour reply; Smale's sharp-featured face was sombre, "He ain't had good news – that's certain."

The elderly butler sat himself down with a groan, "I reckons if summat don't turn up soon we'll all be out of a job! They say down in the village that this Frenchie be the rightful heir to old 'Artington – so all 'is 'igh and mightiness' 'opes are down the drain."

There was a cunning look in the valet's pale eyes as he looked scornfully at the anxious faces turned towards him. "I reckon you'll find Mr Brandon don't give up so easy. There's ways and means, y'know!"

Mrs Arnold looked puzzled, "Marry an heiress, you mean, Mr Smales?" she added with a coarse laugh, "My word, 'e'd 'ave to change his ways then. No more fancy women, eh! Shockin' I calls it, the way 'e carrys on."

At that moment a bell rang in the passageway, "That'll be 'im, Mr Smales!" she filled a jug with chocolate which had been kept warm on the side of the stove and handed him a tray, saying with a chuckle, "Mind as 'ow you don't get it thrown at yer 'ead for yer pains."

The valet tightened his lips repressively, "I believe I know how to handle my gentlemen, Mrs Arnold."

"Turn 'em up sweet, can you?" She eyed him wonderingly, "Beats me why you stay wiv 'im – with your h'abilities an' all!"

Smales disdained to answer. As he mounted the stairs he thought grimly of the many months of wages overdue: that would have to be set to rights before he could contemplate a change. Still, there was no doubt his master did him credit – a fine figure of a man – upon whom his own exceptional talents were not wasted. No-one could set of a coat better than Mr Brandon, and his calves – Smales sighed – what a misfortune that such well-turned legs should support so profligate a gentleman! He had the common sense not to offer more than a softly spoken "Good-morning, sir!" to his master, who, pale and irritable, glowered at him from his pillows, and after opening the shutters and retrieving some garments thrown carelessly to the floor removed himself from the room in silence. It was only later, as he assisted his master into his coat that the opportunity occurred to offer Hugo some solace and some advice.

Beyond a few words regarding his attire, silence had reigned in the dressing-room, until Hugo, goaded into speech by his anger and frustration, remarked savagely, "Hell and damnation, no need to pretend you don't know what's amiss, Smales! No doubt you are as well informed, if not better, as anyone."

"A very distressing turn of events, sir!" He eyed Hugo's handsome face, a scowl distorting its fine lines, and enquired softly "Am I to understand that the young gentleman from France has proved to be your great-uncle's heir?"

"Yes, God dammit, you may!" hatred glared from Hugo's eyes, "And if he dropped down dead tomorrow, I should be the last to shed any tears!"

Smales picked up some discarded cravats and eyed his master thoughtfully, "If I might be permitted to say so, sir, it might be wiser to dissemble somewhat your very natural feelings." He gave a discreet cough, "I remember when I was in service with Mr Henry Preston – he was upon very bad terms with his cousin, the heir to the title – and when that gentleman died, suddenly like, there were such rumours –" he left the sentence unfinished and saw with satisfaction that Hugo was regarding him with a dawning interest.

Encouraged, the valet continued gently, "I've heard from Richards, him as waits upon Mr Francis over at the Grange, that the young lady from France, the sister of this here gentleman, has a deal to recommend her – quite a beauty, Richards says! One would suppose that her grandfather will see her well-endowed." He had caught Hugo's attention now. The dark eyes stared into the looking-glass at Smales's face reflected in its polished surface, and whose pale eyes were gazing blandly back at him.

Hugo crossed to the window and stood for a moment staring out across the ill-kept pleasure-gardens, then turned, a look of resolution upon his countenance. "Tell Hunt to bring the phaeton round!" was all that was said, but it was sufficient to send Smales downstairs to carry out his instructions with a feeling of satisfaction.

CHAPTER 8

"How unfortunate that the announcement must be delayed!" Lady Sedley voiced her thoughts in decided tones, as she threaded her needle.

Louise, her head bent over the fringe that she was knotting, murmured, "Yes, Mama." in a low voice and continued with her work.

Her mother, casting a sharp glance in her direction, was unable to see more than the top of her daughter's head, "So inconsiderate of dear Lady Gresham to have left no forwarding address." she continued in an aggrieved voice. Henrietta, seated by the window with her new workbasket at her side, felt that it was high time to give another direction to Lady Sedley's thoughts. "You have such an excellent eye for colour, ma'am; would you consider this shade of green will blend with the darker colour of the tree?" She brought the silks and her embroidery frame across to Lady Sedley's chair and knelt beside her.

Throughout the previous day, Henrietta had endeavoured to see that her brother and Louise had had no further opportunity to converse in private; that at least she had felt she could safely do without contravening Sir Charles's wishes. It had been noticeable that Louise had been quieter than usual and no doubt Lady Sedley had observed this and had reached her own conclusions, however mistaken they might be.

The piece of embroidery was an unusual one; Henrietta had taken the idea from a print and drawn the figure of a girl wearing a blue and white muslin dress upon the cream-coloured silk: a rod and line in her hand, she was holding up the fish that she had caught. She had already finished the foliage of the background, setting quite neat stitches considering that her own mother had set little store by such accomplishments. Even Lady Sedley had felt called upon to commend her handiwork.

"A charming piece of work, my dear Henrietta, I wish Louise had the same application to her needle."

As Henrietta resumed her seat, heartily hoping that she would not be obliged to spend too much of her time in such a sedentary activity, voices could be heard in the hall, the door opened and the butler announced, "Mr Hugo Brandon has called to see you, my lady."

"Show him in, Haines." Lady Sedley looked surprised. She had heard from her husband of Hugo's furious departure from Mr Forsythe's office and had imagined that some time would have to elapse before his rage and disappointment would have abated sufficiently to allow him to resume normal social intercourse with his new cousins.

"What a charming scene of industry!" Hugo's face betrayed no sign of resentment as he paused in the door-way, his eye-glass raised, then strode across the room to greet the three ladies. Lady Sedley looked approvingly at him, to her mind no good ever came of family quarrels; for Louise it was a pleasure to have some distraction from a task which she found tedious; only Henrietta's response to his greeting was tinged with reserve: since her arrival in England, he had been the one who had first opposed, then bitterly resented their relationship. However, the open admiration that was clearly visible upon his face as he turned to Henrietta in her new sprig-muslin dress went a long way to dissipate any feelings of antagonism.

It was the first time that Hugo had seen her dressed as a fashionable young lady and the warmly appreciative look in his eye as he surveyed her brought a faint colour to her cheeks. For her part, Henrietta became once more aware of the strong family resemblance between Philip and his cousin. Hugo was, of course, several years older than her brother and had an air of sophistication and cynicism which was vastly different to Philip's enthusiastic attitude to life, both were of the same height and colouring, but there was also something in the shape of his nose, the angle of his dark brows that reminded her of her brother.

It was Henrietta whom he first addressed, saying contritely, "I hope you'll find it in your heart to forgive me, Cousin, for I know I have behaved badly towards you and your brother," and adding with a rueful smile, "Perhaps you can imagine how great was the shock when I learned that another was to take my place."

It was said with a disarming frankness that at once appealed to Henrietta's sympathy. "Why, indeed, Cousin Hugo, I can understand it very well – for you, having no knowledge of Philip's existence – how could it be otherwise?"

Hugo turned to Lady Sedley, "I am sure Sir William has told you of my uncivil behaviour in his presence two days ago – I beg you to convey my apologies to him." Before Lady Sedley could reply, the door opened and Sir William, himself, entered the room, followed by Philip, both dressed for riding.

"Well, young fellow, come to your senses, eh?" Sir William clapped him heartily on the back and looked relieved, "It's a sad day when relations fall out with one another."

"Indeed, sir, my apologies to you!" Hugo's gaze fell upon Philip and he stepped forward, extending his hand to the younger man. "I've a devilish temper, as others will bear witness – perhaps you will be good enough to set my behaviour at Forsythe's office down to my intemperate disposition and forget what I said in a moment of anger and frustration."

Accepting his cousin's explanation afforded no especial difficulty to Philip. He had paid little heed to Hugo's threats, and now, his mind far more occupied by the lovely Louise, he had no scruples in taking the hand held out to him in a firm grasp, saying light-heartedly, "Consider it deuced handsome of you, Hugo, – Good God – to lose the expectations of a lifetime – I wish it could have happened differently." He was conscious of Louise's approving face and gave her a warm smile. There was an agreeable feeling of relief amongst all those present.

Henrietta saw Hugo's eyes follow Philip's gaze to Louise's face and thought that she observed a gleam of interest upon his countenance. He was addressing her now, taking the embroidery-frame from her hand and looking admiringly at her handiwork, "I see you are as talented as you are charming, my dear cousin!"

She looked at him in friendly fashion and said, laughing," And you, sir, know how to turn a pretty compliment, however ill-deserved," but she seemed pleased in spite of her disclaimer. At this moment, heralded by two excited spaniels, Francis appeared at the French-window and, acknowledging Hugo's presence with a grin, demanded to know how much longer he was to await his father and Philip at the stables.

"Francis! Those dogs in my drawing-room!" Lady Sedley's voice rose in protest.

"By Jove, yes, Francis!" Sir William urged his son towards the open door to the garden, "Quite forgot we were on our way to join you." He added, pleased to prolong the accord within the family, "Come along all of you – come and see the new mare that I am thinking of buying – hope she'll make a quiet mount for you, Louise."

"For me! Oh, how kind you are, Papa!" Louise rose to her feet with alacrity, "Come, Henrietta! Let us go with them!"

Henrietta needed no second bidding and, as the younger members of the family accompanied Sir William to the stables, she found herself walking between Hugo and Francis, both of whom seemed eager to engage her attention. "When are we to see you out riding, Cousin?" Francis enquired.

"Soon, I hope, for the habit that I ordered in Brighton must soon be ready."

"If you would care to drive out with me in the meantime," Hugo promptly proposed, "it would give me great pleasure to show you this part of Sussex."

"Hugo fancies himself with the ribbons, drives to an inch, y'know – but best beware of meeting a farm-cart in these narrow lanes!" Francis quipped.

The badinage continuing as they made their way across the drive. Henrietta found herself enjoying the novelty of attracting the attention of two young men, one of whom was undoubtedly an extremely modish gentleman, dressed in the height of fashion, and whom one might have supposed to have had more sophisticated tastes in female companionship. Indeed, there was about Hugo a recklessness, which, unlike her brother's impetuosity, seemed to hold an element of danger; something in the expression in his eyes that caused her heart to beat a little faster. About Francis, on the contrary, there was an eminently good-natured air that Henrietta found particularly appealing and she thought to herself with inward amusement that his manner most resembled the friendly attentions of the sporting dogs that always cavorted at his heels.

The groom had led out the mare into the stable-yard, a pretty bay with a good head and an intelligent eye. Sir William was pointing out her virtues to the assembled company, when the sound of hooves made him break off in mid-sentence as a horseman mounted upon a handsome gray could be seen trotting up the driveway. "Why Charles, just the man we want. Come and see the mare I am thinking of buying for Louise." Sir William greeted his future son-in-law with enthusiasm.

Charles, now near enough to see the expressions on the faces turned towards him, saluted them affably. Henrietta thought, as he dismounted, that the role of horseman suited him admirably and casting a hasty glance at Louise, hoped that she was of the same mind. Certainly she greeted him prettily enough.

He seemed, Henrietta thought, quite at his ease and it was impossible to perceive any sign of irritation upon his face at finding Philip close by Louise's side in the group surrounding the mare. Indeed, having examined and admired Sir William's proposed purchase, it was to Philip that he turned, saying in a friendly manner, "I'm planning to shoot this afternoon – wood-pigeon, you know, – which are a pest at this time of year in particular, and maybe the odd rabbit. I could lend you a gun if you would care for it?" It was certainly an invitation that appealed to Philip: he was a good shot and accepted it with enthusiasm, anticipating with pleasure an opportunity to show himself to advantage.

"May George and I join you?" Hugo enquired, "He gets deucedly bored in the holidays, you know, then gets himself into some mischief or other – I know he would be delighted and if I am there I can keep an eye on him – not that he isn't sensible enough with a gun."

Sir Charles, being agreeable to this proposal, arrangements were made as to time and place, "Come to my house about two o'clock and we'll try the wood that adjoins Green Lane, and the fields alongside." So saying, he was about to remount and depart when Philip, who had been regarding with envy the excellent cut of his coat, asked diffidently the name of his tailor, adding, "I feel I must present myself at my grandfather's house at least looking like an Englishman!"

"Weston is my man, but there are only a few of us who patronize him as yet." Charles seemed amused, "Your cousin favours Milne in Grosvenor Street which you may prefer. He probably needs the assistance of two men to get that coat on his back!"

"Nonsense, Charles!" Hugo grinned at him, "No such thing – but Milne is favoured by many of the ton, ain't that right, Sir William?"

"Maybe, maybe, don't consider myself an authority on the subject – comfort is my object, y'know."

Philip, looking with new eyes at the dark green coat, which fitted Hugo's elegant frame like a glove, hesitated.

"Take you to Milne myself, introduce you, if you like – they'll take more interest then." Hugo seemed anxious to demonstrate his friendliness.

The young ladies, meanwhile, were given an excellent opportunity of regarding their male companions without concealment, and each knew which gentleman, in her opinion, would set off his tailor's art to the best advantage.

"Fashionable tailors!" interjected Francis scornfully, "Dashed well make over their customers' figures to suit their own requirements, padding here – pinching-in there – then send you a bill as long as your arm! I've no use for 'em – give me a country tailor every time."

Punctually at two o'clock Charles's guests were assembled. He selected a gun for Philip and, followed by the dogs, they set out for the West wood with the intention of terminating the existence of as many vermin as possible. Entering the wood, Charles directed them to spread themselves out in a well-spaced line extending from the edge of the trees by the road to the field on the east side, and from there to advance towards the pastureland to the south. As he traversed the wood, Philip thought how strange it was to think that only a few days before he had been fleeing for his life from the only home he had ever known. Now, in these peaceful English surroundings, with all the agreeable sights and sounds of nature around him, he mused with pleasure and amazement how unbelievably his life had changed. There was so much new to learn about his father's country, so many new members of his family to meet. He hoped fervently that his grandfather, Lord Hartington, would be pleased to learn of his grandson's existence.

It was about three o'clock as they neared the edge of the trees. Their bag by now consisted of nine wood-pigeon, a jay and two rabbits. Philip, who had accounted for three of the birds, was about to call across to Charles, whom he could hear, but not see, in the thicket alongside him when, suddenly, there was the sound of a gunshot. The blow spun him round and a burning pain seared his shoulder.

His involuntary cry of alarm rent the silence and in a moment Charles, crashing through the undergrowth, was beside him. Leaning, white-faced, against a tree-trunk, Philip was clutching his hand to his shoulder when Charles reached him, "Good God, man, what has happened?" Charles's face was grim. Helping Philip to sit down upon the ground, by which time the rest of the party had appeared, concern and astonishment upon their faces, he directed them to aid him in easing off Philip's coat which was charred and torn on the shoulder.

"Thank God it's no worse! Painful – but a surface wound only!" Charles, no stranger to the sight of gun-shot wounds or blood, let out his breath sharply, as he undid Philip's shirt and disclosed a flesh wound above the collar-bone where the ball had passed through the thicker material at the shoulder.

"But where did the shot come from – and why?" Philip, the colour beginning to return to his face, looked with amazement at the anxious faces surrounding him.

"By the angle it looks as if it may have come from the lane – why, God only knows!" Charles was gently binding the shoulder with his own cravat, "Thank the Lord, the ball has not entered the shoulder."

George, whose youthful ebullience had been momentarily subdued by the accident, broke into excited speech, "There are gypsies encamped a little way down the lane – could it be one of them? Hugo has been trying to get them off our land for ages – maybe they thought Philip was him – from the distance, you know, they could be mistaken."

Hugo looked thoughtful, "It's true they have no love for me – but I wouldn't have thought they would go as far as that –"

"We'll have to report it – but we must get the poor fellow home first." Charles helped Philip to his feet and laid his coat around his shoulders, "Do you feel able to walk back to my house?"

"Why, of course, 'tis not so painful –" He laughed, "Confound it! Here was I believing that I had reached a law-abiding country at last. It seems that I was mistaken.

CHAPTER 9

It was Francis who drove Philip back to the Grange in the gig. Philip had been resolute in refusing to allow Charles to accompany them, though the latter had declared earnestly that he felt under an obligation to do so – the accident – if that was what it was – having taken place upon his property. Agreeing, finally, to let them depart without him, Charles announced his intention of calling the next morning to make sure that all was well and to report the details of their exact location at the time of the shot to Sir William.

Henrietta had reflected afterwards that it had been fortunate that Lady Sedley had not been present with Louise and herself, when Philip and Francis had entered the drawing-room. She and Louise had been discussing the books that they were reading and she had been astonished at Louise's uncritical delight in the most impossible adventures that her novel contained. They both looked up at the young men's unexpected entrance so early in the day. Philip's appearance standing in the door-way, his coat slung around his shoulders and streaks of blood marring the whiteness of his shirt front, was quite enough to arouse alarm in the breasts of both girls. Louise, rising to her feet, her face drained of colour, cried out in horror, "Dear God, what has Charles done?" and fainted at Henrietta's feet. The latter, being made of sterner stuff, endeavoured to stifle her fears and asked her brother anxiously, "Are you badly hurt?" and receiving a reassuring negative, turned to assist her cousin.

Meanwhile, Francis, who had entered the room on Philip's heels, was staring at the recumbent form of his sister in disgust and astonishment, "Girl's got wind-mills in her head! Why the devil should she suppose this is Charles's handiwork?"

Philip, attempting awkwardly to kneel beside Louise, was shooed away by his sister, "Let me attend to her – you are quite in my way, and besides – you look as if you need attention yourself! In a moment I will ask you all about it – when," she added, impatience creeping into her voice, "this foolish creature has recovered her wits."

"Poor little one – she is so sensitive! Alas, that I should have been the cause of her distress."

"For goodness sake, Philip, sit down! And if you, Francis, will fetch me a glass of water, we shall have her recovered in a moment." By now Louise was showing signs of returning consciousness and Henrietta, as she chafed her hands, murmured soothingly, "All is well – let me help you up, and then Philip shall tell us what has happened."

Louise's eyelids fluttered, then opened and her dark eyes, wide with fear, gazed up into Henrietta's face. "Oh, say that he is not mortally wounded, Henrietta!"

"I will say it with infinite pleasure, Louise!" Even in her concern for her brother, Henrietta could not but feel an inward stirring of amusement at Louise's highly developed sense of drama. "If you could, with my assistance, find the strength to rise and lie upon the sofa, I will ask poor Philip to reassure you and I will see what needs to be done to aid *him*."

As soon as she heard these words, Louise rose shakily to her feet and, assisted by her unsympathetic brother, lowered herself upon the sofa. After a few sips of water, the while regarding Philip anxiously, said in a soft voice, "I am so sorry to be so stupid – it is *you* who must be attended to! *You* who are suffering!" She turned to Francis and added, "Should we not send for Dr Thornton immediately?"

"Charles will have already sent a message to him, so, no doubt, he will be here shortly." Francis, feeling that Philip had already had enough to bear, began to recount the story of the startling event that had terminated their afternoon's enjoyment. "– so you see," he finished, "it was a shot that came from the lane; there's little doubt – and a strong possibility – that one of the gypsies mistook Philip for Hugo!"

As he spoke, Henrietta had gently removed Philip's coat and seeing the neat way that his shoulder had been bound and that no fresh blood was soaking through the bandaging, sighed with relief. "It is excellently done – I hope it does not pain you too dreadfully!"

"That's Charles's handiwork, took off his cravat and bound it up as neat as any sawbones – that's the advantage of having a naval man present." Francis's admiration for their neighbour was clear.

Philip, immensely gratified by the effect that his accident had had upon Louise, sought to reassure her, saying gently, "It is no more than a flesh-wound, little cousin, it is nothing." and smiled tenderly at her.

Henrietta was thankful that at that moment Sir William's and Lady Sedley's voices were heard and their entrance speedily put an end to any further exchanges between Philip and Louise. Even Francis, who, she was sure, was not a naturally observant man where the finer passions were concerned, could hardly fail to notice the ardour of Philip's regard, nor Louise's response. Confronted by the sight of their daughter languishing upon the sofa and their guest bespattered with blood, both Sir William and Lady Sedley expressed horror and amazement.

"Good God, what's amiss?" Even Sir William's ruddy countenance had paled.

"My poor child! What has happened?" Lady Sedley took Henrietta's place at Louise's side, her daughter's welfare taking precedence over her new kinsman's, although she cast an anxious glance at Philip.

It was Francis, once again, who told his horrified parents how Philip had come to be wounded, finishing his recital by saying, "– a damned fortunate thing, saving your presence, Mama, that he ain't dead, a few inches to the left and . . .

There was a faint cry from Louise, "Pray, pray don't, Francis!"

Lady Sedley patted her hand, "My dear child, Philip is alive and, thank God, his wound is not too severe or he would not be standing here." She turned to her son and said, "My poor Louise, what has happened to her?"

"Fainted away, Mama, when she saw Philip." Francis spoke with disgust, "Henrietta's the heroine of the hour, never turned a hair – and, deuce take it, he's *her* brother, after all is said and done."

Henrietta, somewhat embarrassed by this unlooked-for encomium, added hastily to the startled Lady Sedley, "Louise is so sensitive, as you know, dear ma'am, – the sight of blood was too much for her –"

Lady Sedley nodded, but there was a sharpening in the gaze that she turned upon her daughter. In the meantime, Sir William had been gently interrogating Philip, having first re-assured himself that Dr Thornton had been summoned.

"It is, I believe, the merest scratch, sir – and well tended by Sir Charles." Philip was anxious to reduce the alarm that his appearance had produced but already the delayed shock was beginning to take its toll. He drew his hand shakily across his brow, where beads of perspiration had begun to form.

"Off to your room with you, my dear fellow!" Sir William ordered, "You'll feel the better for getting away from all this commotion – deuced unfortunate business this – never heard the like. I'll see the constable in the morning and get some enquiries set on foot. Though whether we'll ever get to the bottom of the matter, I have my doubts – if it was a gypsy, they'll stick together and deny it all!"

It was shortly after Philip had retired that Dr Thornton, a neat, spare figure wearing an old-fashioned 'physical' wig, arrived, to the relief of all concerned, and was conducted by Francis to Philip's bed-chamber. While awaiting the medical verdict, Sir William, observing that Henrietta was, herself, looking a good deal shaken, offered her some brandy as a restorative draught, saying kindly, "It's enough to give you a disgust for your country, now that you are returned home at last. And we thinking all the violence and bloodshed was across the Channel!" He rambled on gently, thankful to see a little colour returning to her cheeks.

Lady Sedley, re-arranging the cushion at Louise's back, spoke bracingly to her daughter, "So fortunate that dear Charles was at hand when the shot was fired – just the man to have beside one in a crisis and he would know at once what was best to do. I am sure he will be sorry to hear of the distress it has caused you."

"Oh, Mama, pray do not tell him how foolish I have been!" Louise looked up at her anxiously, "That is if Francis does not take it upon himself to do so." she added bitterly. Her face displayed such a degree of concern that her mother felt obliged to reassure her. "My dear, if you prefer it, I will say nothing upon that head."

Dr Thornton returned to give a satisfactory report upon Philip's condition. "He's had a lucky escape, thank the Lord, Lady Sedley. It's only a surface wound and clean enough – I've dressed it and bound it up again and given the young man a dose of laudanum to take that he may get some sleep tonight. It will ache like the deuce – so he should be sure to take it and not try for any heroics by doing without."

"I'll make sure that he takes it, Doctor!" Henrietta spoke with resolution and Dr Thornton looked at her with some surprise.

"I'm his sister, sir." She continued ruefully, "I know well how obstinate he can be, but, I assure you, there'll be no nonsense."

He smiled at the determined face turned towards him, recording inwardly that the young Brandons were a remarkably handsome couple and likely to cause no small stir in the neighbourhood. As he took his leave of them all, he added that he would return on the morrow to see how the patient progressed and to be sure that no fever had resulted from the wound.

Philip passed a restless night but in the morning his brow was cool and Henrietta, fearing that a battle of wills would be more likely as not to exacerbate her brother's condition, consented to his rising from his bed. Thus, when Sir Charles called to find out how the invalid progressed, he found Philip, his arm in a sling and looking

114

every inch the wounded hero, seated in the drawing-room in the midst of the ladies of the house.

Having exchanged greetings and made searching enquiries as to the doctor's prognosis, Sir Charles took a seat beside Henrietta and said with a wry smile, "I would give anything for this not to have happened – and on my land – it makes me wish that I had never issued the invitation."

"Why, sir, you can not be blamed. But it makes me a little uneasy, I must confess." She looked at him with large, troubled eyes, and said quietly, so that her words were inaudible to the rest of the company, "It hardly seems possible but – can it be that Philip has enemies in this country?"

"I hardly think so – and his whereabouts in England cannot be known in France – you can be sure of that, Miss Brandon." He sounded so confident that Henrietta, looking into his face and beholding his expression, his eyes wearing the kind, calm look that was usual to them, felt herself reassured.

Hard upon Sir Charles's heels came Hugo, who having encountered Sir William in the hall, accompanied him into the room. "Glad to hear, cousin, that you make good progress – who would not, by Jupiter, surrounded by such a bevy of beauty!" Hugo, eyeglass in hand, surveyed the company, and his eyes seemed to linger longest upon Henrietta.

Sir William, taking up his usual stance before the fire-place, revealed that enquiries were being made in the vicinity, "The constable is down at the encampment now and will be asking questions in the village – but I fear it will be in vain." he sighed, "Well, we must be thankful that no great harm has resulted."

"Only that his coat is ruined!" Hugo grinned at Philip, "You'll be more anxious than ever to visit a tailor. I mean to drive to London on Friday – if you are sufficiently recovered and would care to, you could accompany me and I will introduce you to my man." He added in friendly fashion, "You can stay the night at my place – I have rooms in Ryder Street – and we might look in at 'Brooks's."

"By Jove, yes, I should like that extremely." His invitation received an enthusiastic assent from Philip – his fashionable cousin was just the very person to introduce him into the upper ranks of masculine society in the capital, even though the Season was now over. "I've heard my father speak of 'Brooks's. He said that the play was high but well conducted."

"What an agreeable coincidence – I, too, go to London on Friday." Charles joined in the conversation, "Going to Tattersalls, you know – for I'm after a new hunter for next season. Perhaps I'll take a look in at 'Brooks's on my way home." he crossed the room to speak briefly to Louise and her mother upon the subject of the accident. The young girl's subdued manner could not fail to attract Lady Sedley's attention even as she, herself, commiserated with Sir Charles on the unexpected outcome of his shooting party. Having said all that was polite, he was about to take his leave when Philip, stopping him in the doorway, enquired confidentially, "I wonder, sir, if it is possible for you to help me?"

"In what way, dear boy?" Sir Charles, eyebrows raised, responded politely.

"Henrietta and I are anxious to try and convey some message to my mother in Switzerland and to our servants – that we are safe, you understand." Philip added in explanation, "I know that you are acquainted with the local fishermen and I am sure that, inspite of the war, there is some traffic across the Channel, smuggling no doubt – and after all, when all is said done, we, ourselves, made the journey – do you think you could find me a way to send such a message?"

Sir Charles regarded him thoughtfully for a moment, "There seems no harm in making the attempt – I will see what can be done, my dear fellow, but it will not be easy, I fear. Even if one could find some means of conveying a message across to France one could not be sure of it being sent on to Switzerland."

"If it could reach the skipper of the 'Marie-Claire' in Dieppe, I believe he could arrange to pass on the news to Jeanne. One can only hope that she may find a way to advise our mother of our safe arrival in England."

Sir Charles nodded sympathetically, "Well, we shall see what can be arranged. Take care of that arm – if you follow your sister's advice you will not go far wrong." It was in that moment that Philip felt for the first time a twinge of conscience; Sir Charles was, indeed, a most amiable man; how unworthy was it of him to endeavour to engage Louise's affections?

Meanwhile, Henrietta was feeling quite in charity with Hugo after his invitation to her brother – a visit to London would be the very thing to distract Philip from this unfortunate infatuation that he had formed for Louise – and so it was with pleasure and an agreeable flutter of excitement that she accepted an invitation before he left them, to drive out with him the following afternoon.

"Husband, I have fears for the future!"

Sir William, lying beside his wife, for they were sufficiently unfashionable not to sleep in separate bedchambers, turned to stare at her, his face displaying amused perplexity. "What's that, my love? The future – I see naught to concern us in the future."

Lady Sedley, her hair confined in a be-frilled cap, looked at his puzzled face beneath his nightcap and replied sarcastically, "My dear sir, you never see beyond your own nose. It is of Louise that I speak." She continued, not troubling to conceal her irritation, "I should have thought even you could not have failed to observe that our new cousin is well on the way to falling in love with her."

"Dammit, she's a devilish good-looking gal, so it don't surprise me one jot." Sir William's expression softened as he thought of his pretty daughter, "No doubt poor Philip can't help himself. Though I'll admit you're more perceptive than I am – anyway – she's betrothed to Charles – a devilish fine fellow – so what's amiss?"

"What is amiss, my dear sir, is that I fear that Louise begins to reciprocate his feelings."

"Of course she reciprocates his feelings, deuce take it – ain't she betrothed to him?"

"Sir William, are you being wilfully obtuse?" Lady Sedley flushed with indignation, "I refer to Philip Brandon, of course – have you not noticed her manner when he addresses her?" she added inconsequentially, "Of course, he'll be Lord Hartington one day."

Sir William, inspite of his bluff exterior, was a remarkably shrewd man. He knew his wife and looked at her with disapproval, "Setting your sights higher, my lady? Well, I, for one, will have none of it – I'm very fond of Charles and have no wish to serve him a back-hander."

"There's Francis, too."

"Francis!" Sir William's eyes seemed ready to fall from their sockets.

Lady Sedley smiled gently, "Never known him show the smallest interest in any female, at least," she corrected dryly, "not in any eligible female – but he seems to show a partiality for Henrietta's company. And she'll be an heiress one day, I don't doubt."

Sir William smiled, "Taking little thing – I like her – so there's naught to fear there."

Lady Sedley shook her head doubtfully, "Francis has so little address – I've tried my hardest – if only he would model himself upon Hugo, for if Hugo should set his sights upon Henrietta, I fear that dear Francis will suffer a disappointment".

Sir William fell back upon his pillow with something between a groan and a chuckle, "Dear ma'am, from what you have told me, this household has become a veritable hot-bed of intrigue! I trust we shall not rue the day that we extended our hospitality to these young kinsmen."

"Remember, I warned you, Sir William – I warned you when we first set eyes upon them." Whether this was true or not, Sir William was content to let it pass; with a sigh he kissed his wife gently on the brow and, turning upon his side, blew out the candle that stood beside the bed, murmuring to himself as he did so, with a smile into the darkness, "I'm sure you'll find a way to set all to rights, my dear heart."

The next day being Sunday, Henrietta attended Morning service with the Sedley family while Philip remained at home to rest his shoulder. She was interested to observe from her place in the family pew that Sir Charles was also present. No sign of Hugo, however, and she concluded ruefully that his way of life, as portrayed by Louise, was scarcely likely to include church attendance. Curious glances were cast in her direction and as they emerged into the sunlight at the end of the service, Lady Sedley was approached by a large lady, her bonnet nodding with many plumes and ribbons, and accompanied by a stooping, elderly gentleman who followed in her wake.

"My dearest Julia, such rumours as I have been hearing! Can it indeed be true that you have acquired some interesting new cousins from France?"

"Of a certainty it is true, Maria. You will be quite astonished –" Lady Sedley was about to enlarge upon the subject when she observed the frown upon her husband's face. Comprehending that this was hardly the moment to inform the members of the local congregation standing around them of the young Brandons' history, she continued, in lowered tones, "Call upon me tomorrow, my dear, and I will tell you all about it."

Punctually at two o'clock, as promised, Hugo arrived, and nothing could have been more elegant than the appearance he presented as he waited for her in the hall. Glad that she was wearing a particularly becoming hat trimmed with an abundance of ribbons, she greeted him in a friendly manner and was soon sitting beside him on the seat of a high-perch phaeton with towering wheels and yellow wings and bowling along the country lanes. Lady Sedley having agreed that as

Hugo was her cousin there could be no impropriety in such an unaccompanied expedition, stated repressively as she gave her permission, "– for you know a young girl's good name is her most precious possession!"

In no time it was evident that he was, as Francis had told her, a dashing driver. At first she had been conscious of some unease but she soon realized that he had his pair of spirited bays well under control. When they skimmed past a laden wagon with a hair's-breadth to spare, she had to acknowledge that, in the words of her brother, he could drive to an inch. Her lofty seat provided an excellent view of the countryside and Hugo, clearly at pains to please her, pointed out various interesting features of the landscape and the principal houses in the district. It was upon their return journey, while he was entertaining her with a description of the delights that awaited her in London, of balls and routs and expeditions to Vauxhall and Ranelagh and offering with evident sincerity to escort her on such occasions, that they encountered a horseman. He greeted Hugo with a friendly wave of his hand and cast an appreciative glance at Henrietta as he took off his hat to her. She beheld a young, fair-haired gentleman, whose appearance of fashion must cast all others into the shade, though, to Henrietta's more austere taste, he sported an over-profusion of jewelry for one riding in the country.

After introductions and an exchange of civilities, Mr Simon Gosport enquired whether Hugo still had the intention of driving up onto the Downs upon the following Thursday, the object being, so Henrietta learned, to witness the Sham-Fight to be performed by the regiments encamped at Brighton. "M'friends tell me it's to be a grand Field-day – Prinny will be present and the Duke of York of course, and other generals."

"By Jove, yes – wouldn't miss it for the world, and I mean to get there early," Hugo replied with a grin, "for last time there was scarcely room to move." They arranged a time and place to meet and finally Mr Gosport, raising his hat politely, bade them farewell, declaring fervently that he was enchanted to have made Miss Brandon's acquaintance.

As Hugo gave his horses the office to start, Henrietta, who had been listening with the greatest interest, exclaimed impetuously, "Gracious, Cousin Hugo, what wouldn't I give to witness such an event!" adding disconsolately, "But Lady Sedley said, when we were in Brighton, that such occasions are not suitable for young ladies."

Hugo regarded her eager face with amusement, eyebrows raised, and remarked provocatively, "In that case, my dear Henrietta, it scarcely seems possible. If our revered cousin *forbids* it – though I confess I consider her views upon such matters to be positively gothic!"

It was a challenge to which Henrietta could not fail to respond – after all, what right had Lady Sedley to order her life? Her own mother had always encouraged her to form her own judgments. Only the previous year, she remembered Mrs Brandon's satisfaction when her views upon female education and place in society had been strongly confirmed by the newly published book by Mary Wollstonecraft, 'A Vindication of the Rights of Woman'. Henrietta did not feel that there could be any possible objection to her presence with her cousin at such an event. A precept of her mother's teaching had been not only that a woman's education should equal that provided for men but also that they should participate in political and intellectual life.

It would, nevertheless, be wise to employ a degree of secrecy. Lady Sedley, a traditionalist, clearly did not share her mother's open-mindedness. Her eyes wide with excitement, she said breathlessly, "Thursday, the very day that we were all to drive to Henfield to dine with friends of the family. Oh, Cousin Hugo, if I plead a headache, I could remain at home with ease and then – I know I could contrive to leave the house unobserved!" The bright, appealing eyes gazing at him were very persuasive. What had he to lose? To agree to such an escapade would certainly put him in Henrietta's good books and that would be no bad thing and could, indeed, well be turned to his advantage. Unaware of these calculations passing through her companion's mind, Henrietta continued eagerly, "Please, please Cousin Hugo, take me with you – it would be such a splendid chance."

He glanced down again at the face turned towards him – she was a devilish fine-looking girl; a little out of the ordinary perhaps but that only added to her attractions, he liked a woman of spirit. "My dear Henrietta, I should be enchanted to escort you." He saw with gratification her look of delight, "But you must be ready, mind, for I shan't be able to wait around for you."

"Oh yes, I'll be ready." she replied confidently, adding with a smile, "Oh, Hugo, I'll never forget this!"

For the rest of the journey home they laid their plans and when Henrietta was finally set down at the front door of the Grange, all had been arranged. As they parted, Henrietta was conscious of Hugo's eyes resting caressingly upon her. There was something in that look and in the way that he held her hand in farewell that brought a faint colour to her cheeks. If he could have known how eagerly she looked forward to the promise of a day spent with her handsome cousin, he would have been well satisfied.

CHAPTER 10

The following morning Mrs Fortescue called. Her hostess settled her comfortably in an armchair in the drawing-room and offered refreshments. Looking at her expectant guest's face, Lady Sedley was thankful for the absence of her husband, who might have cast a dampener upon her narration. She confided earnestly, "My dear Maria, you cannot conceive how greatly our lives have been turned upside-down!" She glanced out of the window, where across the terrace she could see her daughter and the two newcomers standing together, and added, "It seems as if Fate has taken a hand in our affairs." Then, drawing her chair closer to her visitor, she began to recount the events of the past few days.

Mrs Fortescue, following with some difficulty this complicated history, looked all astonishment. "So this young Philip Brandon is now the heir *and* the future Lord Hartington." She paused, then, in lowered tones, added significantly, "My dear Julia, I declare – he will be the matrimonial catch of the season! Such prospects! And your lovely Louise – how delightful it would be if she should attract his notice!" As if in response to this pronouncement, the door to the garden opened and Louise and the young Brandons entered the room and were presented to the caller.

"We are on our way to the stables, Mama," Louise said, after civilities had been exchanged and Mrs Fortescue had congratulated the Brandons upon their escape from France. "We are going to see the new mare that Papa has given to me," and, excusing themselves, the young party departed.

It was clearly evident that Mrs Fortescue was favourably impressed by this charming and good-looking young man and, after her visitor had left, Lady Sedley acknowledged to herself that it was perhaps *fortunate* that Louise's betrothal was still unannounced. Of Philip's interest in her daughter, there could be no doubt.

The next few days passed peacefully enough at the Grange. Philip, nursing his wounded shoulder, spent the time within the house and garden enjoying the ministrations of Henrietta and Louise. Lady Sedley was also sympathetic and it was evident that she had softened in her attitude towards him. It had not at first been in Philip's mind to pursue Louise with any serious intentions but he had realised almost at once that this enchanting girl was quite un-awakened to any serious passions. In her imagination, she viewed Sir Charles as the embodiment of all her romantic dreams. This was not, perhaps, unexpected in a young girl of Louise's upbringing but, at the same time, Philip was confident that Sir Charles had embarked upon this betrothal without any strong feelings for his neighbour's daughter. Such a course, to Philip, was to inflict a quite shocking wrong upon this charming girl. In the past his mind had been so fully occupied with France's new political ideas and aspirations that he had bestowed little serious attention upon the fair sex other than to indulge in some mild flirtations. Now, the more time he spent in her company, the more he appreciated her gentle innocent ways and felt himself to be becoming daily more attached to her.

He had been sitting in the drawing room, ostensibly reading a book but in reality thinking of Louise, when he heard her voice outside in the garden calling him. He found her on the terrace holding a kitten in her hands and went at once to her side. "Oh, Philip, Francis' wretched dogs! See what they have done! What can we do for this poor creature?" The kitten was mewing piteously but it was not easy to discover the cause of its distress for there seemed to be no apparent injury. To Philip, it was the distress of his cousin, this lovely girl, which was the more poignant sight. He gently took the little animal from her and suggested that they should at once endeavour to find its mother. This was fortunately not a difficult task for, hardly had they turned the corner of the terrace than they saw a tabby cat carrying another kitten in its mouth which it carefully placed behind a bush near the house.

"There, dearest Louise, it will be safe with its mother. She must have decided to move her family after being disturbed by the dogs. No doubt that is all that ails the one you found." Philip laid it down beside the other kitten and returned to Louise's side. He looked down into her upturned face, lovelier than ever in its tender delight at the kitten's rescue, and something of the intensity of his feelings and desires must have touched her for a faint colour rose in her cheeks and when he took her hand and kissed it, she said softly, "It is so very agreeable, indeed delightful, that you have come into our lives."

Meanwhile, Sir Charles was away in Portsmouth visiting a naval family, to whose eldest hopeful he had stood godfather. Henrietta, regretting his absence, felt it could not have occurred at a more inopportune moment for her brother seemed to be growing closer to Louise day by day. As a consequence she took advantage of every possible occasion to extol Charles's virtues to Louise. The picture of him that she painted, portraying him as a romantically wounded hero of intense but hidden passions, would have surprised and amused the gentleman in question if he had been apprised of her opinions. Whether she made any impression on Louise, Henrietta had reason to doubt. An attentive and handsome Philip was there beside her cousin, wounded also, though for less heroic reasons, and making no concealment of his feelings towards his host's daughter.

When Thursday dawned, a faint, early morning mist having provided the promise of a perfect summer's day, Henrietta encountered not the least difficulty in remaining behind when the rest of the party set out for Henfield. Intense excitement had made her quite pale and Lady Sedley, unquestioningly accepting her complaint of an aching head and sore throat, recommended rest in a darkened room and the application of lavender water to her temples. Allowing a decent interval of time to elapse after the departure of the family, with all the attendant excitement and confusion engendered by five persons making a journey of a bare twelve miles, Henrietta summoned a maid to her bed-chamber and desired that she be left undisturbed for the remainder of the day until such time as she, herself, should ring for attention. Then, rising from her bed, she speedily dressed herself in a new, white chemise dress of Moravian worked muslin, closed in front from bosom to hem by a series of ribbon ties of her favourite blue and with which she was particularly pleased. A dashing Dunstable straw bonnet tied under her chin, decorated with matching looped ribbons and feathers, long gloves and a parasol completed her outfit. With a final anxious glance at her reflection in the looking-glass, she took up her reticule and rummaged for a shawl in case it should be breezy upon the Downs. Quickly opening the door to her room, she stole down the stairs, making certain that she was not observed by any member of the household. In a few moments she was out of the house and walking briskly down the drive, congratulating herself on the success of her stratagems and looking forward eagerly to an expedition unique in her experience. The prospect of the company of the rakish Hugo, with his warmly admiring eyes and dashing appearance, added to her inner excitement. Sparkling eyes and faintly flushed cheeks were evident in the glowing face that greeted him when, a few moments later, Hugo rounded the corner in his curricle and drew up beside her. As he assisted her up onto the seat beside him, he felt well satisfied with the fashionable appearance of his companion and with the thought of the day ahead.

"So you contrived your escape without difficulty?" Hugo enquired with a grin as the curricle moved forward.

Henrietta nodded in friendly fashion, saying airily, "In fact, it was the easiest thing in the world. As far as all of the household are concerned, I am now laid upon my bed, with drawn curtains and instructions not to be disturbed. The family will not be returning until the evening so we have a whole day in which to enjoy ourselves."

Amused that no thought of the impropriety of her actions seemed to have entered Henrietta's head, Hugo set himself to entertain her as they drove towards their destination near Piecombe. He found an appreciative audience for his tales of the raffish society that surrounded the Prince of Wales in Brighton, conveniently forgetting at times that some of his anecdotes were scarcely suitable for such young and innocent ears. Soon they found themselves part of an increasingly dense throng making their way up onto the Downs. Barouches, landaus, landaulets, sociables, curricles, gigs, even fish-carts – all of them crammed with spectators – formed a continuous procession and by the time that they reached the group of trees which was Hugo's agreed meeting-point with Mr Gosport, there was an immense number of vehicles drawn up on the hillside with a view of the Devil's Dyke. Mr Gosport greeted them with a flourish of his whip and a bow. Casting an appreciative but surprised glance at Henrietta's radiant countenance, he announced that inspite of their early start they were still too late to obtain a position in the first ranks, "I believe we shall see well enough if we take our places speedily – I have discovered that the regiments have been formed into two columns, with an equal share of artillery to each, and with the object of one or other first gaining the heights of the Devil's Dyke."

They found a place for the two curricles side by side, as near as was practicable to the front rank of vehicles, and were soon exchanging greetings with those in the vicinity. Henrietta now had an opportunity of drinking in the scene around her. It was an astonishing sight. On all sides they were surrounded, for others had by now drawn up behind them, and she thought she had never seen a greater mixture of people and means of transport. From the exquisites in fashionable dress, their female companions arrayed in the very latest confections of the milliners' and dressmakers' arts, to the solid citizens, the shop-keepers and the farmers, accompanied by their wives and daughters in their very best gowns and bonnets, all seemed to be intent upon enjoying themselves to the utmost. Every kind of conveyance was present, even carts and other humble means of transport had been brought into use occupied by members of the lower orders, whose colourful language both amused and startled Henrietta. Below their vantage point, ranks of infantry were drawn up, making a brave sight in their scarlet uniforms, their colours flying. Further to the right, Hugo pointed out to Henrietta a regiment of foot-guards who could just be perceived in the distance.

At that moment a wave of cheering swept along the front ranks of vehicles and a group of mounted officers, resplendent in their uniforms, rode past. "That's Prinny and the Duke of Richmond!" Hugo shouted above the uproar and Henrietta observed that one of the leading horses bore a stout figure upon its back, whose uniform outshone all others in magnificence and who was graciously acknowledging the plaudits of the crowd. She could not avoid a feeling of disappointment. The face she could just glimpse was handsome enough, but oh! How shockingly overweight he was!

The excitement of the crowd around them was now intense and at this moment Mr Gosport found his attention attracted by two ladies who now stood beside his curricle and were addressing him in the friendly manner of old acquaintances. "Oh, Mr Gosport, take pity on us, do!" one of them declared, her vivid, handsome face smiling up at him, "Here's Mrs Daintry and myself finding ourselves without a place to watch the fight, for one of Rupert's horses went lame and we've had to walk the last part of the way."

Henrietta regarded them with interest. They were both elegantly, if brightly, dressed in the latest fashions with splendid, large hats and an astonishing display of curvaceous bosom. Mr Gosport responded gallantly, though casting a dubious glance in Henrietta's direction, "My dear Lizzie, this is indeed a pleasure! Your servant, Mrs Daintry." He assisted them into his curricle, apologizing for the lack of space and announcing that he was 'demned' if he didn't regret not bringing his carriage so that he could have better accommodated them.

Henrietta had caught Hugo's eye while this manœuvre was taking place and saw, to her surprise, a mischievous smile upon his face. He greeted the new arrivals, as soon as they were seated, in the friendliest manner and begged to introduce Henrietta, "Miss Brandon, who has arrived here recently – a refugee from France, you know – Henrietta, may I present Mrs Barnstaple and Mrs Daintry, who are at present honouring Brighton with their presence." At this both ladies burst out laughing to Henrietta's surprise and confusion, not having, herself, the least notion of the cause of their amusement. However they both acknowledged her presence with nods and smiles and cried, "Pleased to make your acquaintance, I'm sure, my dear." They were affable enough, though she was conscious of two pairs of eyes absorbing every detail of her appearance.

Wishing to be sociable and feeling sorry for them in their recent dilemma, Henrietta said smilingly to Mrs Barnstaple, "What an unfortunate event, Ma'am. I trust that your husband will not have any difficulty in rejoining you." She then became aware of two astonished faces regarding her while Hugo and Mr Gosport exchanged amused glances.

"Good gracious, my dear, that's the last thing I shall be wishing for." Mrs Barnstaple tittered, adding in a whisper to Mr Gosport, "What an innocent to be sure. Wherever has Mr Brandon found her?"

Any further conversation was fortunately prevented by the sound of bugles, the shouting of words of command and the firing of muskets. A sudden silence fell on the waiting crowd and there was the distant sound of drums. The plan of battle had, no doubt, been clearly drawn up and understood by its commanders, but to the crowd of onlookers it was by no means so plain: there were advances, and there were retreats and there was a great deal of inactivity, but the sights and sounds could not fail to stir the blood, and no English man or woman present could observe our gallant troops in action, the sun glittering on weapons and uniforms, without experiencing a sensation of pride and patriotism.

Suddenly, from one moment to the next, this scene of splendour was turned to horror and near tragedy – the defending army before them, by a swift move of the cavalry, was forced back into the midst of the front row of spectators, while the so-called enemy pursued them hotly with shouts of "Victory!". The horses harnessed to the various vehicles began to plunge about, becoming hopelessly entangled with one another, the ladies shrieked and fainted and chaos and confusion reigned. Hugo's curricle was one of the first to suffer under the unexpected onslaught, the carriage beside them was forced backwards by its frightened team, the wheel locked with theirs and there was the sound of splintering wood as the curricle tipped sideways.

Henrietta found herself thrown hard against the side of the seat with Hugo's full weight upon her while he struggled to control his horses. For a moment there was pandemonium and she was hard put to it not to cry out with pain and fright – then Hugo pulled himself to his own side of the carriage, Mr Gosport went to the horses' heads and, at length, managed to calm the terrified animals.

Her initial fright over, Henrietta was surprised and a little shocked to hear a string of profanities issue from Hugo's lips. However, she perceived that it was perhaps forgivable under the circumstances; undoubtedly an alarming thing had occurred and had put them in an awkward and ignominious situation.

The two ladies who had attached themselves to their party, having shrieked mightily at the moment of crisis, were now brimming over with solicitude. "You poor child!" Mrs Daintry exclaimed, "What a wicked thing to have happened – 'tis a wonder you weren't thrown out on your head and killed!" Mrs Barnstaple's remarks were of a more practical nature, "Better come up with us in Mr Gosport's carriage, my dear, for you ain't going to be able to return home in that one."

Hugo, scowling ferociously at the damage done to his curricle, was in agreement with this piece of advice. "What a damnably unlucky turn of events. You'd best do as Lizzie suggests, Henrietta, at least then you will have somewhere to sit until I can find us some other means of transport."

The exchange was effected after considerable difficulty in climbing out of the tilted curricle into the arms of the attendant Hugo. It was accompanied by a series of jocular sallies from the ladies, which brought the colour to Henrietta's cheeks. She was already horribly conscious of her rapidly beating heart as Hugo held her for a moment against his chest. His face was so close that she could not but be aware of the expression in his eyes; an expression that filled her with the strangest sensations of excitement delightfully tinged with alarm.

Presently she found herself squeezed onto the seat beside her two companions, whose persons emitted a strong smell of musky perfume. Their brilliant complexions she discovered, being now at such close quarters, owed considerably more to artifice than to nature.

Hugo at once departed with hopeful promises of a speedy return and some means of escaping from the dilemma now confronting them. Hardly had he left them than Mrs Daintry, exchanging a surreptitious grin with Mrs Barnstaple, said knowingly to Henrietta, "You have a very close relationship to young Hugo, no doubt!"

"Yes, he is my cousin." Henrietta replied politely. To her astonishment, this answer threw her companions into gales of laughter. "A cousin, to be sure!" Mrs Daintry responded, "Quite an unusual gentleman that would bring a cousin to such an event as this!" and, to Henrietta's considerable embarrassment, her new acquaintances began to discuss good-naturedly and in intimate detail every part of her person and dress, with fulsome praise for her slim, youthful figure.

That selfsame morning Sir Charles Gresham had returned from Portsmouth. Hearing from Cummings of the Sham-fight to take place that day so near to his property, he decided to drive up onto the Downs to see what he might of that event. He took Benson with him to mind the horses while he, himself, walked forward to obtain a good view of the manoeuvres.

Soon after his arrival, while passing between the close-packed carriages and carts, he had encountered Lieutenant Frensham, who, due to an injury to his arm, was unable to play any part with his regiment in the forthcoming fight. That unenthusiastic military man admitted cheerfully to not being unduly distressed at his inability to participate, "Y'know, Charles, it's a devilish exhausting business – and in this heat! Well, frankly, I had as lief be here as with m'regiment." They were threading their way forward between the vehicles, aware that the manœuvres had begun, when suddenly the alarming incident in the front ranks occurred with all its attendant panic and confusion.

Concerned for those around them, they endeavoured as best as they could to assist those nearest at hand to calm their frightened horses and when some degree of order had been restored were about to proceed to where a view of the troops could be obtained when suddenly Lieutenant Frensham exclaimed with surprise and pleasure, "By Jove, Charles, if that ain't that delightful Miss Brandon whom we met at the 'Ship' the other day!" adding doubtfully, "But she's in devilish bad company, I'd say." Sir Charles, following the direction of Lieutenant Frensham's gaze, stared with disbelief, swiftly followed by outrage, at the ill-assorted group, then, grim-faced, made his way purposefully towards them.

Henrietta had been becoming increasingly uncomfortable in the face of a barrage of inquisitive questions from the two ladies and ever more aware of the keen interest being taken in her situation by those in the carriages surrounding them and the surreptitious glances cast in her direction; glances accompanied by barely suppressed laughter. It was with a sensation of profound relief that she was startled to hear a familiar masculine voice beside her demanding peremptorily, "Good God, Miss Brandon, what in the name of Heaven are *you* doing here?"

Turning to look down into Sir Charles's face, she was surprised to discover a forbidding frown upon his countenance, and replied hastily, "I came with Cousin Hugo, sir, but, as you see, his curricle has met with an accident and he has gone to seek some other conveyance – in the meantime," she continued cheerfully, "these ladies and Mr Gosport are taking care of me."

She looked beyond him to Lieutenant Frensham, who saluted her politely, his youthful face presenting a comic mixture of amusement and concern, then back again to Sir Charles, expecting to discover some sympathy for her plight.

At this moment Mr Gosport, who had been holding the horses' heads, called out, "Most unfortunate accident, Gresham! Poor Hugo's in the devil of a fix – no fault of his mind you."

Mrs Daintry, whose sparkling, black eyes were absorbing with mischievous interest the disapproval of the tall, handsome stranger who had appeared beside them, said provocatively, "'Tis a pleasure to meet such a pretty young lady, sir, so unaffected too, why, I do declare, she'd outshine any of my girls!"

"Good Lord – can't say that, Lizzie, y'know!" even Mr Gosport seemed horrified and, with heightened colour, looked apprehensively at Sir Charles.

The latter regarded the two ladies grimly, contenting himself by saying sarcastically, "Miss Brandon, I'm sure, is grateful to you for your assistance." then turning to Henrietta, said in a harsh voice, "Get down at once, Miss Brandon, and I will drive you home."

His words and attitude had unfortunately quite the opposite effect upon Henrietta to that which he intended. Horribly conscious that she was being addressed as a child, and as a recalcitrant one at that and this in front of four strangers, she replied coldly, "You are most kind, sir, but I should not wish to trouble you. I am quite content to await Cousin Hugo's return – for I am sure he will contrive some means to take me home."

Behind her, Mrs Barnstaple chuckled and whispered in her ear, "That's right, my girl – don't stand any nonsense from his high and mightiness – you'll be alright and tight with us."

Sir Charles, by now very angry indeed, laid his hand on Henrietta's arm and said, "Miss Brandon – if you will not willingly descend from that carriage immediately I will myself ensure that you do so – I trust you will have the prudence not to force me to such an undignified alternative."

During these exchanges several people standing nearby had become aware of the dispute and Henrietta had not the least wish to become a public spectacle; she could see by the expression of grim determination on Sir Charles's face that he would not hesitate to carry out his threat – there was, therefore, nothing else to be done but to submit to his demands. With ill-grace, she rose up from her seat and, taking Sir Charles's out-stretched hand, descended to the ground with as much dignity as she could muster, inwardly seething with indignation at his treatment of her, and turning back defiantly to thank the ladies for their assistance.

Lieutenant Frensham, fully aware of his friend's fury and having no wish to be a witness of the tongue-lashing that he was confident that the adorable Miss Brandon was shortly to receive, now bade them farewell, saying regretfully as he saluted her, "Must leave you now, Miss Brandon – have to dine with m'fellow officers, y'know – very unfortunate situation for you – most regrettable." He half-turned to Charles, his bright, honest eyes fixed on the latter's face, and added in a low voice, "Too young to understand, y'know, my dear fellow – not up to snuff – not by any means." and strode off into the crowd and disappeared.

His remarks seemed to have made little or no impression upon Sir Charles, who, saying curtly to the apprehensive Mr Gosport, "You may tell Hugo that I shall call upon him this evening." pulled Henrietta's arm through his and turning his back on the pair of amused faces gazing derisively at him from Mr Gosport's curricle, set off at a firm pace through the crowded ranks of carriages and spectators.

Speechless with indignation at this high-handed treatment and out of breath from their headlong progress, it was not until they had almost reached Sir Charles's carriage that Henrietta found words to express her outrage.

Stopping short and dragging her arm determinedly from beneath his, she turned upon him, saying in a voice trembling with vexation, "It is too b-bad, Sir Charles, you go too far! How dare you compel me to come with you, – it is Hugo who is my cousin – you – you have no authority to do so."

Sir Charles, having succeeded in mastering the sudden fury that had threatened to overcome him when he had recognized Henrietta and her notorious companions, glanced down at the set, white face beside him and contented himself by replying sarcastically, "If, Miss Brandon, it were I who had the responsibility for you, I should be tempted to beat you soundly for today's escapade. It's inconceivable that Lady Sedley gave her consent. Are you so determined to ruin yourself in the eyes of the world? As for Hugo –" his face hardened, "A man who could permit you to indulge in such a prank is not fit to take care of anyone – that was bad enough – but to expose you to the company of such women – But I will say no more on that head and can only hope and trust you were not recognized."

The knowledge that there might well be some truth in Sir Charles's accusations of impropriety only serving to increase Henrietta's resentment, she retorted indignantly, her blue eyes flashing, "I can only thank heaven, sir, that you are not and never will be in a position of authority over me! I can only pity Louise – to be married to a man, so over-bearing, so – so conscious of his own consequence that he considers himself superior to all others – no doubt that is the reason you hold these ladies in contempt!"

To Henrietta's fury, a glimmer of amusement had crept into Sir Charles's eyes and it was almost with a return to his normal calm manner that he replied austerely, "No doubt you have formed a very poor opinion of me, Miss Brandon, but I can assure you that I have your best interests at heart."

To be laughed at was the final straw, Henrietta was trembling with anger, "Sir, you m-may have rescued me when I arrived in England, for that I am grateful, but that does not give you the right to interfere in my life! No doubt your opinions coincide with those of Lady Sedley, but I am no English-reared bread-and-butter miss, sir." She continued defiantly, "Cousin Hugo is kind and amusing and I enjoy his company."

"And when he has sufficiently compromised you – you would, no doubt, be willing and eager to marry him – that is to say, if he should feel compelled to offer for you!" There was a grim expression upon Sir Charles's countenance as he added, "Perhaps that is what you would wish."

Henrietta, utterly taken aback by this accusation, was for a moment unable to speak, then, in a low voice that shook with emotion, she replied, "I do not know why you wish to insult me – you did not feel obliged to offer for me after I had spent *days* with you in your house – why should Hugo be expected to do so for such a trifling reason?"

He laughed harshly and looked away from her, "If your presence had become known, my dear girl, I would have done so."

She stared at him with disbelief – eyeing his stern profile with amazement, the frowning brows, the well-shaped mouth compressed into a hard line – too astonished to reply.

He must have felt her eyes upon him for he moved his head to look down at her again and for a moment a faint smile curved his lips as he saw her incredulous expression.

"Gracious Heavens, I believe you would indeed have offered me marriage!" Henrietta regarded him with respect; then the recollection of his present insufferable behaviour returned to her forcibly. The man was outrageous, to attempt to order *her* life, to force her to come with him! All the disappointment of having had an enjoyable day in Hugo's company ruined by un-foreseen circumstances and the interference of this self-appointed guardian, burst upon her anew, further fuelled by the suspicion that she had acted imprudently.

"Thank Heavens that I was saved from such a fate!" she exclaimed, with intent to wound, and turned abruptly from him to walk towards the waiting curricle, her head held high in an attempt to stifle a strong inclination to burst into tears. Sir Charles stared after her for a moment with a frown, surveying the uncompromisingly stiff back of the slim figure before him.

If Benson felt any surprise at the arrival of the young lady from France looking to be in the grip of some strong emotion, followed by

Sir Charles, a forbidding expression on his normally good-humoured countenance, he gave no sign of it. From his place at the horses' heads he watched his master assist Miss Brandon onto her seat, noting her averted face and when Sir Charles had mounted beside her and had taken up the reins, he took his seat behind them, expecting to be the interested witness of a severe dressing-down, and feeling some sympathy for its recipient.

He could well remember the boyish figure that they had rescued in Shoreham – behaved like a proper game 'un, she had – it looked now as if the poor young thing was in for a rare scold!

His presence acted, however, as a deterrent to any further remonstrations on Sir Charles's part; Miss Brandon, seething with conflicting emotions, remained obstinately silent as they drove, in an atmosphere of mutual hostility, through the Sussex lanes.

'Sir Charles was impossible – his attitude towards her outrageous – she had never been so deceived by anyone – that calm air, those agreeable manners, had proved to be a deceptive front which concealed a character that was high-handed and positively Gothic in its outlook –' Henrietta stormed inwardly against her companion, aware, as she gave vent silently to her indignation, of the lowering sensation that she had forever sunk herself in his estimation – And what would the dashing Hugo think of her faint-hearted desertion of him? It did not bear thinking of – she was the most miserable creature in the world!'

So preoccupied was Henrietta with her own thoughts that it was with a sensation of shock that she realized, upon recognizing some familiar landmarks, that they were already within a short distance of the Grange; if Lady Sedley should become aware of her part in this ill-starred expedition she would indeed be in disgrace. Hugo would have aided her, as much for his own sake as for hers, in returning unseen to his cousin's house, but she could hardly expect her present companion to be equally obliging; especially as he disapproved so wholeheartedly of the whole escapade. She bit her lip and stole a glance at Sir Charles's face from under her long, dark lashes.

"You are wondering whether I am going to report the whole to Lady Sedley, are you not?" he asked her suddenly, as if he could read her thoughts.

Henrietta almost jumped and stared at him in amazement, "How did you know, sir?"

"You have a very transparent countenance, Miss Brandon."

Thinking crossly that it would quite serve him right if he did possess the ability to uncover her every thought, she admitted, "I was thinking of my return to the Grange, sir – Lady Sedley will be very displeased with me when she discovers where I have been."

"My dear girl, what a very unhandsome person you make me out to be – I shan't squeak beef on you, as they say! You shall alight outside the gates and then you must contrive to make your own way into the house unobserved."

Henrietta looked at him curiously, what a strange mixture the man was. She said stiffly, "For that I am grateful, sir."

He gave a sardonic laugh and remained silent until they drew up at their destination, then, as Henrietta prepared to descend to the ground, Benson having jumped down to assist her, he addressed her in a low voice, looking at her gravely and with those stern eyes upon her she felt again all her rebellious feelings rising up within her.

"My dear Miss Brandon, I beg of you not to put your trust in Hugo – his reputation is bad, to say the least – with women in particular."

He was not allowed to finish – her eyes flashing, Henrietta flung back at him, "Never sir, will I permit you to order my friends or my conduct! Why you should attempt to prejudice me against my cousin, I do not understand." Then, turning from him, haughty outrage visible in every line of her face, she permitted Benson to assist her to alight and having safely descended, looked up at him and said with chilling politeness, "I cannot conceive why you should concern yourself with my affairs but I bid you good-day, sir, and – and thank you for your discretion." she finished lamely.

Inscrutable eyes looked down at her, then, as she turned on her heel, followed her slim figure, head held high, until the trees and shrubs of the driveway concealed her from his sight.

No intelligence of Henrietta's escapade ever reached Lady Sedley's ears. She had been able to regain her bedroom without being detected by the servants and found herself thankful to lie down upon her bed for a while to recover from all the conflicting emotions of the day. She could not, for one moment, regret her adventure with Hugo; never before had she been escorted by such an undoubtedly dashing member of the fashionable world. That he admired her, he had made clear. Sir Charles's interference had been quite uncalled for, positively Gothic, nevertheless, she felt a lowering of her spirits at the thought that she had fallen in his opinion.

The party being returned after dinner, Louise came to Henrietta's bedchamber and rendered her an enthusiastic account of their day.

"Such a delightful family, the Tildens, Henrietta – we have known them for ever. You would like Andrew I'm sure, so high-spirited, such a tease – he had us all in fits! And," she added, her eyes sparkling, "we are all invited for Saturday, an informal dance at the house, just some twelve couples to stand up – and you and Philip are included in the invitation!"

Henrietta's face brightened, this was most welcome news and served instantly to distract her thoughts from the disasters of the day. As Louise continued her recital of the extent of the Tilden's hospitality, Henrietta could not help but observe that Philip's name was frequently upon her lips, his conversation repeated almost verbatim.

"Your brother was quite a favourite, Henrietta, I could see that Jane, she's the Tilden's daughter, you know, was quite taken up with him, she came out two years ago but didn't take – but Philip brings out the best in everyone."

When Louise left her, Henrietta sighed and shook her head doubtfully; Louise appeared to her eyes horribly like a girl who was falling in love – if Sir Charles became aware of it – and how could he fail to do so – he would be wishing Philip and herself a thousand miles away. How bitter his thoughts would be – how absurd and how provoking that he should seem to feel obliged to embroil himself in her affairs.

Sir Charles had held two conversations after depositing Henrietta at the gates of the Grange. The first took place immediately upon his return home. It was not of long duration. As he climbed down from the driving seat and handed the reins to Benson, he said with deliberation, "The young lady that I have just escorted home – you've never set eyes upon her before, have you, Benson?"

"No, sir. Never, sir." The reply was unhesitating, Benson's face expressionless but his eyes were alert as he watched his master's face.

"Just as I thought." Sir Charles nodded, "Best forget the whole incident, Benson."

"Yes, sir – of course, sir. Anything further, Sir Charles?"

"That will be all – and thank you, Benson, I knew I could rely upon you!"

The second interview took place in Hugo's study. A call that evening found Hugo at home, a glass of brandy at his side. Sir Charles, grim-faced, wasted no time in coming to the point, "May I suggest, my dear Hugo, that you do not encourage Miss Brandon in any further adventures."

"What the devil's it got to do with you, dammit?" was the intemperate reply, as Hugo filled a glass for his visitor. "Infernal impudence making her come with you like that – they told me she didn't like it by half."

"As Miss Brandon's first acquaintance in this country, I feel some responsibility for her welfare."

Hugo laughed sarcastically, "The devil you do – got an interest there yourself? My God, ain't one lovely armful enough for you, Charles?"

Sir Charles waived aside the proffered wineglass with a frown and said coldly, "You're a fool, Hugo! And worse than a fool to permit that child to encounter that kind of woman – but I warn you – if you haven't the decency to pay regard to the welfare and honour of such a young and innocent girl, I will not have the least compunction in calling you to account!"

Hugo stared at him with surprise, dark eyebrows raised, "Good God! You mean it too! You're a devilish deep one – a regular firebrand, too. Dammit, man, I only agreed to it to please her, y'know – she's a taking little creature and damnably attractive."

"I have no desire to discuss Miss Brandon." Charles said repressively, "It's best the whole incident is forgotten – I only hope to Heaven that she was not recognized."

"I ain't likely to forget the damage to my curricle." Hugo looked morosely at Charles, and added inconsequentially, "Have to marry an heiress, y'know – fact of the matter is, I'm deep in dun territory."

"Keep away from the tables, that's my advice to you for what it's worth." Charles replied unsympathetically, and taking his leave, left Hugo to his solitary reverie.

CHAPTER 11

By Friday, Philip's shoulder had become sufficiently healed, though still tender, to allow him to accept Hugo's offer. The latter, having borrowed his friend, Mr Gosport's, curricle, his own being still unusable, drove him to London with all his customary speed and dash.

Philip's visit to Milne's establishment in Grosvenor Street had equalled if not rather exceeded his expectations; introduced by Hugo and greeted deferentially, it had been pleasant to be told admiringly, as the little tailor took his measurements, "We shan't require any padding for you, sir, a fine pair of shoulders – if I may be permitted to say so – and the waist – all that one could wish for." It appeared, in some mysterious way, that it would actually be an economy to order two coats and waistcoats rather than one; from this decision it had seemed only a small step to authorize also the making of a dress coat and knee-breeches. The merits of various West of England cloths, Broadcloths and Bath Superfines having been discussed at length, they had been escorted to the door with many bows and expressions of pleasure at being favoured with the future Lord Hartington's custom. Little did they know that, as the door closed behind them, the tailor, raising his eyes to heaven had expressed the pious hope that his new client would settle his accounts more promptly than his cousin.

Outside on the pavement, Philip and Hugo agreed to part company for the moment. To Philip, it was an opportunity not to be missed to see something of the sights of London of which he had heard so much. Having received instructions from Hugo as to how to find Brooks's club in St James's Street, they arranged to meet there soon after dusk and each went his own way; Philip to take a turn or two down Bond Street, a stroll through Piccadilly and, later in the afternoon, a visit to Hyde Park to see the fashionables riding there. Some day soon he hoped to see the entertainments in Vauxhall Gardens but that must wait until another day.

Sir Charles's activities that day had afforded him some considerable satisfaction also. At Tattersall's, he had been fortunate enough to acquire just the very animal that he felt convinced would carry him well in the hunting field in the coming season, and that without being obliged to pay too high a price for the pleasure. There he had encountered an old friend from his days as a midshipman and had invited him to dine at Fladong's hotel in Oxford Street, a hostelry much frequented by naval men. After a good plain dinner and an excellent claret, Henry Marchant had departed and Sir Charles, recollecting that he had expressed the intention of joining Hugo and Philip at 'Brooks's, set out for St James's Street.

That same night the sky was beginning to darken as Lieutenant Wetherby left the Admiralty building but the evening was fine and warm. He stepped out briskly, with a gratifying sense of importance; it was not every day that one was ordered to take an important despatch to Downing Street and as he descended Whitehall his thoughts revolved pleasantly around his future prospects in the service. Downing Street was soon reached but, alas, upon enquiring at No 10 for the First Sea Lord, for whom he had important information, he was directed to White's in St James's Street: the meeting with the Prime Minister had ended an hour earlier and the Earl of Chatham had departed to take supper at his club.

Reflecting ruefully that if he had but known he could have saved himself a great deal of time and energy, Lieutenant Wetherby set off again, this time across the park, towards his new destination.

He was crossing the maze of streets that lie between Pall Mall and St James's, thankful to think that he would soon have completed his business, when he heard hurried footsteps behind him. It was now almost dark, the moon not yet up, and he had just sufficient time to wonder if he had been foolhardy to venture away from the main thoroughfare to this dark, deserted street, when he received a crushing blow upon the shoulder; as he turned with a shout of alarm to face his assailants, further blows rained down upon his head and he fell unconscious to the ground.

A hackney carriage had pulled up near St James's Street and its occupant was alighting, when, as he set foot upon the ground, he heard a cry of alarm and the sound of blows and looking urgently in the direction from which the sounds had come, beheld two figures bending over what appeared to be a body lying upon the ground. Without hesitating, the passenger from the carriage ran towards them, and as he did so drew a pistol from his pocket and fired it into the air above the heads of the attackers. They, taking to their heels in fright, disappeared up a side street, no doubt the self-same one from which they had emerged, and vanished from sight.

The rescuer, a tall, dark-haired man, knelt down beside the figure on the ground; he could dimly see that the man was young, that he was breathing, but unconscious. Meanwhile the hackney driver, seeing that all danger was past and fully aware that he had not yet received his fare, had driven his vehicle forward to pull up beside the victim, grumbling out loud "Gawd help us, it ain't safe to walk abroad these days – very dangerous these 'ere streets around the Park!"

"I don't doubt it!" was the response, "But I need a hand here, if you will. The poor devil's unconscious – he can't be left to lie here."

Obeying the note of authority in the voice that addressed him, the driver climbed down from his seat and assisted his passenger, with some difficulty, to prop up the unconscious man on the seat of the hackney. Having directed the driver to take them to the nearest hostelry in Piccadilly, the gentleman took his seat beside the unfortunate young naval officer and, having re-assured himself that he was still breathing, began to search the victim's person in order to establish his identity, feeling, as he did so, a profound sense of irritation that his evening plans should have been so unexpectedly delayed. It was not long before he drew out of the inner breast-pocket of the young man's coat a folded document bearing a heavy seal. Hoping that it would reveal its owner's identity, he broke the seal and holding the paper up to the light of the flares that illuminated the principal buildings in St James's Street, he realised, with a start, that he held in his hand an important naval despatch. Astounded, he sat back, the document in his hands, staring out of the window as they proceeded along Piccadilly.

Whatever his thoughts may have been, by the time they had pulled up in the inn-yard of the 'White Horse Cellars', he acted with speed and decision. Summoning the landlord, he requested a room for the young man and assistance in getting him within, describing the attack that had rendered him insensible.

The landlord, re-assured by his visitor's gentlemanly appearance, bustled around and soon had the young officer installed in one of his best bedchambers. The gentleman, having paid off the hackney carriage, with a handsome tip into the bargain, mounted to the bed-chamber and seating himself by the bed, read by the light of the candles the paper that the unfortunate lieutenant had been carrying.

That it contained information of vital importance was soon evident; his face betrayed amazement as he read: instructions to Admiral Hood in command of his Majesty's ships in the Mediterranean, times of sailing, the position and timing of a rendezvous, all was information of the utmost secrecy. As he reached the end, and folded the document again, he said softly to himself, "My God, what wouldn't the French give to have this dispatch!" For a few moments he sat, staring before him. On the bed the young officer stirred and a faint groan came from his lips though his eyes remained closed. His rescuer rose to his feet. There was a gleam of satisfaction in his eye as he thrust the paper into his own pocket and left the room.

Downstairs, he called for the landlord and said, "I fear the young fellow is in a bad way and should see a physician as soon as possible." then, pressing a few guineas into the landlord's not unwilling hand, he added, "I know of a doctor who lives close by: I'll go myself to see if I can persuade him to come out at this time of night." and without further words, pushed open the inn door and vanished into the darkness outside.

When Sir Charles entered Brooks's, that home of inveterate gamblers, where the leader of his Majesty's Opposition was so frequently to be found, he discovered Hugo and Philip seated at a table, where a game of Hazard was in progress, surrounded by a group of excited men laying extravagant wagers while a groom-porter called out the odds. Greeted by several of those present with expressions of pleasure, he soon realized, from his flushed face and his manner, that Philip was well in his cups and Hugo scarcely less so, and observed with misgiving that before Philip lay a number of scribbled vowels bearing his signature.

He stood a moment watching the play. "Getting in devilish deep – young Brandon." The Irish peer, Lord Clermont murmured in his ear, "Strange story, ain't it? I mean about his late parent – like father like son, it seems."

Sir Charles frowned and taking his opportunity when play had halted momentarily, said quietly to Hugo, "If you'll get young Brandon to leave the table now, I'll redeem those vowels for him."

"What a killjoy you are, Charles!" Hugo had a reckless look in his eye, "You seem mightily concerned about my relations." Nevertheless, he clapped Philip upon the back and announced his intention of being off to bed, "The luck's not with us, dear boy – let's call it a day – there's always tomorrow, you know!"

Philip looked at him owlishly, "S'good fun, by Jupiter!" He shook his head sadly, "Ain't got the hang of it yet – but you're a good fellow, Hugo, a devilish good fellow! And you, Charles, a devilish good fellow! And –" he looked around him to see whom else he could add to his recital as he was assisted to his feet, and continued murmuring, on his way to the door, "– devilish good fellows –"

Charles remained behind, exchanging a few civilities with his acquaintances and depositing his own note of hand upon the table in exchange for the vowels written by his future wife's cousin, saying, as he observed some raised eyebrows, "Neighbour of mine, y'know – new to the country."

"They say you saved his life. Young Hugo seems to be taking it well." Viscount Debenham remarked, as he picked up the cards to re-commence play, "What a shock for him – he'll find himself hard-pressed now he's no longer the heir – it's said he's up to his eyes in debts."

Charles looked at him from beneath frowning brows, but the tone of his voice was even as he replied, "Hugo's in a deuced difficult situation, there's no doubt – And Philip Brandon, too," he murmured under his breath, "though I surmise he is scarcely aware of it."

CHAPTER 12

When it was discovered at the Admiralty that the First Sea Lord had never received the vital despatch, the gravest alarm and consternation ensued. The Prime Minister was immediately informed and an urgent search began for Lieutenant Wetherby, who had failed to report for duty. By mid-morning the Bow Street Runners had been called upon to investigate what was feared to be a serious breach of security and messages were dispatched post-haste to all ports on the south coast alerting the authorities to exert the maximum vigilance and to intercept, at all costs, anyone who might be attempting to pass information across the Channel.

At the White Horse Cellars, the landlord cursed himself for having been a soft-hearted fool when neither the stranger nor a physician had returned. Anxious for the state of the injured man, he had, himself, sent for a doctor, not wishing to have a corpse, and an unknown one at that, upon his hands. The doctor pronounced the patient's condition to be serious and that on no account should he be moved. "Rest and quiet, that's all that can be done. He looks a fit enough fellow, and may well soon recover consciousness. Let's hope his mind ain't affected.," and with these depressing words had departed. The following morning, a further and closer investigation of the effects of his unwelcome lodger had led to the discovery of the initials P. R. W. inscribed upon the reverse side of his pocket-watch. The landlord's wife, being a woman of a good deal more resolution than her husband, announced her intention of sending to the Admiralty, "For 'e's a naval man, that's for sure – let them take charge of 'im. You'm a sight too tender-hearted, Amos Barker."

Thus it was that late on Saturday night the higher echelons of the Navy learned of Lieutenant Wetherby's whereabouts. It brought them little comfort, for the young naval officer remained insensible. An interrogation of the landlord by the investigating officer the following morning proved more fruitful. At least they were now aware of the events, as described by the gentlemanly stranger to mine host. If the tale was true, it accounted for the present condition of the lieutenant and for his presence at the 'White Horse Cellars'. Who had abstracted the vital despatch and its present whereabouts remained a mystery.

Seated upon a settle alongside the fire in the bar parlour at that busy hostelry, the Bow Street officer lit his long clay pipe with a spill taken from the vase on the mantel-shelf and gave a long-drawn-out sigh. "A very, very difficult case, William, ol' son." His assistant gazed back at him, waiting for more words of wisdom to fall from the pursed lips of his mentor. A prolonged silence ensued. The Runner puffed at his pipe and stared into the fire, his round, blue eyes bearing a look of innocence strangely at odds with his profession. Joshua Prout was altogether a round man: early baldness, a rotund figure and short stature combined to produce the impression of twin spheres mounted upon short sturdy legs. He took a long pull at his tankard, wiped his mouth with the back of his hand and repeated portentously, "A very difficult case."

On the Monday following, while Joshua Prout was pursuing his enquiries in the vicinity of the White Horse Cellars among the hackney carriage drivers who plied their trade in that area, a letter addressed to the First Sea Lord reached the Admiralty. The missive, written in a seemingly unformed hand, was brought instantly to his lordship's attention. Urgently opened, it was found to contain certain astonishing, if imprecise, allegations. These were conveyed immediately to Joshua Prout. As he read, a faint hint of excitement appeared upon his cherubic countenance, but his words expressed a degree of scepticism, "That's as maybe – there's many a spiteful man – or woman for that matter – what's eager an' willin' to put about very unpleasant h'accusations. Howsomever, m'young fellow, this requires h'investigation by yours truly an' the sooner the better – for it's too much of a co-h'incidence that this 'ere letter comes to 'and at this very precise moment!" Procuring a post-chaise was a matter of a moment and, accompanied by his assistant, in less than an hour they were rattling through the streets in the direction of the south coast.

At the Grange the chief topic of conversation amongst the younger generation had been the forthcoming Tilden's dance. Certainly there had been interest in the communication received from Lady Hartington disclosing that her husband's health was slowly improving and expressing the hope that, in the not too far distant future, his newly found grandchildren would pay them a visit. The arrival of the constable was, likewise, a cause for interested speculation. Reporting on his enquiries amongst the gypsies in the encampment on Hugo's land, he had announced his failure to discover any evidence which might throw light on the mysterious shot. "Though," he had added ruefully to Sir William, "them varmints knows more than they'm willin' to admit, sir. One young feller – I do declare 'e were a'laughin' at me – knew summat, 'e did – but there, sir, there ain't a mite of proof –" But the Tilden's dance had surpassed all other subjects in interest and excitement and had been preceded by many absorbing discussions between Louise and Henrietta as to their dresses for the occasion.

Hugo, Henrietta learnt with pleasure, was also invited and had kindly offered to lend Philip the correct evening-wear for an informal dance in the country. Sir Charles, it was anticipated, would also be present. Henrietta hoped fervently that he would not see fit to cast a damper upon her enjoyment of the evening. Well – let him disapprove as much as he liked – he would be far better employed in devoting all his attention to his fiancée! One discovery had softened her attitude to Sir Charles. The day following her expedition with Hugo to see the sham-fight, she had been out riding accompanied by Francis. She had taken the opportunity, as they paused for a moment at the end of an exhilarating gallop, to ask him if he was acquainted with a Mrs Barnstaple and a Mrs Daintry who were staying in Brighton. His reaction had quite startled her. His ruddy complexion attaining an even more vivid hue, his eyes almost starting from his head, he had desired Henrietta to repeat her question, assuming hopefully that he could not have heard aright. Her clearly enunciated reply gave no further grounds for doubt and for a moment Francis had stared at her. Opening and shutting his mouth without uttering a sound, he had finally muttered, "Ain't acquainted with them – not the thing, y'know – not a subject to discuss with a young female –" and had tailed off into silence looking profoundly uncomfortable.

But Henrietta was not to be so easily put off, "Fiddle-sticks, Francis! If you are too craven to tell me who they are, I shall be obliged to ask your Mama."

"By Jove, cousin, don't do that for the Lord's sake! For the life of me I can't imagine how you came to hear their names mentioned –"

"Never mind about that, Francis, – but I mean to find out, so you may as well tell me as not."

One look at her face had been enough to assure him that she was in earnest and glancing around him as if he feared even the trees might conceal someone who could overhear their conversation, he had said flatly, "Mrs Barnstaple is the owner of a 'Bagnio' in Brighton – Mrs Daintry's her sister – they used to keep a like establishment in Covent Garden." Then, seeing to his horror Henrietta's puzzled expression, further questions trembling upon her lips, he had added desperately, "For immoral purposes, y'know, the muslin company – Cyprians – all that!"

"O-oh – I see!" A faint blush had risen to Henrietta's cheeks, "That explains a great deal." Then, to Francis's astonishment, her eyes dancing, she had burst into helpless laughter.

"Well, really, cousin! Can't see for the life of me what's so amusin'. What an odd girl you are to be sure." A frown upon his honest face, he had stared at her for a moment, then said with a grin, "For the

Lord's sake don't go repeating any of this to m'sister, nor to anyone else for that matter." They completed their ride in amicable silence, both deeply engrossed with their thoughts. Francis, who had already formed a liking for Henrietta's company, was more impressed than ever with his young cousin. She seemed a world apart from the young ladies of his acquaintance whose sensibilities were so easily offended. From that moment on he began to think that pursuing a girl like Henrietta would be both agreeable and worthwhile. He even seemed to be making some efforts with his appearance and astonished and disgusted his father by descending that evening wearing a cravat, trimmed with a fine lace edging, tied in a large knot under his chin.

The Tilden's dance took place upon the evening following Hugo and Philip's visit to London and Henrietta found the Tilden family just as delightful as Louise had promised. Mr John Tilden, the host, had been quite a favourite with the ladies in his youth and still prided himself upon his appearance. Tall, not needing stays to preserve his figure, and with his now sparse locks carefully arranged, he was dressed in the height of fashion. He provided a striking contrast to Sir William, whose stout figure looked uncomfortably constricted by his evening dress. He had greeted the Sedley party most cordially, complimenting the ladies upon their appearance and agreeably interested in making the acquaintance of Henrietta, saying to her politely, "So regrettable, Miss Brandon, that you were not well enough to accompany your brother last Thursday." His wife echoed his remarks with the greatest kindness. Mrs Tilden was small, brown-haired and plainly dressed. Henrietta was forcibly reminded of a pair of farmyard birds — Mr Tilden, the strutting cock in all his magnificent plumage, and his spouse, the meek, brown hen. Mrs Tilden clearly held her husband in the greatest admiration but Henrietta had the feeling that she was by no means without a mind of her own.

The room had been cleared for dancing, rugs rolled up and removed, chairs placed along the walls and, in a convenient alcove, a trio of musicians, hired for the evening, were tuning up. There were already a number of guests present, both old and young and amongst them Henrietta was delighted to perceive Hugo, deep in conversation with a pretty, fair-haired girl. At that moment he looked up and saw her and, excusing himself to his companion, came striding across the room to greet the Sedley party. Henrietta could not help feeling a delightful sensation of excitement as he bowed over her hand. There was a gleam of admiration in his dark eyes as he looked into her face then lowered his gaze to the décolletage of the white gauze open-robe, whose neckline to Henrietta's young eyes was cut alarmingly low. To her relief, he seemed not to be in the least offended that she had deserted him on the day of their expedition, only murmuring in her ear, "Enchanting, little cousin! You must allow me the first dance of the evening." Having smilingly granted his request, Henrietta looked around her at the throng of people, wondering how long it would be before they became acquaintances instead of strangers. She was struck by the stark contrast between life in England and the land she had left behind her with all its dark deeds and shattered society.

"Here comes your gallant rescuer!" Hugo murmured quizzically to her. Henrietta turned and saw the tall figure of Sir Charles approaching them. As he drew near she could not but admit to herself, even though he had thoroughly provoked her and deserved her displeasure, that he was the most distinguished gentleman present. There was something in his height and bearing, in the plainess of his well-fitting coat and knee-breeches and in his easy manner that made him stand out amongst the company. But, as he reached her side, Henrietta could not forget his behaviour on the day of the Sham Fight. How could he be so proud, so hide-bound by convention, so disapproving of others? These were attributes which could only lower him in her estimation and increase her pleasure in Hugo's dashing company and conversation. Greeting her in a calm manner which betrayed no sign of any recollection of their last encounter, Sir Charles moved on to speak to Sir William and Lady

Sedley. At that moment, the first notes of the music sounded, he turned to Louise and requested with a smile that she should do him the honour of standing up with him for the country dance about to commence.

Henrietta, watching them, as they all took their places, was shocked to discover so little pleasure in Louise's expression. Her enchanting little face bore rather a look of resignation and, as she began to follow the movements of the dance, she could be seen to glance several times in Philip's direction. He, partnered by a lively little blonde, was clearly enjoying her conversation and her admiration. But her anxieties about Louise were soon dispelled by Hugo's excellent dancing. He appeared to be in good spirits and made her chuckle with his malicious comments upon those present. His attentions were both flattering and intriguing and she found it easy to forgive him for allowing her to encounter such shocking persons at the sham-fight – after all, it had not been of his contriving.

How well he had recovered from his first shock at learning of Philip's existence. It was, she thought, quite admirable that he had so swiftly reconciled himself to the loss of title and wealth. Moreover it was, indeed, very agreeable to receive such delightful compliments from one who clearly was in the first stare of fashion. She had endured enough censure from other quarters!

As the evening progressed, the truth of Francis's remarks about his sister, when she had first arrived at the Sedley's house, were forcibly brought home to Henrietta. There could be no doubt that Louise was the belle of the neighbourhood. Surrounded by attentive young men whenever the music ceased, her hand was eagerly sought by them for each succeeding dance. Henrietta observed Philip, scowling blackly, having to wait his turn to lead her onto the floor. For her own part she was thankful to find that she had her fair share of partners. Mr Andrew Tilden, who to his everlasting regret had inherited his mother's short stature, had presented himself to Henrietta immediately following her dance with Hugo. He had beguiled their dance with a series of anecdotes concerning their fellow-guests thereby fully living up to Louise's description of him as an amusing companion.

Mrs Tilden, an excellent hostess, made certain that Henrietta did not lack for partners and she soon found herself the centre of a small group of both sexes who were eager to meet her and to question her upon her escape from France. Amongst them, Mr Bertram Overly, the Rector's son, declared himself impatient to get at these Frenchies. His ferocious sentiments contrasted strangely with his dandified appearance. It seemed that his great wish was to join the army, a desire that was not approved by his loving parents.

His sister, Anne, the girl to whom Hugo had been speaking when the Sedley party had first arrived, wore her fair curls cropped amazingly short. To Henrietta's horror, she indicated the scarlet ribbon tied around her slim neck and informed her grandly that this style was the very latest fashion in London Society, adding that it was named 'a la victime' in honour of those who had perished upon the guillotine. The notion that the terrible sufferings of many innocent people should be the subject of a fashion was more than distasteful. Henrietta looked and felt shocked and disgusted and said sadly, "I know that it is hard for those here to comprehend the terrible suffering in France." The mild censure provoked Miss Overly. She tossed her head and remarked to the world at large, "I suppose you to be half-French yourself, Miss Brandon – we English are made of sterner stuff."

She was relieved when a tall, quiet girl murmured in her ear, "We are not all so unfeeling, Miss Brandon!" This was her host's daughter and Henrietta regarded her with interest. With her indeterminate features and an abundance of freckles, she was no beauty but there was a look of sharp intelligence in her hazel eyes. Henrietta turned to her gratefully, "For that – I thank you!" she said, a smile lighting up her face.

It was fortunate, perhaps, that at that moment the music started again and Henrietta found Sir Charles at her side requesting her to partner him for the next dance. Surprise overcoming her indignation at Miss Overly's remarks, she took his hand and allowed him to lead

155

her onto the floor. She was not a little astonished that he should wish to dance with someone of whom, she felt sure, he now held a very poor opinion. She was also uncertain in her own mind what her present attitude should be to a gentleman who was so clearly prejudiced against her cousin Hugo. For a while they danced in silence. Sir Charles, an impressively good dancer, glanced now and then at the frosty face beside him, his handsome countenance displaying nothing more than its usual calm, good-natured expression. It was Henrietta who spoke first. Her honesty compelled her, despite her indignation, to retract the accusations she had levelled at his head upon the subject of the persons she had encountered the previous Thursday. "I have discovered, sir, since we last met," she acknowledged, displaying some traces of embarrassment in her downcast eyes, "that you were not at fault in deploring my acquaintance with those – those ladies –"

"You relieve me profoundly, Miss Brandon." he replied, with a look of amusement, "I should not care for you to continue in the belief that I consider myself 'superior to all others'. May I enquire how you discovered your mistake?"

It was provoking to have her own hasty words quoted back to her, nevertheless, Henrietta supposed that he had some just cause for complaint. She glanced up at him innocently, "I asked Francis!" she said, without prevarication. To her indignation the look of amusement deepened as her partner exclaimed, "By Jupiter, what wouldn't I give to have seen Francis's face when you asked him such a question!" It was too much – to be made fun of on top of all else – Henrietta frowned upon him severely and biting back a retort, continued the dance in stony silence.

Her next partner was Francis, himself. Enjoined by Lady Sedley to solicit his Cousin Henrietta's hand for at least one dance, he found himself upon this occasion, for once, not averse to obeying her command. His mastery of the steps was not all that it might have been but his guileless conversation and awkwardly expressed compliments were balm to Henrietta's ruffled feelings. To his mother's delight, as she followed their progress around the dance-floor, she saw Henrietta bestow upon him the friendliest of smiles.

It was at the start of the next country-dance that Henrietta became aware that her host's daughter was still sitting amongst the chaperones. She saw the Rector approach Hugo, who was standing near Miss Tilden, and address a few words to him. Hugo then shook his head and retired to stand near the door to garden where several young men were gathered drinking and laughing. She had to admit to herself that this was not well done and was surprised at the feeling of disappointment that overcame her. However, Miss Tilden was soon rescued. Sir Charles, who had been talking to Lady Sedley, came forward and, bowing politely, begged to have the honour of the next dance. As they took their places for the next set, Henrietta found herself contrasting the actions of the two men and thought sadly that only an exceptional minority of men prized intelligence above beauty in women. At the end of that dance Sir Charles led Miss Tilden to a chair and having procured a glass of cordial for her, sat down beside her and engaged her in lively conversation. Drawn out by his interest in her, the girl had become full of animation. Henrietta, inwardly applauding his thoughtfulness, found herself a little envious of Miss Tilden .It would be, indeed, agreeable to be singled out in this way by Sir Charles. To know that one's thoughts and ideas were of compelling interest.

As the evening progressed the exertions of the dancers and the heat of the warm summer evening had caused the temperature to rise uncomfortably in the room. Mrs Tilden, ever mindful of the comfort of her guests, desired that the long windows facing onto the terrace should be opened. Henrietta had been enjoying a second dance with Hugo. She was secretly pleased to discover that his eyes which had often followed her as she danced with her other partners, were now smiling down into her face. As she fanned herself vigorously, he whispered in her ear, "Let us go out onto the terrace, my enchanting little cousin, for a breath of fresh air." Henrietta needed no second urging, the thought of a cool, refreshing breeze upon her face was a tempting one and Hugo was, after all, no stranger. She slipped past him, as he held the curtain aside for her, and went before him into the garden.

It had not been an evening of unalloyed pleasure for Philip. He had contrived no more than two dances with the girl to whom he now found himself drawn ever more earnestly. True she had responded prettily to his flattering remarks whenever the movements of the dance had permitted conversation but her admirers seemed legion. Even Sir Charles had only been her partner twice and was now standing near him, taking a glass of wine. Several of the young ladies having retired for the moment to an ante-room, the room had emptied. Strolling up to Philip, he suggested a turn upon the terrace to cool themselves. Flattered by the attention, he agreed. He knew Charles to be his chief rival in Louise's affection but he held a youthful admiration for this former naval captain nonetheless. Charles's manner was in fact very friendly considering that he must have been aware of Philip's efforts to win a third dance with Louise.

Outside upon the terrace Henrietta had breathed in appreciatively the delicious scent of jasmine flowers and turning to Hugo said impulsively, "What a delightful evening! I cannot recollect when I have enjoyed myself more – and Mrs Tilden – such a charming hostess – after all, I am but a stranger to them and yet she has been kindness itself."

Hugo moved closer to her, "You will never be lacking for partners, my dear Henrietta." There was something in the tone of his voice, a roughness, that made her look up startled into his face. In the faint light of the moon, she perceived an expression in his eyes that made her suddenly horribly conscious that they were alone. Striving to lighten the atmosphere, she began quickly to chatter about the events of the evening, only to feel Hugo's arm steal about her waist and move caressingly upwards. Both alarmed by his action and surprised by the feelings he aroused, Henrietta attempted to move away, only to find herself forcibly turned back towards him as he murmured, "Lovely creature, what man could resist you!" Glancing shyly up into his face and seeing the purposeful gleam in his eyes, she turned her head sharply away so that the kiss he had intended for her mouth, fell upon her cheek.

It was at this precise moment that Sir Charles and Philip stepped out onto the terrace and found that they were not alone. Sir Charles, raising his eyeglass to survey the couple who stood seemingly locked in an embrace by the steps leading down into the garden, said softly, "I believe, Philip, your sister has more need of your company than I."

At that instant Henrietta broke away from Hugo exclaiming in a flustered voice, "Oh no! Hugo, you must not!" and as she turned towards him, Philip perceived this shockingly forward young female to be his own sister.

"My God! Henrietta!" His horrified tones could leave her in no doubt of his feelings. She looked beyond his shocked face to Sir Charles's expressionless countenance. Scarlet-faced, in an attempt to carry off the situation with some dignity, she said, "For goodness sake, d-don't be so gothic, Philip! Besides, Hugo is our cousin, after all –" Her brave words were somewhat belied by a decided tremor in her voice.

"Come, my dear Philip, don't tell me you have never been tempted to kiss a pretty girl in the moonlight!" There was a strange note of elation in Hugo's voice, "Pray escort your charming sister back into the house, for indeed I have no wish to sully her reputation – it is as dear to me as it is to you."

Somewhat pacified by this declaration, Philip looked from one face to the other in indecision. Hugo's superior knowledge of the ways of English society and his sister's obvious desire to avoid any further altercation was re-enforced by Sir Charles remarking in a detached voice, "I believe for Miss Brandon's sake, Philip, and to avoid unpleasant gossip, it would be advisable to escort your sister back to the ball-room."

"Very well!" He glared again at Hugo, "But this isn't the last you shall hear of this, cousin!" and taking Henrietta's arm in a far from conciliatory fashion, he led her through the curtained doorway back into the house.

There was a moment of silence, broken only by the sounds of music and voices emerging from the ballroom. Hugo was the first to speak, "I tell you, she ain't averse to my attentions, dear boy!" A spark of mischief danced in his eyes as he spoke, "And you will agree, we have no need of your approval!" There was no sign of discomfiture in his bearing as he lounged against the balustrade, a cynical smile upon his lips.

Sir Charles stared at him coldly, "Take care, Hugo, you'll go too far one of these days!" He paused, then added grimly, "If it weren't for the scandal it would cause – but it ain't worth it – even for all the satisfaction it would give me." Turning on his heel he strode back into the house.

Obliged, for the sake of appearances to conceal his indignation, Philip had to content himself with hissing in Henrietta's ear a dire warning as to her fate if she did not mend her ways as he led her to a seat near Lady Sedley. The latter greeted her with a nod and a smile and turned back to continue her interrupted conversation. Thankful to sit quietly for a moment, Henrietta found her mind in a turmoil. Could it be that she was a little in love with Hugo? Was this what she should infer from the strange sensations that he had provoked – and yet – was she not deep down a trifle afraid of him? One thing was certain – she felt herself flush angrily at her thoughts – Sir Charles might deal kindly with others but he was the most odious, the most provoking person she had ever encountered. She could not imagine why she should ever have felt sorry for him. It would serve him right if Philip *did* supplant him in Louise's affections. He was forever present at the most inopportune moments, casting a blight on her happiness and causing the most innocent events to appear to be in some way shameful.

The subject of her animadversions re-entered the room at that moment. Henrietta saw him seek out Miss Tilden and engage her in conversation. However she was not long permitted to indulge her resentful thoughts. Claimed by Mr Bertram Overly to dance the boulangère, she was obliged to set aside her ill-humour and, amused by his pretensions to fashion, soon regained her composure. Of Hugo, she saw little for the remainder of the evening. On his return from the terrace he had danced with Miss Overly, who made no secret of her pleasure in his company. Shortly afterwards, Henrietta observed him make his adieux to his host and depart, leaving her unable to decide whether she felt relief or disappointment.

Midnight soon came and with it the departure of the Tilden's guests. Each member of the Sedley party bore away with them their several impressions, hopes and regrets that would not soon be forgotten. Certainly in the hearts of the younger members present there was a great deal upon which to reflect. Louise could not have failed to enjoy a dance at which, quite clearly, she had been the most admired female present, but she was sadly disappointed with Charles's conduct towards her. Admittedly, he had claimed her twice to stand up with him but he had betrayed only his usual calm, pleasant manner towards her. As they took part in the movements of the dance, there had not been any visible sign of the fervent lover, no endearments or even compliments had fallen from his lips. It was impossible not to contrast this sad lack of passion with Philip's ardour. She had sensed his gaze resting upon her as she danced with her other partners. He was clearly jealous and aggrieved that he had not been able to partner her more than twice during the evening.

Henrietta's mind was in a turmoil. She had never, in her past sheltered existence in France, encountered anyone like Hugo and she did not in the least comprehend her own feelings. Men, she decided, were the strangest of beings. They seemed to combine in their persons all the best and worst of human characteristics. The evening, nevertheless, had opened her eyes to unimagined possibilities. Could Hugo be seriously in love with her?

Philip's thoughts were more direct. Louise embodied everything that he most desired and he found himself daily more enchanted by her. He was cross with Henrietta but her shocking behaviour he attributed chiefly to youthful ignorance. As for Hugo – what he had done had been inexcusable – he felt furious and wished that he could have knocked him down upon the spot.

CHAPTER 13

Early in the week which followed, Sir William was summoned to a meeting in Lewes with the Lord Lieutenant of the county and his fellow magistrates and had returned home in the afternoon in a state of great excitement. The family had assembled in the drawing-room, for Lady Julia, when at the Grange, preferred to keep country hours and they were to dine at four o'clock. The ladies plied their needles and Philip and Francis were engrossed in a game of picquet when Sir William strode into the room and announced in a portentous voice, "French spies, by God!"

Five startled faces were turned towards him. "Spies! Sir William!" Lady Julia's disdainful tone seemed to denote rather that a breach of good manners had occurred than a threat to her country's security.

Francis, a frown on his good-humoured countenance, asked quietly, "What's this, sir? Is it serious?"

Sir William went to stand before the fireplace and looked around him at his family. Despite experiencing the natural anxiety of a patriotic Englishman, he could not help but feel a certain satisfaction at being the bearer of such amazing news. "Serious enough, Francis! Could be damned serious, if you'll pardon me, my lady, for plain speaking!" He paused, "Mind you – this is for your ears alone – no blabbing it about the countryside – though I reckon it will be known soon enough."

"What will be known, Sir William?" Lady Julia looked mystified.

"Old Pendleton told us, he's a fellow magistrate, y'know, there's been word from London – from the Admiralty, no less – that an important naval despatch is missing. Some young officer attacked on Friday night and rescued by an unknown man – the secret paper stolen – whether by the attackers or the rescuer is not known. There's

163

a watch to be kept on all the ports in case of an attempt to get the information across the Channel!"

There were immediate expressions of astonishment and concern amongst the company. Philip and Francis, after exchanging glances, rose to their feet and crossed the room to question Sir William in more detail. Of the ladies, Henrietta was undoubtedly the most distressed. Too recent and too painful had been her experiences in France to permit her to escape a feeling of horror that any person should wish to aid the government of that unhappy country. "It is hard to believe that an Englishman could so betray his country!" she exclaimed, laying down her work, her face displaying the utmost dismay.

"And yet, my dear, there are undoubtedly some who believe the revolution in France to be an excellent thing." Sir William, who had heard her words, shook his head resignedly at the folly of mankind, "Fine philosophical ideas they may be but what shocking events have resulted."

"It is devoutly to be hoped that these villains will be apprehended. Have the authorities no information that will aid them – no descriptions?" Lady Julia enquired of her husband.

"Alas, it seems not, the officer has not so far recovered consciousness. It's a bad business indeed!"

Sir Charles Gresham was to dine with them that day. Haines announced his arrival and Sir Charles entering the drawing-room, was surprised to discover that he had interrupted an animated discussion.

"Such disturbing news, Charles!" his hostess remarked as she greeted him, "Sir William has set us all in alarm."

"Indeed!" Charles looked around him with raised brows at the assembled family, noting the seriousness of the men, the anxiety of Louise, the concern in Henrietta's face. "May I enquire what this news is, that has had such distressing results?"

A confusion of voices greeted him in reply. Sir William took him by the arm and led him aside, recounting to him with a solemn countenance all that he had heard in Lewes. "It's a bad business, Charles, a bad business!"

Of all those present, Charles Gresham must have been the person most aware of the consequences of such a breach of security. If the movements of ships were involved, if future naval plans for action were to become known to the enemy – how many sailors' lives might be lost or endangered? The news brought a pensive look to his face as he pressed Sir William for more details.

Francis said fretfully, "If only there was aught one could do to assist the authorities." Philip, agreeing, suggested hopefully that the two of them should drive to the coast the next day and enquire if there was some useful role that they might play, "Perhaps we should join the Volunteers? I had been thinking of pursuing that course –"

Charles regarded him thoughtfully, "Ironic, is it not, that you should so recently have asked me to find out if I could discover means to convey a message to France."

Philip, his colour a little heightened, said quickly, "Good Lord, no sense in considering that now!" He turned to Henrietta, who was looking at him with some surprise and added, "Just to tell Jeanne that we were safe – I hoped it might be possible!"

After dinner, when the gentlemen had joined the ladies, Charles strolled across the room to join Louise and Henrietta and found both young ladies more preoccupied with the news than with any consideration of their own feelings towards him. Seeing their anxious faces, he set himself to reassure them, remarking confidently as he sat down beside them, "Depend upon it, this villain will be apprehended, I have no doubt, for once the news is known, there's not a man, woman or child who would give aid to such a traitor."

Louise looked relieved and said solemnly, her ingenuous little face turned towards Sir Charles, her lovely eyes gazing meditatively into his face, "How worthy of our esteem and gratitude would be the man who succeeds in discovering this villain.

He responded gravely, "He would be a hero, indeed!" Henrietta, watching their faces, wondered a trifle enviously how any man could resist this charmingly feminine creature. It was no wonder that her brother was falling in love with her too! Sir Charles was regarding Louise appreciatively, his eyes smiling down at her, then he turned to Henrietta and taking up the embroidery frame that lay beside her, raised his eye-glass and closely inspected her handiwork. His recent interference in her affairs still rankled in her mind. She said with a tinge of sarcasm in her voice, "No doubt, sir, you are about to compliment me upon the neatness of my stitches, I can see that you are, like Hugo, an expert in such matters!"

"Doubtless your skill deserves high praise." he replied calmly, "However, it is the subject matter that intrigues me. I seem to collect that fishing is one of your favourite pastimes – though it can have its hazards, alas!"

The quizzical expression in his eyes, the implication of his remarks and her recollection of her flight from the lake into his arms, brought a flush to Henrietta's cheeks and a sparkle to her eyes as she murmured indignantly, "Unworthy, Sir Charles! How could you venture upon such a reminder."

"Can I be permitted, at least, to recollect a pleasant experience!"

Startled, she retorted quickly, "But I thought –" then hesitated and added uncomfortably, "No matter, I can see that you are only funning."

Louise, not following the allusions of this exchange but aware that her new cousin was being teased, gently reproved Sir Charles, "I will not have you make my dear Henrietta uneasy, sir."

"Heaven forbid, my dear Louise that I should do such a thing!" he replied, looking suitably penitent and in such a droll manner that both girls were obliged to laugh. For the moment all thoughts of spies and traitors and past animosities were forgotten. He then added with a smile, "But I believe, however, that it would be difficult to make a person possessed of so much courage to become uneasy." Henrietta felt agreeably flattered. It was pleasant to find herself the recipient of such a compliment. In Lady Sedley's household she felt herself regarded as one who had broken the rules of Polite Society and whose masquerade as a boy had been in some way shameful.

CHAPTER 14

Two days later, riding near the village of West Burton Sir Charles discovered, to his annoyance, that his mount had cast a shoe. Being close to the smithy, he decided to make his way there immediately. Jem Carter, shoeing Dr Thornton's cob, readily agreed that Sir Charles's horse should be attended to forthwith, "O'ill be only a matter o'minutes, sir! Leave un here and he'll be the next." He looked admiringly at the handsome grey, "Fine bit of blood and bone you got there, sir!" and directed his young apprentice to lead the horse to the side of the forge.

"I'll step into the Dog and Duck for a pint of ale while I wait. You're fortunate to have refreshment so handy." Charles added with a smile.

The blacksmith grinned, wiping the sweat off his brow with a grimy hand, "You'll find a stranger to these parts in there, sir. Askin' questions, he be – proper nosey. They say we've a spy like, around here – some sort of Frenchie, 'tis said!"

Bending his head to enter the tap-room, it took Charles a moment or two to adjust to the gloom within. The windows were small and what light might have penetrated the low-beamed room was largely prevented by the pots of geraniums which flourished upon the window-sills. Once his eyes had become accustomed to the absence of light and he had ordered a tankard of ale, he stood at the bar and surveyed the company. The first thing he observed was a notable lack of conversation around him. Instead of the usual hubbub, in which voices had to be raised to be audible, he had the distinct impression that most of those present were straining their ears to hear the one conversation that was taking place, in low tones, in a corner by the fire. The rounded figure of a man, wearing a rough frieze coat and a wide-brimmed hat upon his head, amply filled, a

Windsor armchair. Beside him a pale-faced youth with straw-coloured hair, bore all the marks of a city-dweller making him stand out amongst the ruddy-cheeked inhabitants of West Burton like a ghost at a feast. Charles noted with a frown, that the man in the frieze coat was deep in conversation with one of the locals, a youngish man, who, to Charles's recollection, was a groom from the Grange.

Recognizing two farmer acquaintances of his seated on the other side of the room, Charles crossed the tap-room to join them, saying, as he set his tankard down upon the table, "What the devil's going on here, Andrews? Place is deucedly quiet today."

"Mornin', Sir Charles! Ain't you heard the tales that are going around?"

"I've heard naught, what's amiss?"

The elderly farmer shook his head, "Such strange stories – it's hard to credit them." He leaned forward and added in a lowered voice, "It's all about that young fellow who fled from France, him, that you took in, Sir Charles – that's now said to be Lord Hartington's heir."

Charles raised his eyebrows, "And what story is being told about him?" he enquired.

Old Andrew's voice dropped even lower, "There's folks saying that he's the spy they're seeking." He gestured with his thumb towards the strangers by the fire, "That one over there – the stout one – a Bow Street Runner he is! Asking question of everyone – 'course no-one wants to speak out against Sir William and his family. Well-respected here, as you know, and his wife's mother was a Brandon – deuced awkward it is, if you ask me. But, we're at war now with those damned, blood-thirsty Frogs –"

At that moment Charles, observing that the young groom had risen to his feet and was about to take his leave, excused himself to his companions and moved across to the fireplace to lower himself onto the now vacant seat next to the Runner.

He found himself regarded inquisitively by a pair of round, blue eyes, "And whom might I 'ave the pleasure of h'addressing, might I arsk?"

"Captain Sir Charles Gresham, formerly of his Majesty's Royal Navy," was the courteous reply.

"H'indeed, is that so – is that so – very good indeed, sir. Joshua Prout's m'name and h'investigatin' is m'business, as you might say, if you was minded to."

"Delighted to make your acquaintance! And may I enquire what matter you are presently investigating in this peaceful corner of Sussex?" Sir Charles was at his most urbane.

"Traitors and spies, sir!" The blue eyes were fixed penetratingly upon his face, "An' if you 'as h'information upon this 'ere subject, Joshua Prout would be h'infinitely h'obliged to you."

"And what makes you think that there are traitors and spies in West Burton, my dear fellow?"

"H'information received, sir – all along of a letter! To their Lordships of the Admiralty, no less!"

Sir Charles surveyed him languidly and enquired, "A letter from whom?" Joshua Prout shook his head regretfully, "No signature h'appended, more's the pity – so I comes to 'ear things – very strange things, wot's more."

"Indeed! Most interesting." Sir Charles sighed and was silent for a moment, surveying his companion from beneath frowning brows, then rousing himself from his reverie, continued in a lowered voice, "If you would care to accompany me into the inn-parlour, where we may be private, I should very much like to hear more of this matter. As you can well understand, anything that concerns the Navy is very close to my heart."

The Runner being agreeable, the move was soon made. As the tap-room door closed behind their departing figures, a buzz of excited speculation arose. All manner of theories were postulated, and an air of pleasurable excitement animated the room and provoked a note-worthy increase in the consumption of ale.

Lady Sedley's mantua-maker had made good progress and Henrietta was now the possessor of several gowns. The riding-coat dress of blue Marcella had almost reached completion but it was vexing to discover that Miss Hatley had run out of the matching silk needed for the finishing touches. Louise, entering the nursery at that moment, and hearing of the dilemma, was full of sympathy.

"What a shame, Henrietta, for you could have worn it to attend morning service on Sunday, for it is truly delightful." Her face brightened, "We'll ask Timpson to drive us to the village. Mrs Knight sells thread, as well as everything else one can think of, and she might well have the shade you require."

It made a very pleasant expedition. As they bowled along in the gig, the two girls, in their summer muslins and chip-straw bonnets, attracted considerable attention from the inhabitants of West Burton. Many heads were turned to watch their progress and see them finally alight in the High Street. Mrs Knight's little shop sold everything from tallow candles and mousetraps to packets of pins and feather dusters, and reels of thread there were in abundance. There were already one or two customers in the shop when they entered and it seemed to Henrietta that a sudden hush had fallen upon them as the two young ladies stepped inside the door. Mrs Knight was all affability. When it was their turn to be served, she greeted Louise with smiles and requested to know how she might serve them; casting a sharp look of interest at Henrietta at the same time.

"This is my new cousin, Mrs Knight – Miss Brandon, who recently escaped from France and is staying with us at present. Is it not delightful for me?"

"Yes, Miss, delightful, I'm sure!" Her bright eyes regarded Henrietta intently, "And you were wanting, Miss?"

"Thread, Mrs Knight, a blue to match this material."

Mrs Knight brought down the boxes containing cotton and silk from the crowded shelves behind her, and the young ladies bent their heads eagerly over the contents. While they were thus engaged, the shop door opened and two village women entered, engrossed in animated conversation, "– from France they do say. That's gospel truth! Whoever would have thought as we'd have a spy in our very midst!"

Her companion, glancing at the counter and recognizing Miss Sedley's profile, gave the speaker a hearty nudge and continued in a raised voice, "All talk, I expect, Jemima, that's all it'll be."

Henrietta, who had just discovered with delight a shade of blue which would do very well for her purpose, looked round in surprise at hearing the words 'France' and 'spy'. Louise frowned, "What's this, Mrs Knight, about 'spies' here? Has something happened?"

Mrs Knight, looking acutely uncomfortable, threw a glance of hostility at the two women who were now inspecting some willow baskets at the far end of the shop with an interest that seemed to go far beyond anything that they might merit. "Why, Miss, jest that there be a stranger in the village askin' a mort of questions of folks. And with the war and suchlike –" Her voice died away, and she began to wrap up the reel of thread. As she handed over the package, she leaned across the counter and whispered to Louise and Henrietta, "Don't 'ee take offence, m'dear, but there's such terrible rumours agoin' around – some secret paper gone missing – and as it seems your cousin, the young gentleman, be come recent across the Channel – Folks will talk, Miss, and there's no stopping them."

Louise and Henrietta exchanged glances of astonishment, "Of course you must deny it, Mrs Knight!" Louise was indignant, "I've never heard such nonsense – how could anyone credit such a thing?"

Henrietta, looking with hostility at the backs of the two village women, said distinctly, in her clear voice, "My brother is an Englishman, ma'am, and proud of it!"

"Yes, Miss, I'm sure, Miss!" Mrs Knight curtsied and smiled but it was not hard to see that doubts still lingered in her mind.

The two girls emerged from the village shop in a state of considerable perturbation. This was horribly unwelcome news to both of them. Louise, saying in an undertone, "We cannot discuss this dreadful rumour in front of Timpson," instructed the groom to follow them with the gig as they desired to walk some part of the way home for exercise.

"It must be this Naval dispatch of which Sir William spoke." Henrietta said, as soon as they were out of earshot, her face grave, "But why, oh why, should there be talk of Philip being involved?"

Louise replied hopefully, "No doubt it's a great deal of nonsense, just foolish local gossip, that gets repeated and grows in the telling."

"But who is this person who is asking questions? That's scarcely something that can have been invented."

By this time they were nearing the entrance to the Dog and Duck. To their surprise they saw ahead of them the elegant figure of Sir Charles Gresham emerge from the inn accompanied by a thick-set man wearing a wide-brimmed hat. Engrossed in earnest conversation, they had paused on the steps leading down to the street. Sir Charles had his back to them and as they drew nearer they could hear his deep voice quite plainly, "– and remember, Prout, if there's aught I can do to assist you, I depend upon you to call upon me – for if there's proof needed, perhaps I can help you."

"Very good, sir – I be h'infinitely obliged to you, Captain." The thick-set man touched a stubby finger to his hat in salute, gave a broad wink, and retreated into the inn once more, no doubt to further refresh himself within.

Sir Charles, descending the steps to return to the smithy, discovered Louise and Henrietta within a few yards of him. He bowed politely, expressing his pleasure at this unexpected meeting. The two faces turned towards him bore such a look of anxiety that he at once demanded with concern what was amiss.

Henrietta spoke quickly, "Shocking rumours of a spy, here, in West Burton, sir. And Philip's name mentioned. It is unbelievable!"

Louise added, "They say there's a stranger here, Sir Charles, asking questions." She looked very frightened.

He nodded gravely, "A Bow Street Runner, no less. I have this instant been in conversation with him. It seems that an anonymous letter has been received, directing attention to these parts. I shall feel happier when this despatch is recovered, for the intelligence it contains must not leave the country." He looked at Henrietta, an expression hard to read upon his face, "As for your brother, Miss Brandon, no doubt you are aware that country people are inevitably suspicious of strangers."

Louise agreed eagerly, "Why that's true, Henrietta, and there is so little excitement in a village; depend upon it, it will soon be a nine days' wonder!"

Henrietta shook her head doubtfully, for grave misgivings were stirring in her mind.

CHAPTER 15

While Louise and Henrietta were in West Burton village, Sir William had driven down to Brighton with Francis and Philip. The former was anxious to discover, if he could, how far the enquiry had progressed. He had also arranged to dine with an old friend, a former Admiral, who, he believed might be able to tell them if there was any assistance that they could render to the authorities. It was therefore not until the evening that they returned to the Grange and were at once informed by the ladies of the presence of a Bow Street Runner in the village and of the alarming rumours that had spread there following his arrival.

Sir William was inclined to disregard the seriousness of these events. He was in a mellow mood following an enjoyable dinner with the Admiral and the consumption of a quantity of burgundy, succeeded by an excellent port. "Depend upon it, my dears, 'tis all part of general enquiries in Sussex and Kent. As for the locals – why even a fellow from the adjoining counties is considered a dashed foreigner!"

Francis was highly indignant, and regarded it as positively outrageous that anyone should believe there to be even a grain of truth in the rumours. "Damme, I'll have something to the point to say to them when I'm next in the Dog and Duck!" he declared roundly. "They must have windmills in their heads even to consider such a thing!"

That Philip was appalled was only to be expected. He turned pale when he heard the news and Henrietta, who knew him so well could tell by the look in his eyes that he was deeply disturbed. Nevertheless, he put a good face upon it, saying jokingly, "There, you see, sir, – fact of the matter is, I knew my garments gave me the look of a dashed foreigner! How timely that my new coat has arrived while we were absent in Brighton."

Louise said petulantly, "These ignorant people! I've no patience with them." She gave Philip a reassuring smile.

Henrietta, too, for her brother's sake, tried to make light of the enquiries, "Obviously, it is a serious matter for the Navy, and the authorities have a duty to pursue the matter everywhere. I make nothing of this gossip – it is only human nature to find such news a big excitement in a small village." These comforting words of Henrietta's were, however, very far from reflecting her true feelings. She had been shocked to hear of the rumours in the village, but far graver were her misgivings when she recalled the sight of Sir Charles in conversation with the Runner. His parting words to that officer which she and Louise had overheard puzzled her. What in the world could he have meant?

That evening after she had mounted to her bedchamber, she had sat a long time before her dressing-table, lost in troubled thought. There was, of course, no foundation for these rumours – not for one moment did she even consider the notion that Philip was involved in spying – but how to account for the anonymous letter? That bore all the marks of a plot to discredit him! Could it be that he had an enemy? It was a possibility that she had feared when the shot had been fired at him when he had been out shooting – now it seemed that someone was determined to implicate him in the theft of the despatch. Though her bedchamber was pleasantly warm, she felt herself shiver. Her thoughts grew ever more sombre. That there was a growing attachment between Philip and Louise must be by now evident to anyone who saw them together, even to the most blind. Was it not said that jealousy, like an acid, could eat into a man's very soul? Sir Charles had spoken of proof – but what proof could he have unless – she forced herself to follow her thoughts through to their logical conclusion – unless he had removed the paper himself and retained it. Not with the intention of passing it to the enemy of his country – she could acquit him most certainly of that – but rather with the intention of planting the dispatch at the Grange to prove beyond doubt that his rival was a spy. To cause his arrest, even perhaps his execution as a traitor!

Unwelcome corroborating facts flew to her mind. Sir Charles had been in London on the night of the theft. Sir Charles would know at once what naval information would be of the utmost importance. Moreover, it was he who had invited Philip to shoot pigeon – the accident had happened on Gresham land – how fatally easy for Sir Charles to have bribed some unscrupulous person to fire at and murder Philip! Had she not once heard of his having assisted a gypsy. Everything seemed to point towards him. Sick at heart, she stared blindly into the looking-glass. She remembered how kindly this tall, handsome Englishman had befriended her initially, and although since then he had enraged her by interfering in her affairs he had shown no signs of bearing malice towards her, rather a concern for her well-being.

With a shudder she recognized that his equable manner must conceal a ruthlessness that would strive to gain its objective regardless of others. He had set his heart upon marriage to the exquisitely beautiful Louise and no man should stand in his way. It seemed he had decided to eliminate Philip – now chance had given him a second opportunity of doing so. If she could only find the despatch and destroy it, Philip would be safe – something must be done and it must be done immediately! Impetuously, she rose to her feet and began to search in the cupboard for the garments that had disguised her sex when she had left France, thankful that she had not permitted their destruction. At the back of the shelf she discovered the bundle and began, once more, to dress herself as a boy.

She waited impatiently until all the Sedley household were asleep, then took up her candlestick and cautiously descended the stairs to the hall. All was quiet, only the loud tick of the long-case clock disturbed the silence. Passing through the baize-covered door to the kitchen quarters, she lit a lantern that stood on a table near the back door then taking it in her hand, slipped out of the house and made her way to the stables. Country born and bred, it did not take long to saddle and bridle the quiet, chestnut mare that she had ridden with Francis and Louise, and, with the aid of the mounting block, she was able to climb into the saddle. A full moon was up, only occasionally dimmed by clouds, and she was able to guide her horse out of the stable-yard and into the paddock. Despite its awkwardness she decided to take the lantern with her, and thus set off carefully across the fields that joined the Sedley and Gresham estates.

By now it was well past midnight and as she approached the familiar surroundings of Gresham Place, skirting the lake and the side of the wood, a sensation of disillusionment swept over her and mingled with her apprehension. The dark outline of the rambling old building came into view against the pale indigo sky and, to Henrietta's relief, she observed that no light was visible at any of the windows facing her. Keeping to the grass, she rode up to the gate that cut-off the field-track from the pleasure gardens and slipping from the saddle, tied her horse to the gatepost. Silence enveloped her, broken by the mournful hooting of an owl in the distant wood; a silence so complete that, as she moved towards the house, lantern in hand, her own heart-beats sounded deafening in her ears.

She remembered when the plan had first formed in her mind, that a key to the garden-door hung on a hook beside it, concealed by the honeysuckle that clambered around the doorway. She had often, during her visit to Sir Charles, entered the house by means of that key. Now she had no difficulty in finding it by the light of her lantern and placing it in the lock. She could not avoid there being a slight click as the key was turned but contrived to lift the latch silently. Thankful to discover that the door made no sound as she swung it open, she entered the passageway. She stood motionless for a moment, but all was silence. Then, cautiously, holding her breath, she tiptoed towards the front of the house. She had decided during her ride that the book-room was the most likely place in which to find the missing paper.

There, Sir Charles attended to his correspondence at a large flat-topped desk set before one of the windows. She hardly dared to think what she should do if the search proved unsuccessful. The door of the book-room was ajar and she slipped inside, noting by the dim light of her lantern, that the heavy curtains were drawn and some disorder was evident. A half-empty bottle and a glass stood upon the desk, making her realize with a disagreeably chilling sensation that its owner had recently been present.

Setting the lantern down upon the desk, she tried one of the drawers and, finding it unlocked, began to glance quickly through the numerous papers that lay within. She was so intent upon her task that she was not aware of the creak of a floorboard behind her. Suddenly, without warning, she was seized from behind and before she could utter a sound, a hand was clamped over her mouth while a brutally strong arm was thrust across her chest pinning her arms to her sides so that she could neither move nor speak. Seconds later a familiar voice spoke from above her head, exclaiming in tones of the utmost astonishment, "Good God! What the devil!" There was a moment's pause and the vice-like grip loosened a trifle, the hand was removed from her mouth and she was turned to face her assailant. Henrietta found herself staring up into Sir Charles Gresham's face.

Determined to direct his mind towards more everyday matters, Sir Charles had spent the evening at his desk wrestling with estate affairs of such intolerable dullness that he had found his thoughts wandering in a different direction. So many problems, so many temptations – some of which bore the gravest implications – crowded in upon him. At length he had rung for Cummings. Directing him to bring him a bottle of brandy, he instructed him to tell Morton to go to his bed. He was not by any means, a man who was in the habit of drinking in solitude but that night, troubled by his gloomy thoughts, he had felt a pressing need for some means of raising his spirits and of forgetting the quandary in which he found himself.

Several hours later, his coat discarded, his cravat undone, he heard the sound of a key turning in the garden-door. Hastily putting down his glass and blowing out the candles, he slipped behind the curtains that hung before one of the windows and waited, listening intently. He heard soft footsteps in the hall, then sensed the infinite caution of the intruder pushing open the door and entering the room. Through a gap in the curtains he saw that a lantern had been placed upon his desk and now illumined the figure of a youth who was standing with his back turned towards him quickly scrambling through its drawers.

"So you have once again fallen for the irresistible allure of your masculine garments, Miss Brandon." Sir Charles was frowning down at her, "I could not mistake such a charming armful. But I confess to some surprise that you should feel impelled to visit me at this hour of the night." His sarcastic tones failed to conceal that he was astounded and a good deal shocked by her presence. For her part, even in her agitation at being discovered, she could not fail to notice with amazement his dishevelled appearance. He was still holding her in a grip that was by no means gentle and she felt an idiotic desire to burst into tears. However, inspite of this shameful weakness, she gazed back at him resolutely and said in a halting voice, "N-no doubt you find it somewhat odd that I should be here, sir."

At that he laughed grimly and released her, saying, "Odd! Upon my word! Let us say, I find it a trifle unusual to discover a young lady breaking into my house in the middle of the night like a common thief, to say nothing of her immodest attire! And –" he looked significantly at the open drawer, "apparently in the process of committing a felony!"

Henrietta flushed vividly. She was beginning to regain her composure and, although her heart was still beating alarmingly, her courage was returning and with it the sense of determination and outrage that had led her to this escapade. Nothing now but the truth would serve. Stiff-backed, and looking directly into his face, she said fiercely, "I came to find the Naval dispatch which you have stolen!"

For a moment he stared at her, as if doubting that he had heard aright, then, with narrowed eyes, enquired, "What in God's name makes you believe that I should do such a thing?"

The words came tumbling out, "Obviously it cannot have escaped your notice that Louise begins to have tender feelings for Philip and you fear to lose the one you love to another. You are consumed by jealousy – you are in London and, by a strange chance, you have the opportunity to take the dispatch. To discredit, indeed, to ruin Philip, your rival – you send a letter to the Admiralty to lead them here and then – then, you will place the dispatch at the Grange, so that my brother will be arrested!"

"My dear Miss Brandon, you have the fevered imagination of a writer of gothic romance! Never have I heard such a farrago of nonsense – even Louise could not have bettered such a flight of fancy." His tone was scornful.

The sarcasm stung Henrietta into further angry accusations, "You do not deceive me, sir, not in the least. I know now that you mean to destroy Philip – I did not think it at first, but now I am sure! First you hired an assassin to kill him in your woods – but when that plan failed –"

Now the veiled eyes that looked down at her were cold as ice, "My God, Miss Brandon! It seems that there are no lengths to which you believe that I will not go. You have a very pretty opinion of me to be sure! Have you not thought that perhaps your brother may be the one who took the letter? After all, he holds views by no means hostile to the present French government and has made enquiries about the means to convey information across the Channel."

Henrietta stared at him, her great eyes open wide with amazement, "That is unbelievable! Philip! But you are mad, sir. Philip has no love for the revolutionaries!"

She had to remind herself fiercely that Sir Charles would deny what he had done. To cast doubts in her mind about her brother was clearly in his best interest. She returned resolutely to the attack,

"Sir Charles, if you will destroy the letter now, no-one need ever know of your intentions. Soon we shall be leaving Sir William's house and – and Louise will forget Philip –" her voice trailed away into silence – impossible to tell what thoughts were passing through his mind behind that grim face regarding her –

Had she but known, frustration and anger fought for domination within Sir Charles as he gazed coldly down into the anxious face upturned towards him. The ride, hatless, across the fields had blown Henrietta's curls into a bronze halo. She was very pale and in the dim light of the lantern her eyes, fringed by long, dark lashes under her finely drawn brows, were staring, wide-eyed into his. His gaze fell to the slim, straight figure in the over-large boy's clothes and Henrietta became suddenly aware of the glitter in his eyes, the purposeful set to his well-shaped mouth. She became, all at once, horribly conscious of his close proximity. She made a move to back away from him and found herself pressed up against the desk behind her.

Anger still remained in Sir Charles's face and there was an intensity, a ruthlessness in his look that aroused Henrietta's worst fears. What madness had led her to come here at night? As panic seized her she looked around her for some means of escape. A bitter smile curved his lips briefly, "You little fool!" he murmured softly, then, pulling her close to him with one arm, he put a hand under her chin and tilted her face to look up at him. At that moment there was as much astonishment as fear in her eyes. With a harsh laugh, he bent his head to kiss her hard and lingeringly full upon the mouth. Then, he raised his head and stood looking down at her searchingly, still holding her closely to him.

Henrietta, aware of a succession of bewildering sensations, stared back at him. Never had she been kissed in such a fashion before for Hugo's attempt had fallen wide of its mark. Ashamed to discover a sudden, unbidden desire to respond to his kiss, her face scarlet, she said breathlessly, "Sir! How dare you!" Then, fastening upon the only reason she could perceive for such uncharacteristic behaviour, said accusingly, "Are you drunk, Sir Charles?"

He responded disconcertingly, "Perhaps I have made greater inroads into the brandy bottle than prudence dictates, Miss Brandon, but I assure you that I should have done the same even if I had been sober as a judge!"

She tried to look dignified but failed miserably. She was pressed so closely against him that she could feel the rapid beating of his heart. Coatless, with tousled hair and shirt unbuttoned at the neck, he had a frighteningly intimate air and with the reckless gleam still in his eyes, she found him an over-powering presence. Dismayed by the shakiness of her legs but determined not to betray any sign of her inner quaking, Henrietta eyed him nervously, conscious that she was now entirely at the mercy of a man self confessed as the worse for drink. Moreover, her mission had proved to be a disastrous mistake. She had failed to find the dispatch and it seemed that her appeal to Sir Charles had been in vain.

To her relief, she found herself thrust suddenly aside as Sir Charles, with an angry exclamation turned his back upon her and crossed the room to stand before the fireplace. Regarding her from under frowning brows, he said, "Do you not perceive the utter folly of your actions? It was permissible to adopt a boy's clothing for your flight from France, but quite shocking to dress yourself again in such a fashion. Worst of all to come here alone at night! If you had been observed – nothing in heaven or earth could have restored your reputation." He seemed unable to contain his anger as he continued, in biting tones, "Your improper conduct with Hugo, your foolish escapade –"

Startled by this sudden onslaught, as pale now as she had been flushed before, Henrietta interrupted him fiercely, "Do not trouble, sir, to make further recitation of my sins! At least my presence here tonight was prompted by my desire to save my brother. As to your opinion – I care nothing for it!" Her eyes flashing with scorn, she added, "You speak of my conduct, but yours tonight – a man who is betrothed to my cousin!" She turned her back upon him and wiped away a furious tear with a trembling hand, muttering as she did so, "I would that I might never set eyes upon you again!"

There was a moment's silence, then Sir Charles crossed the room to her side. He said stiffly, "You had best return home, Miss Brandon, before your absence is detected." Taking up her lantern from the desk, made as if to take her arm to conduct her to the door. Childishly, Henrietta shrugged off the hand at her elbow and, head held high, quitted the room. As he opened the garden door for her and fol- lowed her outside, Henrietta could not help remembering sadly the happy few days that she had spent in this house. Now, disillusioned, she saw miserably that the man she had admired was a villain without pity or principles. In silence they reached the field-gate, where Sir Charles untethered her horse. For a moment he stood looking down at her. The wide, anxious eyes in a face that was drained of colour by the moonlight stared back at him defiantly. Suddenly he touched her cheek gently with his fingers and murmured something inaudible under his breath. Then, tossing her up into the saddle with a curt, "Farewell, Miss Brandon – until tomorrow!" he turned on his heel and strode back to the house.

Feeling horribly shaken and most thankful to have escaped from a sit- uation which had seemed to be growing more and more alarming, Henrietta rode slowly back to the Grange. She allowed her mount, who was as anxious to return to her stable as Henrietta was to regain the safety of her bedroom, to find her way across the fields. Her thoughts were bitter. Convinced that Sir Charles was determined to eliminate his rival, she could not help wondering how, if he was so deeply in love with Louise, he could yet kiss her in such a fashion. Even in the cool night air, she felt a blush rise to her cheeks at the rec- ollection of his embrace. Worst of all, she had to acknowledge the strange and, if she was honest, delightfully disturbing feelings it had aroused. She shook her head, puzzled and dismayed – no doubt men were like that – and, moreover, Sir Charles had been drinking. Ruthlessly she attempted to shut all thoughts of her own feelings out of her mind.

CHAPTER 16

"Come, Louise, the morning is drawing on, I believe we shall not wait for Henrietta – she is unconscionably late in arising today and I have several calls to make." Lady Sedley, very aware of her daughter's languid air and pale face, determined to provide a distraction; no sense in moping about the house she decided. Louise, finding herself embroiled in events which were scarcely less dramatic than her own day-dreams, was finding reality considerably harder to bear. Her future, until recently so assured and only requiring her fertile imagination to give it the mystery and excitement that she craved, seemed suddenly uncertain. It was one thing to be ardently wooed by a handsome young man – indeed, to have feelings aroused of which she had hitherto been unaware; additionally pleasant to be loved by two handsome men, though Sir Charles seemed disappointingly unmoved by Philip's unconcealed ardour. But, on the other hand, how little she, or any of her family, knew of her new admirer. She had been genuinely shocked by the rumours that were abounding in the locality. Suddenly Sir Charles, and all the solid virtues he represented in her thoughts, appeared in a new and favourable light. With a wan smile, she agreed with Lady Sedley. The carriage was brought to the door laden with baskets containing fortifying soups, jellies and other delicacies and mother and daughter set forth to deliver comfort and sustenance to several impoverished invalids in the neighbourhood.

Henrietta had passed a restless night and it was not until almost daybreak that she fell into a deep sleep. Scarcely conscious of the housemaid drawing back her curtains or her placing the brass can of water beside her wash-stand, she awoke eventually to find the morning sun streaming through her window and the hour already passed ten o'clock. By the time she was dressed and had descended to the breakfast parlour, she found the house deserted. After having fortified herself with hot chocolate and some slices of bread-and-butter, she put on her bonnet and taking a shawl, walked out into the garden and through the gate at the farthermost end. From there the path led upwards to the crest of a small hill, where Sir William, with the thoughtfulness which was such a feature of his character, had caused a comfortably low bench to be placed. Seated upon it with a delightful view before her of the foothills of the South Downs where the sheep grazed the close-cropped grass, she sighed unhappily. The tranquil scene, far from soothing her troubled thoughts, only seemed to intensify her unease. Convinced that Philip was in danger, she could see no way in which she could aid him. Her adventures of the previous night had proved a disastrous failure and had left her uncertain and afraid.

She had not been sitting there for many minutes when she heard the thud of horse's hoofs on the springy turf and a rider appeared over the brow of the hill. As he drew nearer she recognized that it was Hugo. He pulled his horse to a walk when he saw her and came alongside her, greeting her with a delighted smile, "My lovely Cousin Henrietta! What a charming surprise." Dismounting, he looped his horse's reins over the branch of a nearby tree and came to sit next to her. "I'm on my way to the Grange – your brother and I have arranged to ride over to Saddlescombe this morning – there are some first rate gallops there." His tall figure was displayed to excellent advantage by his dark green riding-coat and immaculately fitting breeches and the unspoken admiration in his eyes went some way to restoring Henrietta's low spirits. He continued, his voice full of sympathy, "I am conscious of the concern that these rumours that I have heard must be causing you – damnable nonsense of course – but this anonymous letter – that's deucedly worrying!" He hesitated and seemed as if he was about to say something more, then shook his head and said, "Have you any notion what lies behind it?"

Henrietta turned towards him eagerly, "Pray tell me anything you know – or suspect – for I am half out of my mind with worry."

He stared at her for a moment as if unsure how to proceed, then taking one of her hands in his, he said slowly, "I cannot bear to see you so distressed – I have no certain knowledge – only I am afraid that jealousy may have driven someone to unpardonable lengths of duplicity."

Her eyes grew round with horror, whom else could he be referring to but Sir Charles! She was not then the only one who suspected him – and Hugo knew him better than she did – "You mean Sir Charles?" she faltered.

"One can scarcely credit it – and yet –" Hugo was regarding her searchingly, "My poor little cousin, my heart bleeds for you."

"Alas, it is all just as I feared – how I have been deceived!" There was a spark of anger now in Henrietta's eye.

Watching her face, he raised her hand to his lips and kissed it, saying softly, "I wish that I could help you, my enchanting Henrietta."

She looked at him as if she was hardly aware of what he said or did, her mind filled with foreboding and snatching her hand away, she jumped to her feet, saying breathlessly, "I must return at once to the house, cousin." Then, recollecting her manners, she added swiftly, "You are all kindness, Hugo – it will be good for Philip to have some occupation – I only hope and trust that he is unaware of our suspicions." Together, they walked back to the house, and Hugo, having consigned his mount into the care of a groom in the stable-yard, accompanied Henrietta into the drawing room.

"If you will wait here, I will find Philip and tell him you are waiting for him." Henrietta bestowed an abstracted smile upon him and quitted the room hurriedly.

Morton had found his master to be uncommonly silent that morning, and had reflected, with an inward smile, of which no trace was permitted to show upon his elderly countenance, that Sir Charles was enduring the inevitable consequences of imbibing too freely the previous evening. After breakfasting with a preoccupied air, Sir Charles had called for his horse to be brought round to the door and had set out for the Grange with a look of resolution upon his countenance.

He found, to his surprise, having been ushered into the drawing-room by Haines, that Hugo was its sole occupant. The latter came forward from the window-seat where he had been sitting and greeted Charles in an easy manner, saying, "I'm to ride out with Philip this morning – Henrietta has this instant left me to summon him." He eyed Charles speculatively, observing the rigid set of his jaw, his frowning brows, and enquired laughingly, "Ain't still in a fury about what occurred at the Tilden's dance, I trust? You've a devilish long face this morning."

Charles eyed him sombrely and turned to confirm that the door to the hall was closed. Then, looking gravely at Hugo, he said quietly, "Forget that for the moment – I'm damnably uneasy." He hesitated, then added, "This despatch – fact of the matter is, I can't for the life of me, help remembering that young Philip has a great deal of sympathy with the present regime in France and he was in London the night it was stolen. Were you both in each other's company all that evening?"

"As it chanced we were not. For Philip was set upon seeing some of the sights and we met again in my rooms before leaving for Brooks's. But, Good God, man – that notion is inconceivable! I won't believe it for a moment." Hardly had he spoken than the door opened and the subject of their discussions strode into the room, a broad grin on his face as he saw the two men, and greeted them warmly.

"By Jove, what a piece of good fortune that you are both here together." He was dressed in a coat of dark blue superfine, whose exquisite cut set off his slim figure. He seemed to be in excellent spirits, though Charles observed that dark lines lay under his eyes, as if sleep had been elusive. "What do you think, Sir Charles?" Philip spun round before him, "Damme, if I don't believe Milne has excelled himself. These cuffs, now," He held out his arm before them, "Voila! The very latest!"

Hugo grinned appreciatively and laid his own sleeve alongside Philip's, "What say you, Charles, do you prefer two buttons or three?"

Endeavouring to conceal his suspicions of the youth, Charles raised his quizzing glass and bestowed his serious consideration upon the two examples of the tailor's art. Plucking a loose thread from Hugo's sleeve, he examined the finish of the stitching upon Philip's cuff and pronounced his verdict in favour of the younger man. "I like the extra button," and could not resist adding, "had Weston make mine with three for the past year or more."

"Excellent, sir!" Philip was delighted and Hugo raising his eyes to the heavens, exclaimed, "By Jove, Charles, I'd no idea that you were such a fribble as to be conscious of these finer points!" Then, clapping Philip on the back, he suggested that they should depart, "If we're to reach Saddlecombe, we'd best be on our way."

Philip nodded and looked towards Charles, his young face suddenly serious, "Has there been any news? Has this missing paper been found?"

Charles shook his head, "I've heard nothing as yet – it's damnably disturbing."

For a moment no-one spoke, then Hugo made a move towards the door, "Will you join us, Charles?"

Sir Charles declined politely, "I shall await Miss Brandon, – I've a message I wish her to convey to Sir William, since the rest of the family are absent. Then I have pressing business to attend to."

Several minutes had passed before Henrietta re-entered the drawing-room. Deep in thought, she was startled to discover Sir Charles's tall figure outlined against the sunlight pouring in through the windows. He turned at the sound of her approach and for one instant she hesitated, as if she would withdraw. Then, struck suddenly with foreboding, for Hugo's remarks had horribly strengthened her suspicions, she came forward. Scanning her face, a frown creasing his brow, Sir Charles beheld a countenance upon which a restless night had left its mark. Dark hollows lay beneath her troubled eyes, her cheeks were pale and drawn and there was an air of exhaustion about her person which contrasted sharply with her normal liveliness and optimism.

"Why have you come here, Sir Charles?" There was a challenging light in her eyes but he could see the fear and uncertainty that lay behind her demand.

His reply was stiff and formal, "I have come, Miss Brandon, to leave a message for Sir William, who, I understand, is away from home until later today. Would you be kind enough to tell him, in private, that I will wait upon him this evening, about six o'clock, upon urgent business?"

She was frowning now, wondering what this could mean. Impelled almost against her will to make one last effort to save Philip she approached him more nearly saying urgently, "Do not destroy my brother, sir, I beseech you!"

He stared down into her face with such a stern expression that she felt her heart miss a beat, "Alas, my dear girl, what must be, must be. It is out of my hands – God knows, for my part, I would not willingly cause you distress." Thoroughly frightened by his strange words, she backed away from him and it was with relief that she heard the sound of voices in the hall and Lady Sedley's voice declaring her surprise and pleasure to learn of the visitor. The door opened and her hostess swept into the room with Louise in her wake, bringing with her a welcome atmosphere of normality.

"My dear Charles, an unexpected pleasure!" Lady Sedley's keen eye had quickly observed the constraint that existed between the two persons within the room she had entered and had instantly determined to ignore it. "Louise and I have been upon an errand of mercy, dear sir – so unfortunate that the poor have so little idea how to go on in cases of sickness."

Sir Charles nodded gravely and announced the object of his visit, "If it would not inconvenience Sir William, I should be grateful if he could spare me a few minutes of his time this evening."

Lady Sedley cast a sharp glance at his face and, gaining no further information from his expression, declared at once that Sir William would be delighted, adding pointedly, "We count you already quite as one of the family, you know." for Sir Charles, in her eyes, had now been restored to his prime position as her future son-in-law; there could be no doubt as to his loyalty to his country. Following these terrible rumours, Philip no longer seemed an eligible candidate for her daughter's hand.

Henrietta had moved away from the window and Louise, after a gentle enquiry as to how she had occupied her morning in their absence, returned to Charles's side and asked him eagerly if he had heard any further news of the Runner, her face alight with pleasure at his visit.

He smiled down at her and shook his head, only remarking in reply, "It seems he is still in the village – I hear he has taken a room at the Dog and Duck and is pursuing his enquiries from there."

Watching their faces from her vantage point on the window-seat, Henrietta felt a shiver of apprehension. Was her dear, dear Philip to be sacrificed to provide a tranquil future for this lovely girl? What real depth of feeling existed beneath that charming exterior. Or did she only live in a world of make-believe – a world devoid of real passion? If Sir Charles succeeded with the plot that she suspected he planned to execute, Louise, she supposed, would regard him as a hero and fall into his arms. She, herself, had come to believe that Philip's love for Louise was far more than the passing fancy that she had at first suspected. Of Sir Charles's love for Louise there could be now no doubt.

CHAPTER 17

Dinner that day was an awkward affair. Conversation was mostly sustained by Sir William and Lady Sedley, with a few light-hearted contributions from Francis, who had returned from a visit to a friend in Surrey with glowing tales of a cricket match he had witnessed. Neither Louise nor Henrietta were in the mood for conversation and Philip, though valiantly attempting to enter into Francis's enthusiastic descriptions, bore a strained expression and soon lapsed into silence, his eyes seldom leaving Louise's face. They had repaired to the drawing-room when, punctually at six o'clock, Haines announced the arrival of Sir Charles to see his master and ushered him into the room.

"Evening, Charles!" Sir William rose quickly to his feet and crossed the room to greet him with his usual bluff kindliness, but even he seemed to be affected by the atmosphere of unease in his house. "Come along to my study right away, dear boy, then you can do the civil to the ladies when we are done."

Closeted in the book-lined study, where papers, whips and other sporting impedimenta jostled each other for a place, Sir William turned to his guest with a worried countenance, thoughts of Charles and Louise's betrothal uppermost in his mind, and demanded, "What's amiss, Charles? Tell me without roundaboutation – and if there's anything I can do, I will do it, by God – if it lies within my power."

It was a moment or two before Charles answered him. He looked at the honest, rugged face regarding him hopefully and inwardly cursed himself for having to bring a multitude of troubles upon this honourable man. "God knows, I wish it could be otherwise – but I feel obliged to warn you that Prout, that's the Bow Street Runner's name, sir, has a warrant to search this house." He saw the incredulous expression on Sir William's face and added quickly, "It's the Naval despatch of course. Prout believes, and I fear he has grounds for his suspicions, that Philip Brandon is the perpetrator of this theft."

Sir William, crimson with outrage, glared at Charles and expostulated, "Good God, sir what's this nonsense! Don't tell me that you are a party to this piece of impertinence?"

"No, sir, only that Prout has confided his intentions to me." He looked grave. "I confess he has some reasons for his search. You may not be aware of it – but Philip is not as averse to the revolutionaries as one would naturally expect. It gives one cause for unease."

"But a Brandon! And a pleasant enough young fellow – I'll not countenance the idea for one moment."

Hardly had he uttered these words than there was an imperious peal on the door-bell followed by several loud knocks. Both men listened in silence as Haines' footsteps could be heard crossing the hall. Upon his opening the front-door, a confident voice demanded, "Tell your master that Joshua Prout be 'ere on very h'important business for, and on behalf of, his Majesty."

A moment later the study door opened and Haines, striving to maintain his customary stolidity, enquired whether Sir William was at home to his visitor, "A 'Joshua Prout', sir," adding repressively, "It appears that he is here upon official business, sir."

"Show him in, show him in!" Sir William exchanged glances with Charles and went to stand behind his desk, a look of displeasure on his rubicund countenance.

The butler announced disparagingly, "Prout, sir!" and the well-rounded figure of Joshua Prout appeared in the doorway, hat in hand, the solemn face of his assistant peeping over his shoulder.

"Evenin', Sir William!" The Runner turned to regard Charles and nodded pleasantly, "Evenin' Sir Charles." He advanced into the room, ignoring Sir William's expression, and withdrew a crumpled piece of paper from his side-pocket. "No sense in beatin' about the bush!"

He proffered it to Sir William, who took it with disdain and glanced at it before replying in a grim voice, "And what the devil do you expect to find here?" It was, to Sir William, beyond belief that a man in his position could be suspected of harbouring a traitor and should be subjected, with his household, to this intolerable indignity.

The round, blue eyes stared back at him innocently, "Why, this very same naval despatch as is causin' their lordships sich a mort of trouble at the Admiralty, sir. H'and from h'information received, I 'as reason to believe that it may very well be in this 'ere 'ouse of yourn – all along of your 'aving a young gennelman astayin' 'ere who be come from France recent like, sir."

Sir William, beside himself with fury, glared at him but failed to evoke any response from his visitor, who continued to regard him calmly. Recollecting his official status as Justice of the Peace, he came from behind his desk, saying contemptuously, "Well – you have your duty to do, Prout, no doubt – though you're making a rare fool of yourself. I shall make it my business to see that your superiors are made aware of this outrage." He turned towards Charles, "We'd best acquaint her ladyship and the rest of my family with this disgraceful news. For they'll need to know, before any search can take place," then led the way to the drawing-room.

Lady Sedley, in the act of pouring tea, paused, elegant tea-pot in hand, as the door opened and stared with amazement at the group revealed in the doorway. Louise had been playing the piano and the sounds in the hall of the latest arrivals had not been audible to the company in the drawing-room. One look at Sir William's face was sufficient to convey to her that something disagreeable had disturbed her husband. She set down the pot, raised her eyebrows with hauteur, and demanded to know in peremptory tones, what was meant by this extraordinary invasion.

"It's a warrant to search the house, my lady!" Sir William replied grimly, "And this," he indicated the stout man at his side, "this is a Bow Street officer, who has got it into his thick head, God knows why, that he can find this damned despatch in my house!"

General consternation swiftly followed this announcement. Lady Sedley, for once at a loss for words, seemed hardly able to believe her ears and her colour rose alarmingly. Francis, exclaiming, "Good God!" got to his feet, his eyes on his father's face, and Louise looked pitifully towards her mother, her little face pale with shock. Philip remained standing by the piano, only the rigidity of his pose displayed his feelings, and his face, save for a tightening of the muscles by his mouth, remained inscrutable.

Henrietta, with the nightmare sensation that her worst fears were about to be realised, jumped to her feet, a stormy expression in her eyes. The sweep of her skirts dislodged the work-bag which lay beside her on the window-seat, spilling it's contents to the floor in the full view of the company. A cascade of multi-coloured silks descended upon the carpet and amidst the soft browns and vivid greens and blues there tumbled a folded paper bearing a broken seal.

For a stout man, Joshua Prout could move surprisingly quickly. Even before this trivial event had had time to register any surprise or alarm in those around him, he had stepped forward and extracted the document from amongst the skeins of silk. Clutching it in his stubby fingers, he looked about him at their startled faces, a beaming smile upon his countenance. "Very interestin'!" he remarked, and taking a pair of spectacles from one of his many pockets, he perched them upon his nose and unfolding the paper began to read.

Silence suffocated the room as if all present held their breath, only Louise, with an involuntary movement, put her hand out towards Philip where he stood beside her. Henrietta stared at Charles. Joshua Prout raised his head at last, and the wide, blue eyes were turned to Sir William, looking at him over his spectacles, "Jest the very item as we was a'searchin' for, Sir William! And a deal less painful than huntin' high and low for it in this very 'andsome 'ouse of yours."

Sir William's mouth had fallen open and he suddenly looked ten years older. "The n-naval despatch?" he stuttered, hardly able to get the words out.

"The h'identical document!" Prout paused and looked around him, "An' if you would be so good as to h'identify Mr Philip Brandon, I'd be h'uncommonly grateful, sir."

Suddenly there was an interruption. Henrietta stepped forward, her face paper-white, her eyes flashing with anger. It was not to the Bow Street officer that she addressed herself but to Sir Charles, saying in tones of the utmost loathing, "So you have stooped to this shameful act! But you shall not achieve your object." In an agony of fear for her brother and wretchedly conscious that this man whom she had formerly admired was as unscrupulous and unprincipled as the merest rogue, she continued contemptuously, "You must indeed be lost to all sense of honour to attempt to implicate an innocent man!" Adding to her feeling of horror, she observed that Sir Charles, far from displaying any sign of shame or regret had a look of absorbed interest, almost of elation. She was frightened and disgusted.

Sir William, already shaken by the Runner's discovery, was taken aback at Henrietta's outburst, "What the devil! Have you run mad, child?"

Ignoring him, she turned to Prout, fighting back her tears, "This is your thief! Sir Charles Gresham!" She pointed towards him, "He has placed this paper in my work-bag to incriminate my brother!"

Philip, who had listened to his sister with mounting astonishment, broke in at this point, "Sir William, as God's my witness, I know nothing of this despatch!" Lips compressed and very pale, he was clearly labouring under strong emotion.

Joshua Prout, following with interest these exchanges, placed the document in his pocket and cleared his throat impressively. There was an instant silence. He looked at the varied expressions upon the faces around him: fear, amazement, anger, confusion, distress: all were displayed. Only Sir Charles remained aloof and thoughtful. After a moment's pause, the officer spoke, "H'it don't exactly h'astonish me that this young gennelman," he indicated Philip with a jerk of his thumb towards him, "denies this 'orrible deed, nor does h'it surprise me, bein' a keen stoodent of 'uman nature, as I am, that 'is sister," he looked towards Henrietta, "makes h'accusations agin another party." He glanced briefly at Sir Charles, "H'accusations which I find very 'ard to believe!" He shook his head wonderingly, "But which will be h'investigated in due course. However –" here he paused significantly, and advanced towards Philip and laying his hand upon the latter's shoulder, announced in a raised voice, "Philip Brandon, I arrest you in the name of the law! And am h'obliged to ask you to h'accompany me to London forthwith!"

Before anyone had time to recover from the shock created by these words, Sir Charles had strolled forward from his place by the door, "All very well, Prout, but I fear that there exists an impediment to your actions, which I believe you have forgotten in the natural excitement caused by your discovery of the missing papers.

"H'and what might that be, Sir Charles?" The officer's face betrayed perplexity.

"You are not, I believe, in possession of a warrant to arrest Mr Philip Brandon, only of a warrant to search this house!"

Joshua Prout stood for a moment dumb-founded, staring at Sir Charles, then declared reproachfully, "Well, I'll be jiggered, if this ain't the darnedest thing! And comin' from the very man wot's been a'helpin' me."

Sir William, who had been slowly recovering his wits and his dignity, joined his voice to the discussion. "As a magistrate, my man, I must insist that, however urgent the circumstances, all proceeds in a proper and lawful manner. You will have to approach my colleague in Brighton, from whom you obtained the warrant to search my house."

"An' supposin' this young feller decides to slip anchor, as you might say, during the night?"

Sir William looked his amazement, "If Mr Brandon gives his word that he will remain within my house you may rest assured that he will do so."

He looked towards Philip, who, biting his lip, nodded his head in agreement and said quickly to Sir William, "I give you my word, upon my honour, sir!"

The Runner, by now looking singularly aggrieved, regarded Philip suspiciously and shook his head, "H'if 'e be a traitor – wot honour be there in that, I asks myself?" He turned to Sir William, "I'll leave my h'assistant 'ere, sir, if you 'ave no h'objection, to see that all's right and tight." He clapped his wide-brimmed hat on his head, gazed around him once more. With the ominous words, "I'll return tomorrow, with the necessary!" he took his assistant by the arm and muttering instructions in his ear walked with him out of the room.

Before the door had even closed upon his retreating form, Charles drew Sir William aside: "Forgive me, sir, but I must leave here immediately. There is much still to be done to bring the solution of this crime to its proper conclusion – and I must have a word with Prout before he leaves." Charles's expression was grim, "Pray give my apologies to Lady Sedley."

Sir William regarded him with surprise and some displeasure: surely his daughter's betrothed might have been expected to offer some moral support in this moment of crisis in all their lives. He said grudgingly, "Well, no doubt you know best what you're about . . ."

Going to the door, Charles turned to take one last look at the room's occupants and encountered Henrietta's gaze. Bestowing upon him one scorching glance, hatred and contempt in her eyes, she turned her back upon him.

Succeeding the initial shock that the finding of the despatch had engendered, there came a gradual, unhappy division of those present into their respective families. Henrietta came swiftly to her brother's side and putting her arms around him, said passionately, "I know you are no traitor! It is Sir Charles!" she spoke his name with contempt, "His jealousy of you has driven him to this terrible deception!" Philip, confusion in his face, looked down at her and drew some comfort from her single-hearted confidence in him; it was painful for him to observe that the Sedley family had withdrawn from him, unable to conceal their doubts and fears.

Lady Sedley had led her daughter, by now in tears, to sit beside her on the sofa, where Sir William and Francis now stood before them. After a brief, low-voiced conversation, she rose to her feet, and with a look of contempt towards Philip, announced that she and Louise would retire for the night, and, moving to the door, suggested coldly to Henrietta that it would be appropriate if she followed their example. As Louise passed by Philip she gave him a pathetic, scared glance from tear-filled eyes.

Henrietta, gathering together the ill-fated skeins of silk and thrusting them in confusion into her work-bag, spoke defiantly to Sir William, "It is not possible, sir, that Philip could do this thing! Besides, anyone could hide that paper in my bag – Sir Charles, himself, was alone in this room this morning – he could have placed it there!" Her eyes looked pleadingly into his set face, searching for some sign that he acknowledged the possibility, but he dismissed the idea with a slow shake of his head. There was a shocked expression on his face and it was clear that in his mind there remained little, if any, doubt of Philip's guilt.

When Henrietta had gone, he turned to her brother, and said stiffly, "I should prefer that you ascend now to your bed-chamber, sir, for there can be nothing to say between us. I have your word that you will not attempt to leave this house and I trust that I can have confidence in your honouring that undertaking. In any case," he added, "This man, Prout, has left his assistant to keep guard."

Philip, white-faced, met his host's eye proudly, "Sir, I have given my word." His gaze flew to Francis's face and his jaw hardened, the contempt in that amiable young man's countenance was painful to bear; with a polite bow, he walked stiffly to the door and left them.

CHAPTER 18

After a restless night, Henrietta elected to have her breakfast brought to her room. It was, she felt, more than she could bear to sit at the same table with those who appeared to accept without question her dear brother's guilt. Having dressed hastily she went at once to Philip's bedchamber to offer him her comfort and support.

Downstairs in the drawing-room, Sir William and Lady Sedley returned again to the vexed subject of their kinsman's treachery, a subject that had occupied their minds and conversation until late into the previous night. For the thousandth time Lady Sedley bemoaned the hospitality that they had extended to the brother and sister. "To think, Sir William, that we have given aid and comfort to a traitor!"

"With hindsight, it was a mistake, but how were we to know your cousin was a spy?" Sir William, burdened by the consciousness that others might not take such a charitable view of their actions and foreseeing the possibility of having to resign his seat upon the Bench and other disagreeable consequences, spoke with an irritation quite unlike his usual mild manner.

"And Henrietta's accusations about Charles – how disgraceful that she should try to involve him in this affair. I wish, Sir William, that I had never set eyes upon either of them."

Sir William groaned inwardly knowing, as surely as night succeeds day, what would follow. His fears proved justified.

"I knew how it would be – I said so at the time, Sir William, as no doubt you will remember."

Having been allowed no possibility of forgetting, Sir William took a pinch of snuff and listened patiently. Lady Sedley was still expatiating upon this theme when Louise and Francis entered the room from the garden, bringing with them the news that Sir Charles's curricle was approaching the house followed by Prout and a stranger in the Dog and Duck's gig. Louise's wan face was quite shocking to her father. Clinging to Francis's arm, she asked faintly, "Oh, Papa, where is Philip?"

Her worried parent came forward and put his arm around her, "He has kept to his room this morning, my love. Best thing in the circumstances – but he'll have to be sent for now." Hardly had he spoken than the butler opened the door and announced the arrival of Sir Charles Gresham and the officer from Bow Street. Lady Sedley, her lips compressed with disapproval, ordered them to be shown into the drawing-room and requested that a message be sent upstairs to Mr Brandon demanding his presence downstairs.

Sir Charles was looking dusty and tired as he strolled unhurriedly across the room, but there was no sign of weariness in his manner as he bowed in greeting and looked swiftly around him. Joshua Prout, hat in hand, followed him. He, at least, seemed to be enjoying the occasion and there was a gleeful twinkle in his eye as he indicated the stranger beside him, upon whom all eyes were fixed. "Sir Charles, after consultation with yours truly, as 'ad the kindness to drive his-self to London last night, Sir William, and 'as returned this mornin' with the very same landlord, one, Amos Barker, of the White Horse Cellars as perhaps you've a'heard spoken of." Amos Barker, a thin, lugubrious looking man, shuffled his feet and looked suitably impressed by the exalted company into which he had been thrust. Prout continued, relishing his position centre-stage, "It was to this 'ere White Horse Cellars that the young naval lieutenant was brought by a stranger – a very traitorous stranger – a'cos 'e took the h'opportunity of purloining this 'ere despatch from the lieutenant's pocket while 'e was h'unconscious, an' 'avin' done so – he vanishes!" he paused dramatically and then continued in measured tones, "Therefore – h'if this 'ere Amos Barker can h'identify this very traitorous stranger, we 'as proof positive of his guilt – an' you can't say fairer than that!"

As if on cue, the door opened and Henrietta entered the room with Philip close behind her. He had clearly taken considerable pains with his appearance as if by doing so he could distance himself from the shameful accusations that had been levelled against him. His cravat had been tied with care and his dark locks combed in orderly fashion. The brother and sister paused in the doorway, conscious that all eyes were turned towards them. Henrietta, valiantly suppressing her feelings of panic, stared back defiantly, the light of battle sparkling in her eyes while Philip's gaze having circled the room, came to rest upon Louise and remained there, a quiet dignity in his bearing.

"Well, Amos?" Prout broke the silence, "Look around you and tell us if you see that there stranger amongst this 'ere company?"

The landlord, a look of puzzlement on his face, regarded Philip searchingly, stared around him at the rest of the occupants of the room, then turned back to him. "This 'ere gentleman – it could be he!" he said doubtfully, pointing at Philip, "There's a likeness, that I must say." He scratched his head and shook it wonderingly, "But there's one thing I knows for sure and certain – and that's that this gentleman, wot came to my inn, 'e wore a ring on 'is little finger – with a lion on it, and this 'ere lion was a'holdin' of a bow and arrers. It caught m'eye like when 'e gave me the money – for archery, that's an 'obby of mine, so it stuck in me mind!"

There was a murmur of horror. Henrietta, white as a sheet, stood motionless, staring at her brother. Philip a shocked look in his eyes, gazed at those around him defiantly, but it was to Louise that he addressed himself in a firm voice, "Who this man is, I know not but – it is true that I have the very crest this man has described engraved upon my ring. But I swear to you, as God is my witness, that I never met this naval officer, I was never at the – how do you call it – the White Horse Cellars – I did not take this despatch. Why should I? I am no traitor!"

Louise was looking at him, her eyes bright with tears, as if her very life depended on his words. Before she or anyone could speak, Prout stepped forward and began again the familiar formula, "Philip

Brandon, I arrest you –" He was not permitted to finish his sentence. Crying, "Oh, no, no Papa! You must stop him. Philip is surely innocent!" Louise freed herself frantically from her father's supporting arm and came to Philip's side. There was an exclamation of horrified dissent from her mother, which she ignored. Never, Henrietta could not help thinking, had Louise looked more lovely than at that moment – there was a dignified womanliness in her manner, the slight figure very straight as she spoke to them, her young voice filled with emotion. "In spite of all that has been said, I believe Philip to be innocent! It is impossible that it could be otherwise." She turned now to face Sir Charles, her huge eyes fixed accusingly upon him, "Henrietta was right! Oh, Charles, how could you? Somehow you have contrived to incriminate him and for that it is impossible for me to forgive you!" she paused dramatically, "I can never marry you, Charles! Our engagement is at an end!" She looked towards Philip with a shy smile, then, turning back to Charles, she added slowly, "I think I never loved you."

"My dear Louise, what are you saying? Have you taken leave of your senses!" Lady Sedley looked appalled at the turn of events. Sir William, eyeing his daughter with consternation, cast a deprecating glance at her erstwhile fiancé.

Sir Charles, regarding Louise calmly, eyebrows raised, said evenly, "Better by far to discover your true feelings now than later, my dear Louise." He met Henrietta's incredulous gaze with a faintly ironic smile and continued calmly, "However, I must deny totally the charge that I have incriminated your cousin."

Philip had caught his breath in astonishment and joy at Louise's brave declaration. Forgetting his own situation for the moment, he gazed at her with wonder, as if some miracle had taken place. The only person who appeared to be quite unmoved by this exchange was the law-officer. Even the landlord of the 'White Horse Cellars' seemed touched by the human drama taking place before his eyes. With a singleness of purpose, which did credit to his profession, Josiah Prout laid his hand again upon Philip's shoulder, only to find himself once more interrupted. The windows to the garden swung open and Hugo Brandon entered, and going straight to Lady Sedley's side, said apologetically as he did so, "Cousin Julia, I received a message from Charles requesting me to call here, upon a matter of urgency, so he said – pray forgive me entering from the garden, but I took a short cut across the fields and left my horse in the stable-yard." Coming from the brilliant sunshine outside, his eyes had not at first adjusted to the light indoors and he was unaware of the group by the door to the hall, where Prout, his hand still upon Philip's shoulder, was staring at the intruder. As Hugo turned and saw the Bow Street Runner and took in the implications of his attitude, his expression hardened, "So this is the traitor!" he said contemptuously, "Has the despatch been found?"

Henrietta was on the point of protesting indignantly. Had this man not implied only yesterday that he believed, like her, that Charles had had a hand in directing suspicion to her brother – when there was a sudden, loud exclamation. "Why bless my soul – if that ain't the *very* same man wot came that night to the inn!" The landlord stepped forward, his face the picture of astonishment and pointed an accusing finger at Hugo – no doubt appearing to exist in his mind now. "T'other gentleman, 'e looked summat like 'im – but too young-like 'e seemed to me. But this 'ere cove, 'e's the one you want, Officer – I reckernise 'im alright – take my oath on it!"

Hugo's dark brows drew together in a frown as he stared back at the landlord disdainfully, "What fellow is this?" he enquired of Sir William, "Good God, the man's raving!"

Prout's round eyes were looking from one face to the other – that there was a strong likeness between the two men was evident – sufficient perhaps to confuse the landlord. Resourceful as ever, he temporised, "And 'oo may this gennelman be, Sir William?"

Sir William, who was feeling with every succeeding moment that he was enmeshed in a nightmare from which he devoutly hoped he would shortly awake, replied briefly, "Mr Hugo Brandon – cousin of my wife – lives a mile or two from here."

"An' may I ask, sir," The officer had removed his hand from Philip's shoulder, "seein' as you sports a ring on your finger, wot may be h'engraved upon this 'ere ring?"

"What the devil do you want to know for?" Hugo was clearly furious, "The Brandon crest, of course. But that's enough of these questions – what in God's name has all this to do with me?"

"More than sufficient, I fear, Hugo!" All eyes turned to Sir Charles, who, having taken a pinch of snuff, was restoring the enamel box to his pocket in a leisurely manner. He regarded their startled faces with a calm smile, "You see, Hugo," and now there was a hard light in those brilliantly blue eyes, "I chanced to observe a thread of a particular green silk – an unusual shade – on the sleeve of your coat yesterday morning, and when this officer found the dispatch amongst the silks in Miss Brandon's work-bag that same evening, I recognized the colour and it was at once clear to me that you might well be the one who had placed it there."

"Good God!" Sir William, his face suffused with colour, was all astonishment – Lady Sedley, as calamity succeeded calamity, was stricken into silence. Francis swore under his breath and Louise and Philip seemed stunned.

Only Henrietta spoke, joyous certainty in her voice as she whispered, "You are safe, Philip!" and hugged him fondly.

"Charles! You can't mean this nonsense! This landlord fellow is mistaken or mad!" Hugo protested, but he was very pale and a muscle twitched in his cheek.

"Alas, my dear fellow, I haven't the least doubt of your guilt! That's the reason that I drove to London to bring this man here to confront you." He turned to the Runner, "You will notice that he is convicted out of his own mouth, Prout, for no-one here has said in Hugo Brandon's presence that Amos Barker is the landlord of the White Horse Cellars!"

"Very good, Sir Charles – a very fine piece of deduction, sir!" There was a gleam of laughter mixed with triumph in the Runner's eyes, "H'I couldn't a'done better m'self." As he advanced towards

Hugo, the latter turned swiftly as if to make a dive for the garden door but Francis was too quick for him. There was a brief scuffle before he was overpowered and his arms held by Prout and his assistant.

Hatred burnt like fire in Hugo's eyes as he faced them all defiantly, "God damn you to hell!" he spat at Philip, "Did you really think that I would take it lying down when you came to this country and destroyed all my hopes – all my expectations? My God, how I wish that that bullet had done for you that day, but the damned fool missed! Then none of this charade would have been necessary!"

It was amidst a shocked silence that Hugo was charged and escorted from the room. Josiah Prout touched his forelock as he passed by Sir Charles on his way to the door, "Very grateful to you, sir, I am, an' that's a fact. Cleared this little matter up somethin' wunnerful, you 'as – an' no 'arm done to the country, thank Gawd, seein' as it's all on account of family affairs, and not a spy, h'as suspected."

Following the departure of the Bow Street Runner with his assistant and his prisoner the silence continued, then Lady Sedley's voice broke it plaintively, "I wish, Sir William, that you would enlighten me. So much has occurred this morning that I, for one, am quite at a loss –" her voice trailed away. With a gratified smile, Sir William came to her side. As he began an exposition of the events of the morning, he could not avoid a certain complacency. It was not often that his dear wife was at a loss for words.

Francis had hurried across the room to felicitate Philip upon his deliverance from the terrible charge. He had liked his young cousin from the first and had been deeply shocked by the accusations levelled against him, which had seemed so plausible at first. He shook him warmly by the hand, saying, "By Jove, you owe something to Charles! Deuced clever of him, eh! I was never more pleased in my life – but it's damnable to contemplate what Hugo attempted." He looked at Louise, who stood shyly beside Philip, and added ruefully, "Poor Charles! He saves Philip and gets jilted for his pains."

Louise blushed, "I confess I misjudged him – poor Charles!" She was playing with the flowered border of her shawl and did not look up.

Philip smiled down lovingly at the cluster of curls on top of her head which was all that was visible to him and said simply, "Yes, my love, poor Charles! And I owe him everything – but, your betrothal – it wouldn't have done you know!" He paused, then continued significantly, "I shall ask for an interview with your father later today."

This was too obscure for Francis's uncomplicated thinking, he looked puzzled, murmured, "Quite, – exactly so!" and went to join his parents by the fireplace.

It was plain enough, however, to Louise. She raised her soft, blue eyes to Philip's face for a moment and there was an expression of wonder on her gentle face. He took her hand and kissed it, saying laughingly as he did so, "What courage, sweetheart! You were a veritable lioness!"

So great was Henrietta's relief when Philip was proved to be innocent that, for a space, she felt herself positively light-headed, caught up in over-whelming joy. But reaction was not long in setting in. Guiltily, she remembered all the cruel accusations that she had hurled at Sir Charles's head. It was he, and he alone, who had discovered the truth and had acted with such commendable promptitude. With a sharp pang of remorse, she reminded herself that by doing so he had lost the girl whom he wished to marry.

About Hugo she shuddered to think – how she had been deceived by his attentions to her when all the time he was planning her brother's death or ruin. As these and other confused thoughts were jostling each other in her head, she found Sir Charles approaching her. With a sardonic smile upon his face, he said, "Are you satisfied now, Miss Brandon? Or am I still the scoundrel that you made me out to be?"

Her face had flushed scarlet and she felt an over whelming desire for the ground to swallow her up. Troubled dark, brown eyes stared up into vividly blue ones as she said, "I admit I have been wrong, utterly wrong! You have every right to revile me. But the motive seemed so strong –", she added quickly, "Nothing can excuse me – to have suspected you of such dishonourable actions – you must think me sunk beneath contempt. But I do thank you, and –" she hesitated and looked down at her clasped hands, "and wish that this whole sorry episode had not been the cause of pain to you."

She did not see the expression in his eyes as he retorted, "Miss Brandon, of your courage, there can be no doubt – but, alas, your judgment has proved on more than one occasion to be sadly at fault!" Turning from her, he crossed the room to take his leave of Sir William and Lady Sedley, saying, "If you will excuse me, my lady, I confess to an urgent need for sleep and must leave you. Hugo's shocking attempts on Philip's life have, thank Heaven, not succeeded and Philip has my wholehearted good wishes for his future."

Lady Sedley was about to speak when Sir William stopped her. "My love, Charles must be permitted to depart immediately. We are all considerably in his debt. Let him leave without further delay." Lady Sedley nodded graciously, admitting secretly to herself that the events of the past hour had changed a great many of her assumptions.

CHAPTER 19

The days that followed soon found the Sedley household restored to its normal tranquil existence. It had not taken Lady Sedley long to accustom herself to the notion that her daughter was to be united to a future member of the peerage. The morning following the revelations of Hugo's infamy, Philip had made his request, in form, to Sir William for permission to address his daughter. This had been granted most willingly and the touching scene that had followed in the drawing-room must have equalled and even excelled any ideas of Louise as to how a proposal should be made. Philip did indeed fall upon one knee before her and covering her hands with kisses had declared his love for her in such terms as brought a blush to her cheeks. Since that moment they had had eyes only for each other and even Henrietta, so pleased to see their evident happiness and delight in each other's society, had begun to feel a trifle bored with their company.

Francis had departed for a few days to visit friends. He was now devoted to Henrietta, and Lady Sedley, beginning to feel her hopes in that direction might well be fulfilled, could not but be guiltily thankful that Hugo had been removed from their midst, his partiality for Henrietta having been increasingly apparent. Hugo's eclipse had been a shock. Like Philip – a kinsman – his arrest had been, however, at least in some measure, less shameful, for his motive had been greed and a desire to discredit and destroy his usurping cousin; not, Lady Sedley reflected thankfully, as dishonourable a crime in the eyes of the world as to betray one's country. Sir William had his own reasons to be pleased. To see his daughter so transparently happy gave him infinite pleasure and he was thankful that her previous betrothal had not been announced. It would not have been agreeable for Charles to be publicly jilted by Louise, for he was fond of his neighbour and wished him well.

The least contented member of the household was Henrietta. She was delighted that Philip was safe and happy and that their future was assured. Only the continued ill health of Lord Hartington prevented the formation of permanent plans. Nevertheless, she found herself increasingly dissatisfied and restless. It had been flattering and exciting at the time to enjoy the wicked Hugo's evident admiration but all his actions were now seen to be motivated by his desire to retain his succession to the title. It was a lowering thought that she had probably been admired by him not for her charms but rather for the wealth that she would one day inherit. Certainly, Francis was an agreeable companion, but, above all, she realized that she missed the company of Sir Charles. He had been almost a daily visitor at the Grange and it was only now that he had no reason to call that she began to comprehend how much, in spite of his interference in her life, she had come to depend upon his friendship. She thought wretchedly that he would probably never forgive her for her mistrust of him. She had been wrong from start to finish ever since she had seen him with Josiah Prout. Her subsequent behaviour, the accusations that she had levelled at his head, must surely have given him a disgust for her. No doubt she was justly punished by his ignoring her now.

He, on the other hand, had acted in an exemplary manner, honourable throughout. Once convinced of Philip's innocence he had left no stone unturned to prove that the latter was guiltless, even though, by so doing, he had saved the man who was so clearly his rival in Louise's affections. Perhaps it was because he was her brother and therefore she saw him in a different light, that Henrietta could not help wondering how Louise could prefer Philip to this handsome man, upon whom one could rely in all circumstances. A man of infinite kindness, whose outwardly calm manner, she believed, concealed a depth of feeling that perhaps even Philip, with all his romanticism did not possess.

She had found it impossible to forget how strangely and disturbingly he had kissed her on the night that she had broken into his house and she could still vividly recall the bewildering sensations that it had aroused in her breast. As she reflected upon her own feelings that night she realized with a sudden, startling awareness that her liking for him had been imperceptibly changing, that she, herself, was falling in love with her rescuer.

It was she thought sadly, indeed unlikely that he should ever come to love *her*. Much time would have to pass for him to forget the lovely girl whom he had wished to marry and soon she, herself, would have left the Sedley household and would have removed from the neighbourhood.

It was several days later that Sir William returned home one evening after dining with friends in Brighton and conveyed to them the interesting news that Lady Gresham had returned home. After her sojourn with her Welsh friends, she had returned to Bath and Sir Charles had joined her there and had spent a week there in her company before escorting her on the long journey home. Thankful that no announcement had ever appeared of Louise's betrothal to Sir Charles, Lady Sedley looked forward to discussing her daughter's engagement to the new heir of Lord Hartington. "I shall call upon her tomorrow, Sir William." she announced, "Her health has not been good and we must hope that her stay in Bath has benefited her. I believe it will be best if I go alone this time. The younger members of the family can call on her tomorrow if that is agreeable to her."

The visit had been an unqualified success. Lady Gresham having shown the keenest interest in all Lady Sedley's news and plans and had invited Louise and Philip to call the next day and hoped that Henrietta would also accompany them. "Lady Gresham seemed in the best of spirits, and stronger than I have seen her for some time now." Lady Sedley reported, "Charles is away for a few days, visiting friends in London. Maybe it is as well that he is absent. It might, perhaps, be a trifle awkward for you, Louise, if he was present for your first meeting with his mother after all that has passed."

The next morning the three young Brandons set off in the carriage for Gresham Place. Henrietta felt a mixture of relief and disappointment at the news that Sir Charles was away from home. She was, however, looking forward to meeting Lady Gresham and to visiting Gresham Place again – a house that held for her so many memories. They found Lady Gresham seated in her drawing-room, a stick at her side and a spaniel lying at her feet. A stoutish lady, somewhat untidy in appearance and with a kindly expression, stood beside her. "My dears, forgive me for not rising to greet you but I am a little stiff this morning." She had such a warm smile upon her face and eyes so like Sir Charles' that Henrietta felt an immediate liking for this frail figure.

Henrietta and Philip having been duly presented, Lady Gresham introduced her companion saying, "This is my cousin, Miss Norton, who bears patiently with all my moods in the kindest fashion." Then, turning to Louise and Philip, she extended to them her best wishes, saying warmly, "Your dear mother is so delighted with your betrothal, my dears. It is a source of great joy to her."

Miss Norton, clearly interested, immediately enquired from Louise about their wedding plans and Henrietta had the opportunity to take a seat near Lady Gresham. "I have such fond memories of my stay here, my lady," Henrietta said quickly, "If it had not been for Sir Charles, I do not believe that I should be alive now! I owe him so much."

"He has a kind heart, my dear, I am only too well aware of that you know." Lady Gresham sighed and added thoughtfully, "I often feel so guilty that my dear husband and I caused him to give up his career in the Navy. He has never complained but I am sure it was a cruel blow to him. He manages the estate so well but it is a dull life in comparison. I pray that he will some day soon marry and bring up a family here." She smiled mistily at Henrietta and patted her hand. "I am sure that you were a most delightful distraction and I greatly admire your courage, my dear, I have heard all about it. You have been through terrible times. Now that all has fallen out so well for your brother, I hope that your future too will be filled with the same happiness as it seems his will be." There was such warmth in Lady Gresham's manner that Henrietta could not help contrast it with the acerbic treatment that she had at first received from Lady Sedley. There, too, there had been great kindness but delivered so very differently. She thought sadly how disappointed Sir Charles' mother would have been if she had known of his betrothal to Louise and then of its sudden ending. There did seem, however, to be something in the tone of Lady Gresham's voice that made Henrietta wonder if she had had some inkling of her son's intentions. Something in her expression told of hidden thoughts.

At this point, Cummings brought in a tray bearing refreshments for the callers and Henrietta relinquished her seat to Louise and Philip. Lady Gresham, remarking upon the likeness between Philip and his cousin Hugo, was anxious to hear more of the desperate measures that the latter had taken to prevent Philip receiving his future inheritance.

Henrietta had heard a great deal about Bath and the fashionable world that gathered there and, moving across to join Miss Norton, eagerly asked her if she had enjoyed her visit. "Yes, Miss Brandon, it was most agreeable. I really believe it has proved quite excellent for dear Lady Gresham's health. Of course it was Sir Charles's visit when we returned to Bath which has so greatly raised her spirits." Her plump face was wreathed in smiles as she added in lowered, conspiratorial tones, "I believe she has great hopes for his future – I have heard talk of a marriage. But no more of that now, indeed, I have no direct knowledge on the subject – just putting together things that I have heard!" Henrietta could hardly believe her ears. Where was the disappointed lover of Louise now? She felt, to her astonishment, a feeling of pain rather than pleasure at this astonishing news. Who could this person be? Had Sir Charles met someone in Bath so fascinating and so agreeable that he now had new plans?

Miss Norton was regarding her closely and she felt that she had to make some response. "Indeed, I believe that would give Lady Gresham great pleasure," she managed to say, hoping that she had not betrayed her own feelings. Quickly enquiring in what part of the country Miss Norton had spent her childhood, she led that lady to embark upon a series of reminiscences.

On their journey home, no mention was made by Louise or Philip of Sir Charles, nor of any plans that he might have for the future and when, after luncheon, they announced their intention of riding on the Downs, Henrietta declined to accompany them, preferring, she said, to spend a lazy afternoon in the garden reading a novel. Her novel did not, however, prove to be sufficiently absorbing. She felt a profound restlessness and was a little shocked to realize to what extent her feelings towards Sir Charles had changed.

With a frown, she rose to her feet. Useless to repine! She must occupy herself in some fashion. Some distraction was necessary if she was not to fall into a fit of the dismals. She looked out of the window and saw that the early morning sunshine had vanished. An overcast sky and gentle breeze brought to her mind the idea that here was excellent weather for fishing. A pity that Francis was not here – he would have enjoyed the sport. She shrugged her shoulders and decided that she would venture forth alone and made her way to the gunroom, where all the rods and tackle were stored.

One of the several ponds in the valley, a bare quarter of a mile away, was extensive enough to be designated a lake by the family. Sir William had enhanced its picturesque appearance from the house and a small boat-house had been erected, many years before, by its side. It was here that Henrietta established herself and was soon gratified to get a rise. Within a short time she had already placed two quite reasonably sized gudgeon in her basket. Admittedly it was a disagreeable business getting the hook from their mouths, but her satisfaction in landing them safely was sufficient to overcome her distaste. By now the clouds had departed and a surprisingly hot sun re-emerged. She cast aside her spencer and looked ruefully at her muslin dress, which had become distinctly muddy at the hem. How fortunate that Lady Sedley was out calling upon a neighbour and that no-one was present to witness her disarray! It was a few minutes later that she entangled her line in some over-hanging branches not far from the bank and despite of all her efforts, it refused to free itself. After struggling in vain for several minutes, she sat down on the bank to remove her shoes and stockings. She hitched up her skirts with one hand and stepped bravely forward into the shallow water by the side of the lake. The water had nearly reached her knees when she was close enough to stretch up and attempt to disentangle her line from the branch. It proved to be easier than she had expected but, alas, when success was near, a gust of wind blew the lightweight cast over her shoulder. The hook caught in the back of the muslin fichu that encircled her neck. It was an awkward, not to say alarming predicament. With one hand clutching her skirts and rod, she was quite unable to remove the hook, whose barb had penetrated the thin material. She found herself the prisoner of her own line. Muttering an unladylike curse under her breath, she was twisting her head round to look over her shoulder and groping single-handed to discover the whereabouts of the hook when a distinctly masculine chuckle assailed her ears from the bank.

Turning with a start in the direction of the sound, she saw with surprise that Sir Charles was standing on the bank regarding her efforts with considerable amusement.

He called out cheerfully to her, "Hoist by your own petard, Miss Brandon!" Rather than making a move to assist her, he appeared to be enjoying the spectacle that she presented.

Despite of her changed feelings towards him, she replied indignantly, "For heavens sake, sir, don't stand there laughing, but come and help me!"

In response to this ungracious appeal, he laid down his hat and whip upon the grass and descended into the shallow water, ignoring the ill-effects that must result from the muddy water upon the gleaming surface of his riding-boots.

Horribly conscious of her ridiculous plight and feeling a sudden awkwardness in his company, Henrietta said brusquely, as he approached, "The hook has caught behind me!" and turned her back towards him, clutching her skirts and rod with both hands.

Sir Charles looked down at the chestnut-brown curls that clustered above the nape of her neck whose slenderness seemed to embody all the charming innocence of the young girl, smiled enigmatically and applied himself to his task. Long, sunburned fingers moved deftly amidst the folds of muslin, and Henrietta, her head bent forward, felt suddenly very conscious of his nearness. She could feel his warm breath upon the back of her neck and the pressure of his fingers and was startled once more by her own unaccustomed feelings.

"It can't be done. I fear the fichu will have to be removed!" Despite his efforts, the barb remained caught and without tearing the material it was impossible to release it. Henrietta, twisting her head round to try to see the difficulty, caught a glimpse of a lean handsome face looking down at her. Blue eyes twinkled, the laughter lines etched around them very visible. Turning quickly away, conscious that her heart was beating in a strangely irregular fashion, she tried with one free hand to undo the coral brooch that held the fichu in place.

Charles watched her efforts for a moment with amusement. Perfectly aware of her heightened colour, he murmured a polite "Allow me". Turning her round towards him, he easily unpinned the brooch at her breast and removed the offending article. Once the fichu had been unfastened, it was only a matter of seconds to disentangle the line from the branch leaving the white muslin, like a flag of surrender, still attached to the cast.

Nobly endeavouring to preserve her dignity, while feeling excessively foolish in her ridiculous predicament, Henrietta said politely, "Thank you, sir, I am indeed grateful!" Then, conscious that he was openly regarding her bare neck and shoulders with an admiring gleam in his eyes, rather ruined the effect by exclaiming crossly, "If you were a true gentleman, Sir Charles, you would not stare so at me!"

"Perfectly true, Miss Brandon!" he replied courteously, adding with a wicked grin, "But perhaps you are not conscious of the picture you present!"

Henrietta glanced down at herself, shoulders and neck uncovered, bedraggled muslin skirts, now copiously muddied, held high above her slim legs and, overcome by the absurdity of the situation, burst into laughter. That there was a streak of mud upon her cheek, she was not even aware.

Before she could form any reply, Charles had bent forward and picked her up easily in his arms, rod and all, and was striding with her towards the bank. Set down breathless upon the grass, the rod removed from her fingers, Henrietta gazed up at her rescuer, eyes wide with reproach, and said stiffly, "There was no need, sir, to put yourself to so much trouble, I could just as well have walked back."

He shrugged but did not answer, merely remarking casually, "How odd that 'fishing' seems to be a motif which continues to repeat itself in our dealings!"

She had a strong presentiment that he was laughing at her but as he preserved a perfectly straight face, it was impossible to be sure. Now he was regarding her wet feet and ankles through his eyeglass in a fashion that made her hurriedly pull down her damp skirts. Then, drawing out a large, white cambric hankerchief from his pocket, he knelt down before her, saying calmly, "I believe it would be advisable for your feet to be dried before replacing your shoes and stockings!" and before she could move her foot, had grasped one ankle firmly and begun the task.

Blushing profusely, Henrietta expostulated wildly, striving to release herself, "You have no right, Sir Charles!"

He interrupted her, still retaining hold of one slim foot, and said, with amusement, "I should infinitely prefer to call it a privilege to which I might aspire!"

Henrietta stared at the top of his bent head, hardly able to believe her ears. Surely this time he could not have been drinking – it was, after all, only mid-day! What could he mean? Where was the disappointed lover? Where was the man with perhaps new plans for matrimony who, she had convinced herself, must hold her in dislike after all that she had said?

Her sudden silence, made him look up at her face and, seeing the confusion in her eyes, he said bracingly, "Come, it is not so bad after all! There – I am done – and you may replace your shoes and stockings! Rising to his feet, he turned his back on her and, picking up the fichu, began to renew his attempts to remove the hook. Henrietta hastily pulled on her stockings, adjusted her garters, and slipped her feet into her shoes, looking now and then to make sure that his back was still turned. Now dressed with more propriety, though still exceedingly muddied, she felt her confidence returning and standing up she approached him and watched his efforts in silence. Patient sailor's hands ultimately achieved success by untying the hook and drawing it through the muslin. He gave her the fichu and Henrietta replaced it around her neck, re-pinning it in place under the appreciative eyes of her rescuer. This done, she looked up at him, and surprised a glint in his eyes that was strangely confusing. Could he be teasing her to get his revenge? As she looked quickly away, she realized with complete conviction that it would be indeed wonderful if he truly cared for her. But how could it be possible that he could forget the lovely Louise so quickly?

Sir Charles was confident that he knew very well what puzzled thoughts were racing through his companion's head. He indicated the bench beside the boat-house and said persuasively, "Miss Brandon, let us sit down here, for I was on my way to the Grange for the purpose of holding some conversation with you." Surprised, she moved forward and seated herself. Looking expectantly towards him as he sat down beside her, traces of perplexity were still visible on her face. He began by saying gently, "I know that it is profoundly disagreeable to discover that one has been mistaken in one's judgment –"

Before he could finish, Henrietta interrupted defensively, her candid eyes fixed on his face, "I admit that I was wrong, sir, but in the circumstances – you must see that it was understandable."

Sir Charles regarded her thoughtfully, "My dearest girl, we are talking of two different things – I am referring to your misapprehension in believing that I was jealous of your brother. Nothing, I can assure you was ever further from my thoughts!"

"You were not jealous! But, sir – that is not possible!"

He smiled calmly at her disbelieving face and said ruefully, "I see that I shall have to explain all from the beginning. You must understand, I was never in love with Louise, charming girl though she is. I believed it right that I should marry – and she, the daughter of my neighbour, seemed the most suitable choice."

Henrietta was frowning, her disapproval very evident, "Pardon me, sir, but I cannot comprehend how you could make such a decision – poor Louise – indeed, I know there are such marriages of convenience – but a girl with her head full of romance –"

"Exactly so! Although I made no protestations of love – nor could I have in all honesty done so – Louise assumed, aided by all the powers of a vivid imagination, that I had been concealing my passion for her. She accepted my proposal under this misapprehension, and I confess I was greatly disturbed, for I had not the least wish to deceive her." He looked away, and seemed to be lost in recollection of the past.

"And, sir –?" Henrietta prompted eagerly. How different reality was proving to be, how utterly wrong all her own assumptions and ideas.

Sir Charles turned back to her, and now there was laughter in his eyes as he said, "And then I met you, Miss Brandon!"

Her eyes widened with surprise and she stared back at him in astonishment, exclaiming, "But sir – then I was a boy!"

He nodded his head in agreement, "True – at first it was your plight that intrigued me and the strange coincidence of your relationship with the Sedleys. Then there came the morning when you threw yourself into my arms to escape from George and his friends!"

He grinned at her provokingly, "I could not then mistake your sex, my love!" Her face a little flushed, Henrietta's thoughts flew back to those days in Sir Charles's house. So, all the time – from that moment – he had known she was a girl! Shocked by his duplicity, she regarded him doubtfully – but he *had* called her 'his love'. "When your brother showed so clearly that he had fallen in love with Louise and, when it became apparent that she was responding to his ardour, far from being jealous, I rejoiced, for now there seemed to exist the possibility that she would end our engagement. I could not honourably have broken it off myself."

"How you must have laughed at my efforts to further your cause with Louise." Henrietta interposed indignantly.

"How could I have disclosed my real feelings? It would have been infamous." he replied.

"So it was Philip's arrival that relieved you from your dilemma?" Henrietta was conscious of disappointment and confusion. She had, evidently, only been an accessory, and in the end, an unhelpful one to his release from a fatally mistaken engagement.

He shook his head wonderingly, "My dearest Henrietta, can you still not comprehend? It was meeting you. Becoming so intimately acquainted with you in all the strange circumstances of your stay in my house made me realize the utter folly of the marriage I was contemplating. How could I marry Louise when I was falling head over heels in love with you!"

Hardly daring to believe her ears, she stared back into his handsome face, her eyes searching it for any sign that he was teasing her. Could it really be true? What had Miss Norton meant? She said awkwardly, "I think, sir you must be quizzing me! Pray don't! For I think rather that you must despise me."

Charles looked lovingly at her puzzled face, the slim brows drawn together in a frown, and said with a smile, "My adorable idiot! I never spoke more truly in all my life. But I see that I shall have to prove my words to you for, indeed, you told me once that I should be more 'ardent' as a lover!" Putting his arm around her shoulders he kissed her lightly on the eyelids, then the tip of her nose and finally, drawing her closer to him, at first gently, then with increasing pressure, upon her mouth.

Somehow Henrietta found that her arms had stolen around his neck and, when he released her, she looked shyly into his eyes. She said wonderingly, "Although I admired you and felt at ease in your company, I never thought of you as a lover whilst you were betrothed to Louise – indeed I bitterly resented your interference!"

He laughed and took her hand in his and kissed it tenderly, "Sweetheart, it is as a husband that you must think of me! And as soon as is possible – for I don't believe that I could wait long!"

"As a husband –" Henrietta, suddenly remembering Miss Norton and all that she had said, asked, with a worried expression upon her face, "Did you talk to your mother of a future marriage?"

"When I went to visit her in Bath, I told her of you and of my intentions – I explained to her what had happened about Louise."

"And was your mother pleased?" she enquired anxiously.

"Yes, she was very pleased and after meeting you she was delighted."

Smiling happily, she said, "I think you need not wait long, sir, for I shall like it above all things to be your wife!"

Several delightful moments later, as he loosened his embrace and looked down into her face, she saw that he was laughing at her and stiffened, sudden fear in her eyes, "Sir Charles! You are hoaxing me!"

He shook his head, still chuckling, and withdrawing his some-what damp hankerchief from his pocket, gently wiped the streaks of dirt from her cheek, "You look, my treasure, as if you had been rolling in the mud – I think you must change your dress before Philip sees you, or I shall be called to account by him for assaulting your virtue!"

She looked down at herself and laughed with relief, and leaning her head back against his shoulder with a contented sigh, said, her eyes twinkling, "Gracious, I foresee that I must strive to behave with more propriety if I am to be married!"

He gave a mock groan, "Somehow, my love, I cannot believe that you will find that possible! But perhaps it would be as well if I confiscated your breeches!"

"Impossible, sir! I shall keep them always as my most precious souvenir!"